MAIDENHOME
Ding Xiaoqi

translated by:
Chris Berry
Cathy Silber

aunt lute books
SAN FRANCISCO

First Edition
10 9 8 7 6 5 4 3 2 1

Aunt Lute Books
P.O. Box 410687
San Francisco, CA 94141-0687

Cover Art: "Red Scarf" by Hung Liu (pencil, tempera and acrylic)
Cover Design: Pamela Wilson Design Studio
Calligraphy: Hung Liu
Typesetting: Debra DeBondt

Senior Editor: Joan Pinkvoss
Managing Editor: Christine Lymbertos

Production: Cristina Azócar   Cathy Nestor
             Danielle Dobel   Indigo Som
             Jonna K. Eagle   Kathleen Wilkinson
             Vita Iskandar

Production Support: Siobhan Brooks   Rebecca deGuzman
                     Lisa Louise   Jamie Lee Evans
                     Fabienne McPhail   Melissa Levin

This collection first published in 1993 by Hyland House Publishing Pty Limited, Melbourne, Australia.

This book was funded in part by a grant from the National Endowment for the Arts.

Library of Congress Cataloging-in-Publication Data

Ding, Xiaoqi, 1959–
    Maidenhome / Ding Xiaoqi. -- 1st ed.
        p.   cm.
    Translated into English by Chris Berry and Cathy Silber.
    ISBN 1-879960-36-2   (pbk. : alk. paper) : 8.95
    1. Ding, Xiaoqi, 1959– --Translations into English. 2. Women
    --China--Fiction. I. Title.
        PL2855.I64A23 1994
        895.1'352--dc20   94-15414
                                                              CIP

Acknowledgments

The history of this book goes back over five years, when I met Chris Berry and Cathy Silber. They were both working in China at the time, and Chris was translating a film I had scripted. They became my good friends and excellent translators, and their long efforts have laid the foundations for the publication of this book.

In May 1990, I joined the Cinema Studies Division of La Trobe University in Melbourne, Australia as a Visiting Fellow. During my second month in the country, I got to know Helen Chamberlain. I was looking for work and was recommended to clean her house. Who could have known that within two meetings she would become my first Australian literary agent? Helen recommended my work to the editor of *Australian Short Stories*, Bruce Pascoe, and he published my first work to appear in Australia, 'Indica, Indica', and then 'If You Were Still Alive'. Thanks to Cathy Silber's efforts, an abridged version of 'Indica, Indica' had already been published by *Mother Jones* in the United States. It was also because of Ms. Silber's efforts that this book is being published by Aunt Lute Books, in the U.S.

One day, Chris phoned me up, shouting that Dr. Joan Grant of the Monash Asia Institute at Monash University had decided to recommend a collection of my work for publication by Hyland House. Hyland House's publishers, Anne Godden, Al Knight and Andrew Wilkins, have given me a lot of help and shown great empathy towards my work from the word go.

I am very pleased to have this opportunity to express my profound gratitude to Gim Wah Yeo, President of the Chinese Arts Festival of Melbourne. Without his selfless and generous support and help, I would never have been able to achieve as much as I have during the short time I have been in Australia.

I am also very happy to be able to express my sincere thanks to La Trobe University, the Division of Cinema Studies there, and my friends Merrilee Moss, Barbara Creed, Helen Moore, Mary Farquhar, Vernoica O'Yong, Bill Au, Dinny O'Hearn, Freda Freiberg, Anne McLaren, Hass Dellal, Bill Routt, Liz Jones, Professor Kong Lee Dow, Dr. Daniel Kane, Dr. Jenna Mead, Dr. Lucy Frost and Derek Elsworth for all their help and sincere friendship.

Finally, thanks to the women of Aunt Lute Books for publishing my work in the United States, and a special thanks to Vita Iskandar for negotiating its U.S. publication with Hyland House.

Ding Xiaoqi
April 1994
Melbourne

Publisher's Note

We thank Cathy Silber for bringing this collection to the attention of Aunt Lute Books, and gratefully acknowledge Hyland House for making this edition possible.

These stories remain as they first appeared in the original Australian edition, with minor exceptions. Because Cathy Silber and Chris Berry are from the United States and Australia respectively, each translated into the idosyncratic English of her/his home country. Hyland House edited the translations with consideration for the Australian readership. Under Cathy Silber's direction, we reversed the process, retaining her original translation and transforming Chris Berry's for U.S. readership.

Where not intrusive, we have left British or Australian conventions in tact. Our guiding concern was to bring to U.S. readers, without distraction, the energy and originality of Ding Xiaoqi's work.

Translators' Note

The *pinyin* romanization system preferred in mainland China has been used for the transliteration of all Chinese names and terms in this volume. In accordance with standard Chinese practice, personal names are rendered with the family name first and given name second.

Each piece in this volume has been translated independently by one or other translator, as indicated, and each translator retains full responsibility for individual translations. However, we have exchanged translations and comments, and undertaken extensive revision procedures, not only in an effort to ensure correct translation, but also to produce consistency of style and tone across the volume.

Table of Contents

Foreword

The stories in this collection come out of one of the most exciting phases of literary activity in China. With the end of the Cultural Revolution in 1976 and subsequent political and economic reform, writers in the post-Mao period began to test boundaries, as the state loosened its grip on literature and the arts. After nearly four decades of 'revolutionary' literature, during which writers either followed Mao's mandate to produce socialist realist works for the masses or fell silent entirely, the literary scene in the late 1970s and throughout the '80s exploded with new writers taking up new (or long suppressed) themes, experimenting with new forms, and publishing in new magazines. Of the many literary developments in this time, one of the most significant has been the emergence of scores of women writers taking on the description of female experience and re-opening explorations of gender issues in new fiction.

Ding Xioaqi, whose work in English translation is collected here for the first time, has not simply followed this trend. She ranks as one of the most daring of its shapers for her treatment of taboo subjects like rape and adultery, and as one of its most sophisticated stylists for her intense renderings of highly subjective states—what she likes to call her psychological realism. The stories collected here—many of which were first published, and later republished, in literary magazines in China—come from Ding's two collections of short and mid-length fiction: *Maidenhome* (1986) and *The Other Woman* (1989). Her work appears in several recent anthologies of contemporary women's fiction. Though she is also known in China for her popular songs, TV scripts, and the script based on 'Maidenhome' that she wrote for the film, known in English as *Army Nurse*, her reputation as a fiction writer is assured.

For readers unfamiliar with China, Ding's work opens windows onto a world that may seem strikingly different in some stories and surprisingly old hat in others. For instance, 'The Other Woman', Ding's favorite of all her work (and the one she fervently hoped would be the title story of this collection), may at first strike a U.S. reader as entirely unremarkable—another story about a young woman's love affair with a married man. Yet the story was widely popular—and highly controversial—in China. The issue of the literary magazine in which it first appeared in 1987 sold out quickly, and handwritten copies began circulating among women college students. For its frank depictions of female desire, and sexual desire in particular, 'The Other Woman' may have been racy by the standards of its day, but the significance of this story is more political than prurient. We need to read Ding's work in its own particular socio-political context to understand how issues absent from feminist agendas elsewhere become salient for Chinese feminist movement.

The rallying cry for women's rights (abolition of footbinding and arranged marriage, access to education), sounded by women and men alike in the early decades of this century in China, was inseparable from a broader outcry, over the decades of national humiliation at the hands of imperialist powers, and from anguished debates over tradition and modernity. The oppressed Chinese woman became a potent symbol of national impotence; 'women's liberation' became only one of many levers applied in efforts to dismantle Confucian social hierarchies and to save the nation. Women's rights were included in the Communist platform, but gender quickly became subordinated to class as the nexus of struggle. After the establishment of the People's Republic in 1949, women were officially proclaimed equal to men. The communists had earned popularity and a power base by championing the oppressed, but as rulers of the state they appointed themselves official sponsors of the voices of the oppressed. With the state already promulgating feminism and controlling its terms, this left women little position of their own from which to speak of women's issues. Work outside the home became a duty, not a right, and so-called 'gender equality' became largely a matter of erasing women's difference. Women could be 'just like men' in the public sphere while domestic relations remained largely unchanged. Women took on heavy factory jobs and adopted male dress, but they continued to do most of the work at home. In socialist China, women remained subordinate to men, but everybody was subordinate to the Party and its paternalistic State. Women were masculinized, but everybody was emasculated. In socialist fiction, didactic to the extreme, characters were model types whose identities were political, not personal, and whose passions were patriotic, not romantic. Love and revolution did not mix. Thus writers in the '80s were reacting to these conditions in taking up issues of gender, personal identity, and sexuality. In the profound disillusionment following the Cultural Revolution, the West became highly fashionable, and writers searching for new narrative forms frequently turned to Western fiction and individualism for models. That the Party reacted with campaigns against 'spiritual pollution' and 'bourgeoisie liberalism' shows what political threats these developments were.

While questions of femininity and masculinity preoccupied both male and female writers in the '80s, many male writers have cast the search for their lost masculinity in frankly misogynistic terms. Meanwhile, women writers like Ding Xiaoqi have insisted on the validity of female experience. Stories like 'The Other Woman' and 'Maidenhome' are thus important explorations of female subjectivity.

For their narrative innovations and thematic boldness, the stories collected here stand as significant contributions to contemporary Chinese fiction. For readers outside China, they provide glimpses of contemporary Chinese society through representations of female experience so resonant for women readers in China.

In 'The Other Woman', we also see a playwright's struggle for artistic freedom from Party control, and in 'Maidenhome' we witness a young woman's struggle with the conflicting demands of political duty and personal desire. 'Killing Mom' makes a rather macabre contribution to national discussions of the social and psychological implications of an entire generation of only children resulting from the one-child-per-family policy.

Through 'Indica, Indica' we follow the experiences of a village girl sold by her family into marriage far away from home. This practice, or perhaps more commonly the kidnapping and sale of young rural women, continues today. In 'Black Cat' we see some of the turmoil wreaked upon families during the Cultural Revolution through the eyes of a schoolgirl whose parents have been sent away for political reform, and the lasting impact of such troubled times on the same character as an adult struggling to come to terms with the terrors of her past. The second-person narration in both these stories highlights the alienation these characters feel from themselves at the same time that it implicates the reader in their experiences.

With 'The Angry Kettle' (and the two plays she wrote in Australia), Ding joins other writers of the post-Tiananmen diaspora in inscribing Chinese experience abroad, using humor to voice frustration at the expectation dominant cultures place upon immigrants to assimilate.

Because she is always incisive and never at a loss for words, we have not heard the last from Ding Xiaoqi. These stories mark the beginning of what promises to be a long and fruitful career.

Cathy Silber

MAIDENHOME

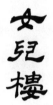

女兒樓

Maidenhome

1

Thank goodness it was over at last, this year's awards ceremony. It was already twenty minutes into lunchtime, but she didn't follow the crowd towards the canteen. Everyone was grumbling because the meeting had gone on so long, so wouldn't it be asking to be snubbed if you went to eat carrying an armful of trophies and certificates?

Since she'd entered Hospital 547, put on the oversized army uniform and gone up on stage to get the collar and cap badges, she'd already been to thirteen of these ceremonies. No, including today's it was fourteen. She'd long stopped feeling the way she did that year, calm on the surface, but in fact ears pricked, straining to hear every sentence from the stage, so nervous her palms were sweaty. She'd known for a long time her name was on the awards list, but she couldn't restrain herself. She had to actually hear the three syllables, 'Qiao Xiaoyu'. Really, it wasn't like your name at all coming from that sacred stage, amplified through the mike, booming through the room and bouncing back off the walls.

To the definite pulse of the music, those whose names had been read out by Lu Zengxiang, the political commissar, went up to get their prizes, faces red, hearts pumping. Everyone applauded in time to the music. She sat in the back row, still thinking about the transfer request she'd folded up and put in her pocket twenty-four hours ago. Should she give it to her section head, or hand it directly to the hospital Party committee? Maybe it would be safer to give it straight to the Party committee. No, she would give it to the section head first, that would be more by the book, but…

'Would the third class merit award winner, second surgical team matron Qiao Xiaoyu, come up to accept her award, please?'

It was only twenty yards or so down the aisle, but she still felt she wouldn't make it. They were talking about her, chattering away. She knew what they were saying. She didn't need to listen, she could tell from their eyes: that Qiao Xiaoyu, she's so hot for awards she doesn't even want a husband. That's right, her feelings aren't worth more than a fifty-buck award. A woman like that shouldn't get married, she doesn't know the first thing about love. She knew there were people saying things like that about her. Look—Ji Yamei was there, jabbering away and looking at her as though she was a stranger. She should walk a bit faster; the leaders were waiting for her on the stage. They were applauding her, too. Look at their kind, trusting eyes; comrades like Xiaoyu really are hard to come by. For her work, for the cause, she even cut her honeymoon short. We really have to encourage young people like that.

It was true, she did deserve the award. All these years, she hadn't been spoiled by the leaders' good treatment of her; she still worked as hard as ever. Why else would the hospital Party committee have given her a third class merit award? Still, it was also true that she hadn't done anything particularly out of the ordinary!

God! How come he's here, too? She hadn't expected to see Ding Zhu at the end of the front row. He was still wearing a patient's white pajamas, and they made him stick out like a sore thumb. Well, do you hear what they're saying? What are you thinking? You're still recovering, so why have you come to the meeting? To laugh at me? No, you haven't laughed or even smirked. Your eyes are staring at me, but blankly, just like back then. Do you really know me? How I'd love things to be just the way they say and imagine them to be. It would be wonderful to be as ungrateful, ruthlessly ambitious and cold-blooded as some people say I am. It would be great to be as conscientious and totally dedicated as the leaders say I am, too. It's all the same to me. That way, at least I would be able to walk up to the stage relaxed and at ease, and to throw off the heavy stone pressing on my heart.

Commissar Lu, your hands are always so warm and strong.

But can those hands of yours help me move the stone from my heart? Do you know what I've got in my pocket? If you knew, would you still smile at me as though you were looking at a work of art you'd created with your own hands?

The dormitory was in the innermost part of the hospital compound. Don't think you can see this little red building that stands out at the foot of the mountain from the main gate; you still have to walk some distance to get to it. Legend has it a famous old author came to visit 547 during the Korean War, walked around the little red two-story building and, inspired by it, composed a couplet on the spot:

Femininity hidden in the green mountains,
A little red maidens' home.

From then on, this dormitory for single women doctors and nurses became know as Maidenhome. Maybe because it had such a beautiful name, although its old-fashioned roof and brick walls were patchy and discolored now, it still seemed as tranquil and attractive as ever at the foot of the lush, green mountains. When the women soldiers walked in, they felt proud, safe and free, a sense of ownership that came with stepping into their own world. When the men soldiers passed by, the brave ones glanced over with a look that suggested they were seeing something completely beyond their grasp, and the timid ones didn't even dare look up at all, as though they were passing a sacred site. Maidenhome didn't have a balcony, just a little, Chinese-style porch at the main entrance with a pointed roof and round columns. According to the old comrades, there used to be some bright folk designs painted on its beams and eaves. I don't remember what year, but when Maidenhome was renovated, maybe because they couldn't find a painter or else because the leaders couldn't be bothered, the whole porch was painted red, like a Chinese bride changing into her red dress. Crude bits of iron wire stuck out of the porch, and women's laundry hung from all of them. There were uniforms, long white gowns and patterned blouses, and there were also bras and underpants. Nylon, frilly, the colors of the rainbow, like flags of all the nations. However, Qiao Xiaoyu never did anything like that. Even though Su Meng-hong had told her repeatedly that underclothes had to be dried in the sun and not in the dark of a room to really sanitize them, she still felt it was a little too ... you know. That year, Menghong and Commissar Lu, who was director of the political section, had quarreled over whether or not underclothes could be hung out in the sun like that. Commissar Lu said one had to think about the effect they would have. Menghong said, this is Maidenhome, so why can't we hang out women's clothes? Commissar Lu said, this is a military hospital, not an ordinary apartment compound. Menghong said, a military hospital should look after the women soldiers' rights even more; women soldiers are soldiers, and they are people too ... At the time, she felt Commissar Lu was in the right, because not long afterwards the women soldiers began complaining that their underclothes were disappearing, and later they were discovered with a convalescent in one of the wards.

'If you hadn't hung them out, would they have been stolen?' asked Commissar Lu.

'He steals things but we're in the wrong—that's the same sort of nonsense as saying the creation of women was a mistake.' Menghong really had a sharp tongue. Qiao Xiaoyu didn't agree with Su Menghong when she said Commissar Lu had become a 'hypocrite'. If Commissar Lu hadn't excused the women soldiers from morning exercises the first day of their periods, nobody in Maidenhome would even have thought about sleeping in a little at those times. That system continued today, making 547's kindness to its soldiers legendary. Still, she didn't approve of Commissar Lu making a mountain out of a molehill, either. He even had it discussed at a Party committee meeting, and then an ironclad rule came down: it is forbidden to hang out any clothes to dry on the porch of Maidenhome.

Now, ten years later, the women soldiers ignored the rule altogether. All sorts of things were hung out there, almost as though it was a competition.

The back of her head throbbed with pain. Really, it was one thing after another. She'd been on night shift yesterday, and only finished at six this morning. There was a film this afternoon—that was what the tickets they'd given out at the general meeting were for—but she'd given her ticket to a young patient at the entrance to the auditorium. He was only seventeen, and he called her Auntie Qiao.

Since she was fifteen—no, to be accurate, since she was fourteen-and-a-half—she'd climbed this steep path every day.

It used to be gravel, and one section used to turn into a puddle whenever it rained, so you could only avoid getting your shoes soaked by jumping. Not anymore. Now it was concrete from one end to the other, and lined with neat hedges. Still, she'd never found the path so difficult before; it was really a struggle. She was out of breath and her forehead was dripping sweat before she even got into the building. Maybe she really was getting old; in a couple of months she'd be thirty. When she first came to 547, she had called nurses of thirty or so Auntie, but now she was an Auntie too.

She lived on the third floor, although she'd only moved up there when she became a matron. She'd lived in almost every room in the building. When she'd first enlisted, she lived in the biggest room on the first floor, a bedding and clothing storeroom that had been cleared out for new recruits. Twelve girls to a bed, and she'd lived there for three-and-a-half years.

When she opened the door to room 307, the warmth that only your own room can have flowed over her, filling her with a sense of comfort and tenderness that was beyond words. Pulling the cardboard suitcase out from under the bed, she dumped the certificate and the trophy into it. She used to flick through her stack of certificates, an inch thick already, every time she opened the suitcase, but not today. She shoved it back under the bed quickly, as though it wasn't hers but someone else's, Commissar Lu's or...

Collapsing onto the bed, she felt as though every bone in her body had gone soft. Someone opened the door and peeked in, but she ignored her. Those girls, they crashed in and out whenever they felt like it. If they were around, it was no use hoping for a moment's peace. Her belly started to hurt again. People said no medicine would cure menstrual cramps; the only thing for it was marriage. Once you married, they were sure to get better. And what about you? She felt full of grievances—inexpressible, nameless grievances that were held back as though somebody was hanging onto them.

She came from a small town in Hebei Province, and her father was the vice-director of an army warehouse. In 1968, when she'd only just started high school, they started messing about with revolution in the school, and although she went to class, there weren't any other students there. She hid in the stairwell with some other girls and watched the boys in the final year pasting accusation notices onto a teacher. She could still remember, it was the woman who taught foreign languages. Seeing strips of paper hanging like tails from the teacher, she felt both worried and excited. To be honest, she didn't like that teacher; those letters and vocabulary words of hers really were a pain in the neck. Now she'd never have to worry about going to her class again.

'Qiao Xiaoyu, your dad's here.' There was a girl behind her, tugging at her sleeve.

'My dad?' She panicked, because if he saw she was getting involved in this nonsense at school too, she'd be sure to get a beating. She was a bit afraid of her father, even though he liked her best of the three children in the family. He'd smacked both her younger brothers more often than anyone could remember.

'There's something important at home.' Dad wouldn't say anything at school.

'What?' she asked quietly. She didn't really want to leave right now. Dad frowned and didn't answer, and she didn't dare ask again.

Dad didn't take her along the usual route home from school. His stride was long, probably a habit from forced marches during the war. She hurried behind him, sometimes running a few steps. He took her to the District Military Headquarters. She knew the place; her father's good friend, Uncle Zhou, worked there. Dad's making me enlist, it dawned on her.

'Qiao Xiaoyu! How come you're here, too?'

'Ji Yamei!' She hadn't expected to run into a classmate here. She relaxed a little. I've got a friend. That's very important to young girls. Actually, they weren't good friends at all in school. There was something odd about that Ji Yamei. She was too outspoken. For instance, if someone's headband was nicer than hers, she'd call her vain, or if the teacher said someone's homework was good, she'd be sure to say a brother or sister had helped.

She passed the medical without any problem. She'd never thought something as sacred and mysterious as this could be wrapped up so quickly. It left her feeling nonplussed. She used to dream of being in uniform and having two bright red collar badges setting off her pointy chin. But now it was really happening, she felt something wasn't quite right. She couldn't say what, but she didn't feel as happy and excited as she'd expected to.

Mom had packed up all her things. Dad said the army issued everything, so it wouldn't look good to take too much. After weeding a lot out, the biggest thing left was a woolen vest, and she made her father swap her scarlet one for her eldest brother's aqua one. Once they'd put everything together, it didn't even fill the smallest travel bag. Mom was in the kitchen cooking, and today she was making more noise with the pots and pans than usual. Dad went out again to deal with some of Xiaoyu's paperwork for her, and he said the train would leave that evening. Her two younger brothers were playing marbles in the yard downstairs, apparently unaware their elder sister was about to leave.

Mom cut her hair, which used to reach her waist when she let it down. Now it made two little braids that only just touched the base of her neck. They were neat and stiff, a bit awkward, but she knew she looked good. There was the sound of the main gate again, and she ran from the mirror to the window. This time it was him. She knew his steps, one and then the other, first fast then slow. She rushed out as though she had just thought of something, bumping into him in the corridor. He slipped past her, but hesitated for a moment. She'd grown up together with this boy since they were toddlers, but for the past three or four years, they'd been a bit lost for words whenever they met.

'Maomao, I'm going away.' She struggled to keep calm, to act as though she'd run into him by accident and just thought of something she wanted to tell him.

'I know.' He stopped and turned to look at her. In the light of that fifteen watt bulb in the corridor, his eyes shone black and serious. 'You're off tonight, to enlist.'

He knew. He was quick. And he was wearing that faded army jacket with the big, soft collar that hid the shirt underneath it completely.

'Goodbye. There'll be time later.' He took control so quickly, as though he was the one leaving to enlist.

He pulled a notebook with a red plastic cover out of the yellow book bag slung over his shoulder. He had prepared for this. The notebook cover had the word 'Friendship' embossed in gold; it was really pretty. Nobody had ever given her anything so solemnly before. She wished she'd thought of something, too. Opening the title page, there was an inscription in neat handwriting: 'Xiaoyu: I wish you every happiness.

Maomao.' She looked up at him and remembered how small and thin he'd once been. When had he shot up so tall? She couldn't even see his dark eyes without craning her neck. Suddenly, she felt anxious and at a loss. Resolutely, he put his hand out and, hurriedly adopting his manner, she did the same. They were as formal as delegates at a summit meeting. And why not? We're grown up now.

She went back inside, and hid the notebook at the very bottom of her bag. She let out a long sigh, as though she had just accomplished a great mission. She wasn't sure whether she felt regret or contentment. And then, just like that, she left home, and boarded a southbound train with a bunch of other girls all about her own age. Mom cried at the station. She said Xiaoyu was prone to chapped hands through to spring and bought her four boxes of the largest scented soap at a shop near the station. Goodness, she'd be using that for awhile. Dad didn't say anything, but just before she boarded he gave her braids a tug.

Perhaps it was just then that she realized something, leaving home this time was different from going to Granny's for the summer. Her eyes filled with tears, and she wanted to hug her parents, to tell them she didn't want to leave, she wanted to stay home. But she didn't do these things, she just thought them. She couldn't act like she did at home when she didn't want to go to school and faked a headache, or...A whistle blew. It was the soldier who'd come to meet them. Then the train whistle blew, too. They followed the soldier, the group leaders and everyone else towards the train turning to look back all the way. Actually, at that point you still didn't know what leaving home really meant, or what sort of a future was waiting for you. You didn't realize this was the turning point in your life. From now on, you would never be a child at your parents' side again. From now on, the boat on the long river of life was in your hands alone. In the future, you were going to lose a lot, including Maomao. If you'd known all that then, if you'd understood, would you still have brought your childhood to such an abrupt and premature end, and boarded that southbound train?

In her third year as a soldier, when she was eighteen, she got her first home leave. Her age, her uniform, her rosy cheeks and her bearing would make anyone stare with envy. When she got home, she found herself short of breath at the door, but not because she was tired. It would be good to run into him now, like just before she left, sort of on purpose and sort of by accident. This time I'll put my hand out first for sure! Suddenly, she discovered a secret about herself: the real reason you rushed home was because you wanted to see him. What does he look like now? Will he still recognize me? Will his bright eyes open wide with surprise? Two days passed, and she longed to hear his steps, now quick, now slow, out in the corridor, but there wasn't a trace of him.

'Just a few days after you left, Maomao enlisted, too. His Dad was transferred to Xinjiang Military District, and so the whole family moved.' Mom was standing behind her, so she couldn't tell if she was saying this deliberately or not. She didn't dare turn from the window. She knew her face was sure to be red and that there had to be tears in her eyes too. She'd been deceived. Just like when they played hide-and-seek as children. She'd hidden, tense and nervous, behind the big dark front gate, waiting for him to find her. But he didn't come. She waited there for such a long time, until it was dark and eventually she fell asleep. Mom went calling for her all over the building, almost beside herself with worry. In the end, it was him who found her behind the gate. It turned out he'd run off with the older kids to see a movie, the Russian film *Chapayev*—the one with the old guy with a handlebar mous-tache. He'd forgotten about their game of hide-and-seek altogether. 'There'll be time later.' When? She wished it had occurred to her to say she wanted to write to him when they parted. And why hadn't he thought of that simple but reliable method either? She'd always put her trust in him, he was so smart.

What about that notebook? What about the brocade-covered notebook she'd brought all the way back? She'd bought it herself with her first month's pay. Back then, she'd imagined how this day would be—she'd be like him, handing him the notebook as though she'd suddenly remembered something. It would seem more natural that way. She had kept it under her pillow three whole years.

Now she locked it in her little green box at home. Dad had made it specially for her when she was little, and in it were her treasures from when she was at home: a red hair ribbon, a little glass doll, things like that.

2

She lay there, half-awake and half-asleep, half-remembering and half-dreaming, until the sound of voices suddenly caught her attention. Right at noon, who could it be talking outside, not watching the movie, and not taking a nap either? Of course it's him. Don't pretend you don't know. In fact, you knew it in your heart all along.

She got up and went to the window. It was him, standing by the red-brick raised flowerbed in front of Maidenhome. But at this time of year there wouldn't be weeds, never mind flowers, so he had to be waiting for you, waiting for you to notice him and call out to him. No, she instinctively hid behind the curtains.

She had only found out yesterday that he was in the hospital. This time, he was in the internal medicine ward. Ji Yamei had told her a patient was looking for her the minute she returned from the northwest. He'd heard Yamei had gotten married, and he'd asked her about her husband.

'That guy's cute,' was how Yamei described the patient. She knew what Yamei was getting at. But she'd been upset ever since she got back, so she hadn't really taken it in. She certainly hadn't expected that the man looking for her would be Ding Zhu. If he hadn't already spoken to her face to face yesterday, she would never have thought it was him. Once she'd looked for him, waited for him. She'd kept that little note of his all this time, but of course he couldn't know that. And that feeling, that sense, only she could know that.

'Why didn't you come looking for me earlier?' she'd asked him yesterday.

He'd smiled and said, 'Are you talking about then or now?' He seemed very calm. Yes, it was over and gone; why mention it now? What's the use? She smiled back just as calm.

Relationships are strange. Who can explain them? Why are they always like the horizon? When you move, it moves too, and when you stop, it stops too. If you want to get closer to it, it runs away, putting a thousand miles between you. But when you want to get away from it, then it follows right behind you.

She peeked through the curtains but he was gone. No one was anywhere near the empty flowerbed. When had he left?

On her way to answer the phone, Nurse Chen asked her to finish distributing the medicine in ward six.

The list read Bed Four, Ding something. She wasn't sure whether the character should be pronounced *zhe* like the top half of the character, or *yu* like the bottom half. 'Ding Zhe.' No response. There were only five beds in ward six, and only one new patient, so it had to be him. 'Ding Yu.' She tried the other option, but still no one answered. 'Bed Four!' She blushed, but fortunately she was wearing a large gauze mask. She wasn't going to lose too much face, so she just called the bed number out. What on earth was that damned character?

'My name is Ding *Zhu*.' His voice was steady, but there was something in his tone. Was it sarcasm or attitude? Anyway, it wasn't what you'd normally expect.

She didn't dare meet his eyes. She was sure they were haughty. One glance at those sharply defined lips and she knew he was incredibly arrogant. Someone sniggered; that soldier from Tangshan again. Damn you and your dirty sniggering! You wouldn't know how to pronounce that character, either. She put the medicine on number four's bedside table, still not daring to look up. If Maomao was his age, would he look like that, too? She found herself making an unexpected association.

When she finished her shift she went back to the dorm. The first thing she did was look it up in the dictionary: '*Zhu*. (Of birds) to soar.' His eyes were just like a bird's, no, an eagle's. She found herself going back to look at his record. She never used to bother about that sort of thing. It had nothing to do with a nurse's routine work, and besides, the director didn't let them go leafing through records at will. 'Ding Zhu, truck company vice-platoon leader. Traffic accident. External chest injuries. Chest and sternum intact...' She spat. For one record she'd been through nearly every record in the second external medicine section to show she wasn't singling anyone out. Maybe she only did it to fool herself: I have the same level of concern for everyone.

Whenever she got close to ward six, she felt uncomfortable. Normally, she could do her work with her eyes closed, but when she got there she fell apart. When cleaning other rooms she longed to be in ward six, but once there she hovered about not wanting to enter. She could feel those eyes following her all the time, deliberately or not. Whenever you look up, there they are. And those slightly downturned, sharply defined lips. Avoid that look! You can't even tell if it's taunting you or promising to open his heart! But you can't avoid it. You want to feel it, don't you? You want to feel it following you, catching you. Look, your neck's gone stiff again. You know there's a ruthless pair of eyes waiting for you.

Instead of taking her break, she washed test tubes at the section sink. The sound of the rushing water seemed to help rinse away her troubles. Things in the hospital really had turned out the way Su Menghong said; Li Lingling had been sent to medical university for training in electrocardiography. Lingling had hugged her and cried bitterly when she'd left yesterday, saying how much she wished they could have gone together, but when the car came to collect her she still left alone. Her parents really weren't going to let their daughter spend her whole life as a nurse in this mountain gully. But Menghong was also right when she said Lingling hadn't actually used up the hospital's quota of university places when she left. What about you? Still washing out test tubes one by one and sending needles and syringes off to be sterilized, just like every other day. And then, of course, there's... There was someone behind her, and he hadn't just come in.

'There's no one on duty.' She stuck by the sink, not even turning her head. From her reaction, she knew who it was; she wouldn't act this way with anyone else. If he wants to change his bandages, why does he have to pick a time when there aren't any doctors or nurses on duty?

'There's no one on duty,' she repeated.

'What about you? I *could* do it myself.' He was angry that she didn't understand him.

She didn't say another word, and she didn't dare do more than glance at his face. She unwrapped the bandage around his chest and removed the dressing. Since a scab had formed over the wound already, there was no need to bandage it again. She hesitated after changing the dressing, and decided to use adhesive tape.

'Better bandage it again.' His voice was very deep, his look tender. It was as though she'd become a tool in someone else's hands, at someone else's disposal. Why are you doing this? It clearly doesn't need a bandage, this is against hospital procedure.

As she wound the bandage around his back, she could hear his heart thumping as though it was going to jump out of his chest. No doubt he could hear her heartbeat, too. She sensed his breathing becoming more labored, and wished she hadn't agreed to put the bandage on. Her hands shook so she couldn't get the bandage around his back. His shoulder blade jutted out. Suddenly, his outstretched arms bumped her and stiffened. She could even feel his biceps pulsing. Waves of heat swept over her; waves of youth and vigor that made her dizzy. They were surging out from his chest.

She didn't know what would happen next; she just knew she wasn't breathing, her heartbeat had stopped, and the rest of the world had ceased to exist. She shut her eyes, her mind already empty of all thought. Was it a minute? No, longer; it seemed a lifetime in which she no longer belonged to herself. Yet it was so short, maybe only ten seconds, or even less; less time than it took for a single breath. A hand gently and calmly nudged her shoulder.

'Xiaoyu, hurry up!' She felt as though she was being woken from a dream. She would never forget those words. An intimate low whisper, but at the same time it sounded like a voice from above. She never thought her name could sound so beautiful. As though really waking from a dream, she quickly finished putting on the bandage. She thanked him and meant it, because just then Nurse Chen and a whole crowd came in chattering away; she didn't dare think what might have happened.

'Thank you, Comrade Qiao.' He addressed her differently now and left. That was their second conversation.

For some reason, he never looked at her that way again. His laughter wasn't as loud, and he even spoke less. The soldier from Tangshan said, Ding Zhu's a real pain in the neck, he always tosses and turns at night, making the bed squeak. She knew it was because he couldn't sleep. Keeping a secret from everyone could be a worry. Now it was her chasing after his gaze.

She remembered a song sheet Menghong had lent her:

Where do the frogs in the river come from?
From that paddy field, they come swimming into the river.
Where does sweet love come from?
From the eyes to the heart.

That tune had been running through her head for several days now. Yesterday, she'd sung nearly all the songs she'd copied into her notebook, not knowing what she was hoping to find in them. What on earth's the matter with you? You've even started wandering around outside the wards after dinner. Are you hoping he'll notice you? You never used to laugh so loudly in the corridors. Is it because you want him to hear your voice? You know he wants to see you, to hear you; his eyes have told you as much.

She started to break the rules because of him. When she heard the soldier from Tangshan say Ding Zhu could play the harmonica, she borrowed one from the hospital club and put it on the bench in the corridor outside the wards. Sure enough, he saw it and got the soldier from Tangshan to borrow it for him. One time, when she was passing by ward six, she heard him saying he was a 'carnivore'. She thought it was hilarious, but when it came to doling out the food, half the braised eggplant dish she ladled out for him was meat.

In no time at all, he was discharged. They sent her to see him off. It was something she had to do quite often. At the bus stop on the outskirts of town, he pretended he had to do up his shoelaces and let one bus go by. It was midday in the summer, and really quiet. They stood in the sun together for forty-five minutes. It didn't occur to either of them to find a place in the shade. When they had left everybody behind at the hospital gate, it was as though they had become strangers and a gap had opened between them. She carried his yellow satchel, trying to casually keep her eyes on the hills ahead. He managed a few formalities—thank you, sorry for the bother, but even he found them too strained to go on. Savagely, he kicked a pebble into the distance. She couldn't help laughing, and he laughed, too. Their laughter blended, echoing from the slopes rising on both sides of the road as though it wasn't their own. It sounded great. Even they didn't really know what they were laughing about, but it was genuine laughter, and for a moment they were so close there was no need to speak. When he laughed, his eyes were full; not like an eagle's at all, but a lamb's.

'Xiaoyu, you're a lot of fun.' Look at him, what was he saying? Inexplicably, they started laughing again. Say it, quick! If you have something to say, hurry up and say it! Quick, start one of those youthful heart-to-hearts!

The ground started to tremble. It was the bus. If he didn't take this one, he'd miss that day's train. He took his satchel and shook her hand firmly. But then he let go just as quick, pressing a little ball of paper into her hand. He'd been prepared. She looked up and saw yearning shining from his eyes. It had been so long; why hadn't he done it sooner? The people on the bus were looking at them, so she nodded nervously, unsure herself whether it was a promise or farewell. The heartless bus door separated them with a bang, but hopefully not forever. The bus set off along the winding mountain road, leaving a cloud of yellow dust and foul-smelling exhaust.

She didn't dare unfold the piece of paper on the road; she didn't even have the courage to put it into her jacket pocket. Nobody could have seen, nobody, she reassured herself. He'd probably been clutching that ball of paper in his hand since they left the hospital, and with the heat of the midday sun and her holding it for awhile too, the sweat from their palms had almost turned it into papier-mâché. Fortunately, he'd used a ballpoint. If it had been a fountain pen, it probably would have been impossible to make anything out.

Damn, all that scrap of paper had on it was his military address and his given name. She turned it over; there wasn't anything else. She felt a bit disappointed, even wronged, but at the same time relieved and happy. You didn't do anything to be ashamed of, and neither did he. You're being too sensitive. What can an address prove? You nursed him, gave him his food, changed his dressings, and so he's left his address. That would make sense to anyone. She took the song book out from under the pillow and unwrapped it, putting the flimsy little piece of creased paper inside, as if it were a song.

A whole week had gone by, but she was always distracted, as though something was still troubling her, or she was waiting for something to happen. In the afternoon someone brought her a letter. It wasn't from home, or from Lingling. In the space on the envelope for a return address, it said 'enclosed'. Her head felt as though it was swelling, and her heart leaped into her throat—it was from him! Wasn't this what she'd been waiting for, yearning for, the thing that made her so distracted?

She slipped into a toilet stall, bolted the door, and stood there reading the letter. It wasn't very long, and it was very simple, but her eyes were watering. She wiped them with the back of her hand, but they blurred again at once.

Dear Xiaoyu,
    How are you?

From the moment I laid eyes on you, I wanted to see you every moment of the day. You're so honest, so pure, so conscientious. Sometimes I even wished my injury was more serious, so I could stay in ward six a few days longer.

I keep remembering those days. I don't know why, but I feel that several times you passed by ward six just so I might see you, and that you laughed so sharply so I might hear your voice. Am I right? You won't be mad at me for thinking like this, will you?

I've been very busy since I rejoined the company. The clanging of iron and steel is everywhere. We move those trucks and oil drums around like chess pieces.

Xiaoyu, won't you write back? I can't believe you don't know why I gave you my address.

That's all for now. I've got to get to work.

Zhu
August 29th, 1972.

Someone came into the toilet and knocked on the door to her stall. She'll never forgive herself for what she did next. Without even finishing the last line she panicked and took the letter—his first letter and also his last—crumpled it, and chucked it down the toilet. She flushed the toilet in a daze, like someone trying to get rid of stolen goods. She may have regretted it that very instant, wishing the letter back, or at least to read it again. But it was too late; the ball of paper rode the whirling current in the pan, and slipped down the dark hole.

As if she had committed some unspeakable crime, she dashed out blindly, not even daring to look up to see who was outside. For some reason, her first instinct was to run back to Maidenhome. She needed to be in Maidenhome, to hear the sounds there and see her friends before her panicking, pounding heart would calm down. No one's noticed anything odd; you're still one of them, you can still sing with them, and you can still all roll around on the bed together. She had more fun than usual with her friends in the dorm that day, and she laughed until her stomach hurt.

For the first time since she'd enlisted, she couldn't sleep that night. She went over his letter again and again in her mind, second-guessing every line she could remember. Should she reply or not? He's waiting for your letter; if he doesn't get it, he'll be anxious and disappointed. But you haven't been made a cadre yet. What if someone finds out? Soldiers aren't allowed to fall in love, but can you call this love? She felt like her head would burst. Also, you've just applied for Party membership; what if...? Maybe you'd better report this to the Party Secretary. You should rely on the Party for everything. No, best go look for Vice-Political Commissar Lu. He understands you best.

'You've done the right thing!' Commissar Lu patted her on the shoulder, making her sit down with his unusually warm and powerful hand. 'A young person like you must put study and work first. You should want to get ahead in life. Love is important too, but that's for later.'

'I'd best not get married!' she blushed at the mention of love, as though she really had experienced it already.

'When the time comes, even if you're not thinking about marriage, the leaders and the Party will be thinking about you. When my time came, the Party took care of everything for me...' Commissar Lu gave a hearty laugh. He was such a good man; he could make you feel so much better right away.

'Xiaoyu, you haven't been made a cadre or entered the Party yet. Don't allow a little thing like this to ruin everything. You've got a future ahead of you, you should demand the most from yourself in everything. Besides, you girls tend to mess these things up and get yourselves into trouble all too easily, so you should take every problem to the leaders and the Party first...' Looking at his kind and understanding face, her heart melted, as though such powerful support made her less upset.

She didn't write back. He didn't write again, either. He was a very proud young man. But she did open that song book of hers more frequently, and only she knew why.

Six months later, she went to nursing school for a year and five months. She studied very hard, and all her grades were excellent. As soon as she got back to 547 the order for her promotion to cadre came, quicker than either Su Menghong's or Li Lingling's. They weren't back from their studies yet. She was twenty-two that year. The first thing she thought of was to write to him. In fact, she had already written the letter in her head many times.

There was no one else in the dorm that day. She wasn't sleeping in the communal bed on the first floor anymore; she had moved to the second floor, where there were six people to a room. Now she had a whole bed and half a desk to herself. What luxury! She really didn't have that many things anyway.

It was unusual to get the room to herself, and she bolted the door after she opened up her writing paper. She was still afraid someone might see her. But as soon as she was ready to write, she got up again and unbolted the door; she was even more afraid someone might ask questions. When could she relax and be happy? As she bent over the desk, her heart skipped a beat at every sound in the corridor. Aren't you a cadre now? What are you afraid of? But it didn't work, and so she put the letter under an envelope addressed to her parents, covering each line as she wrote it.

She didn't mention his letter from over two years ago. She was very restrained, and just asked how his studies and his work were going. And she hinted that she'd been made a cadré. She thought, he's smart, he'll get it. And even if he'd been angry last time, he'd still be happy to get her letter. At the end of the letter, she didn't mention anything about him writing back, because she was sure she'd get a letter from him very soon. Very soon, that was certain.

For the next few days she felt a kind of happiness and fulfillment she'd never felt before and she smiled at everyone. Two new recruits argued until they were sobbing in the big first floor room where she used to live, and although she didn't even know their names yet, she rushed right in to mediate. She even took one of them to her room and peeled her an apple. She almost felt it was wrong for her to be so happy at such a time. She welcomed everything with a smile, even Yamei's sarcasm. Mentally and physically, she felt as beautiful and free as the white clouds in the blue sky. She wanted to pass her mood on to all the girls in Maidenhome, so everyone could share her happiness.

After three days, she was waiting for someone to bring her the letter. After five days, she started taking lunch late to wait for the mail. After nine days, she could not stop herself from running to the main gate to wait for the mail van. It must be that he's still angry that I didn't write back last time. He's getting revenge. How small-minded, but that's a man for you. She was a bit angry. On the tenth day, she sent a second letter, in a different style of handwriting. She wanted to sound tough, but when it came to putting pen to paper, that's not how it turned out at all. She said she was anxiously waiting for his letter.

She was no longer as confident as when she sent the first letter. In fact, she was quite uneasy. It's really hard to take, day after day. Now she was going through what he'd gone through then.

Eight more days passed, and there were two letters stamped 'return to sender' on the desk of the office. She no longer cared about her comrades' quizzical looks. Each letter had been forwarded, but over the return stamp was written 'no such person'.

Was it really the case that once you've made a mistake there's no way to put it right? Like two people who missed each other when their paths crossed and are doomed to go their own ways, never to meet again?

She didn't eat that day. After work, she cocooned herself into bed very early. She wished Ding Zhu had written another letter at the start. She would have answered it for sure. She was angry Commissar Lu hadn't understood her feelings and had told her to have nothing more to do with him. She hated herself most of all. Why had she casually, rashly, given up what was most beautiful and precious? She cried. When Yamei came looking for her, she just said she had a headache.

3

She didn't know how long she'd lain there and she was curled up in a ball, probably in an effort to control her cramps.

'Xiaoyu! Xiaoyu! Wake up! Come on, it's time to eat!' Someone was shaking her shoulder. 'Why's your hand so hot? You aren't sick, are you? Stay there. I'll go and get something from the canteen, and then we'll eat together.'

She made an effort to open her eyes, but it still felt like she was dreaming. Her stomach was a bit better, but her arms and legs still ached. She thought hard: what time is it now? Morning? Evening? Who was that talking to me just now? She pulled back a blanket she didn't know who had covered her with or when. It was Yamei's. Her shoes had been taken off, too, and placed neatly by the bed. She raised herself a little, and saw an army satchel and a bundle wrapped in red patterned fake silk on the bed across from hers. Su Menghong was back. She was overwhelmed by conflicting emotions, unsure whether she wanted to see her or not.

She had moved into this room on the third floor five years ago. There were four of them then: herself, Ji Yamei, Li Lingling back from training at medical college, and a trainee who had just graduated from an army medical school. After her return, Lingling had become an ECG technician. They got on as well as ever, but Lingling had gotten married less than six months later, and within two months she was transferred to the hospital at her husband's unit. Her family had arranged everything for her, even her marriage. That was what Yamei most despised about her. Su Menghong only squeezed in after Li Lingling left. She'd only just been reassigned after graduating from army medical school. It had been five whole years since she'd left 547 to attend college, but as soon as she was back she had everyone convinced she was the best. She had a knack for that. Su Menghong dismantled the spare bed the afternoon of the same day the trainee left the hospital, pulled all the trunks, boxes and suitcases out from under the beds, and piled them up in its space. She said that way no one else could move in. As a result, the three of them had had the room to themselves for four years now.

Actually, no sooner had Lingling gone than Ji Yamei fell in love, and within a few months she was married too. Her husband was a doctor in the records department of the same hospital. Su Menghong called him 'idiot' behind his back and to his face, but he didn't mind. Although Yamei's bed and various odds and ends were still in room 307, she only stayed over when she had a fight with that 'idiot' doctor. It was Menghong's idea that Yamei shouldn't move her things out. That way, she would have an emergency bed of her own away from home. Her own apartment was just a room, ten meters square, and if she had a disagreement with 'idiot', this way she still had somewhere to stay in Maidenhome, her own space.

Su Menghong had enlisted a year after her. One of them worked in the first surgical section, the other in the second, and although they were both on the same floor, they seldom spoke to each other. Xiaoyu was a real perfectionist about her job; the corridor alone got mopped seven or eight times a day. On her breaks, if she wasn't helping someone wash clothes, then she would be helping another person wash the windows. Commissar Lu was always going on about her: 'This soldier I recruited...' But as for Su Menghong, the corridor got mopped once in the morning, once in the afternoon, not a bit more, and she muttered all the way, as though reciting from memory. The few times Xiaoyu accidentally mopped Menghong's territory, Menghong never thanked her, but just smiled and said, 'You're so diligent'. Somehow, she felt that although her smile was genuine, maybe it came a bit too easily. It made her feel a bit odd. It was as though Menghong had helped mop someone else's floor, not her.

Once, Commissar Lu brought Menghong to her wards to see how she worked. She thought Menghong wouldn't be very pleased, she thought so much of herself. But she certainly hadn't expected she would just smile as usual and say, 'You can't always be mopping the floor. First, it isn't necessary, so it's a waste of time and effort. If you just keep things clean, that's enough. Second, one must keep the air dry in the wards; if it's dripping wet all day, people are liable to get arthritis, and it's not good for the medical equipment, either.'

'But I want you to learn Xiaoyu's spirit.' Commissar Lu hadn't expected all this theory from Su Menghong.

Menghong nodded her head modestly. Perhaps it was because she knew that after the last time she had a disagreement with Commissar Lu over hanging out laundry in the little porch, he wouldn't leave if she didn't nod her head this time. Sure enough, he left a happy man.

'He really should go and head up Pediatrics. He acts as though nobody else has a brain.' Menghong shrugged and left.

She was really conceited. But Commissar Lu was a bit fussy too, she thought. Of course, she wouldn't lower her standards because of what Menghong had said.

Menghong spoke fluent standard Chinese, was a good singer and dancer, good-looking, and liked to paint, too. Her works covered almost every wall of their dorm room. She didn't know whether Menghong painted well or not, but at least when she painted something you knew what it was.

Her interests weren't as broad as Menghong's, but she had her own hobbies, although they weren't worth comparing. Maybe she didn't want to share those little pleasures of hers with others. Many of her colleagues didn't know about that pretty little notebook with all those songs carefully copied into it. It was true; every holiday or Sunday, when there was no one else in the room and she copied a good song into that book with 'Friendship' stamped on the cover, she felt indescribably happy. She wouldn't lend the book to anyone, and if someone really wanted to look at it she stood by on guard, as though they might eat it. When she was alone and had nothing to do, she liked to take it out and read it through, starting from the beginning. She didn't sing the songs; she just wanted to read, beginning with Maomao's childish but diligent handwriting on the first page: 'Xiaoyu, I wish you every happiness, Maomao.' A few years later, there was a scrap of paper with an address on it, too.

She didn't know how Su Menghong found out that she liked copying out lyrics, but she lent her some song sheets a couple of times. Quite a few of the songs were foreign, hard to come by in those days. 'Katyusha', 'Hawthorn', and 'Where Do the Frogs in the River Come From?'. She felt nervous copying them, afraid someone might see them, but still wishing they were a bit longer. She even stopped every few verses to read them over from the beginning.

Later, Menghong was transferred to the operating theaters for awhile because Doctor Lou said they were short of nurses trained to use the surgical appliances. He had graduated from medical school in 1966, and was now the most promising of the young surgeons in Hospital 547. Why did he insist on Menghong? There were eight or nine others older than her in surgery. Yamei couldn't stop herself from commenting, 'It's bound to lead to something'. But Qiao Xiaoyu didn't see it that way. Menghong wasn't that sort of woman; she always said one should keep both feet firmly on the ground. She had the job down pat within a few days of moving to the theaters. As for Xiaoyu, she'd been in surgery three years now and even a slightly serious wound still scared her.

She couldn't decide whether she should hate Su Menghong because she posed a threat to her future and her career. In 1972, 547 was allocated a place at university and the Party committee decided to select a woman soldier from surgery. The first surgical section recommended Li Lingling, and the second recommended her. She was no dreamer, but for a few days there she envisioned a truly glorious future for herself.

Li Lingling was the daughter of high-ranking cadres. Normally, they got on very well together, but Ji Yamei took her aside and said, 'Don't be so stupid. Go and talk to the leaders again, or you won't stand a chance. You can't treat it like it's an unimportant class test or something. If you don't do it right, you'll only be on the short list for the sake of appearances'. She half-believed Yamei, but she believed she ought to have faith in the Party. Commissar Lu knew all about her and the whole hospital knew how hard she'd worked the last few years, so the Party committee would weigh it all up and come to a fair decision. Besides, Lingling usually did very well too, and although her father was a high-ranking cadre, she wasn't stuck up. She liked yelling and shouting about though, and if she bumped into Yamei, nine times out of ten they'd be at it until they were red in the face. As a result, she felt Yamei was a bit biased. She actually got on much better with Lingling, as though there was something drawing them to each other. Everyone congratulated them both, and they smiled together, as though it would make no difference which of them went.

However, it turned out in a completely unexpected way. No one had thought Su Menghong would be the one sent to university. Right away, it went around the hospital that Su Menghong had strong backers, and that someone high up had reserved the quota for her. Others said she knew the recruiter and had used her connection, or that she had cried and made a scene in front of the leaders. In any case, Su Menghong was going, a car would come to get her the next day, and now she was packing her things in the room next door.

Lingling came looking for her. Her eyes were swollen from crying, and her lips were pouting too. 'Xiaoyu, I'm not sad because I didn't get into university. But isn't it vexing?' Yes, she felt it was upsetting that something so full of hope had fallen through, and for no discernible reason.

'Xiaoyu, did you know? The quota was only given to surgery because my father phoned them, but…' Lingling couldn't go on. She'd probably never experienced such injustice before.

'Don't cry, Lingling.' What else could she say?

Someone came in, and much to their surprise it was Menghong. She'd overheard them, but she didn't look at all angry. She even squeezed between them, sitting down and putting her arms around their shoulders, as though she was totally uninvolved.

'Okay now, Lingling. What's the use of crying? Don't you worry. Your dad's such a big shot, I don't believe he's just going to sit by and leave you here as a nurse for the rest of your life. I bet you'll be off studying within six months anyway, so why should you need a chance like this that could only come to 547 once in a blue moon? If I'm wrong, I'll leave school and you can take my place. Okay?' As though coaxing small children, Menghong put her arms around their shoulders. Lingling smiled, her dignity satisfied.

Menghong left the room, and early the next morning she left the hospital, too. She went to university. It was only after she'd gone that someone explained what had really happened: the recruiter was an old classmate of Doctor Lou's, and Doctor Lou had written a private letter of recommendation for Menghong. Menghong rushed into town, found the recruiter and told him, 'If you really want to train army doctors, then pick me. There's no one more suitable for university in our whole hospital'. Apparently, her directness attracted the interest of the recruiter's colleagues, and she also discussed various professional topics with them in English, composed several chemistry questions more complex than those in the entrance exams, and even made some suggestions about autopsies. As a result, the recruiters went to the hospital Party committee and told them they would give 547 an extra place, because they wanted Menghong. That meant one more army doctor was being trained for 547, so the Party committee agreed. But in the end, the extra place they had promised disappeared somewhere up the line.

Later, Lingling's mother made a special visit to 547 because of what had happened. She said it wasn't so important that her daughter had been wronged, but that it showed disrespect to a high-ranking officer. However, no matter what she said, it was too late now. It was all water under the bridge; Su Menghong had already started classes.

Xiaoyu had cried too. If it wasn't just because she hadn't gotten into university, what else could it be? At first, she couldn't say, either, but she was terribly upset. She started to believe what Yamei had said. For the first time in the three or four years since she'd enlisted, she took a good, hard look at herself. It's true, you don't have staunch supporters like Li Lingling does, and you don't have Su Menghong's guts, so what will your future be?

She didn't think any further than that. Maybe it was because she hadn't really learned how to think about personal problems; maybe it was because she hadn't had the time. Commissar Lu and the leaders of her section all came to talk to her, and they laid out a very good path for her to follow. Commissar Lu said one had to take a proper attitude to going off to study, and that this was also a test the Party was giving her. She calmed down very quickly; the Party cared about her and understood her, she shouldn't think anything else. Besides, she felt it was better for Menghong to go to school than Lingling, even though she was usually closer to Lingling. Menghong had to rely on her own wits, but what about Lingling? She felt perfectly justified in feeling superior to others, as though the world was her birthright just because her father was a high-ranking officer.

She wrote a thought report, a frank and sincere one. She worked and studied as she always had. Six months later, she entered the Party. Just before, she got a letter from Menghong.

Dear Xiaoyu,

How are you? Still angry with me? I don't know what to say to you. Do you realize that? If I hadn't gone to see the recruiters and fought for the place, I'd probably never have gone to university. Besides, I'd been preparing myself for years, so I was more suitable than either of you. I'm absolutely sure of that. Xiaoyu, I've asked myself whether what I did was immoral, and my answer is no because, for me, going to university isn't like a commendation for hard work or a gift. It was the career break I'd been waiting for for so long. Don't they say, 'Go to university for the Revolution'? Who's got most of what it takes for army medicine, for being a doctor — me or Li Lingling?

It's not as though I haven't thought about you. But I'm sure you didn't stand a chance. The only one who did was Li Lingling. Since that's the way it was, isn't it best that I went and had a try, given that you didn't have the power or the means to get a chance? Xiaoyu, I'm really not trying to let myself off the hook. In fact I'm not absolutely sure even now if I did the right thing. However, I think that since it was a matter of recommendation rather than grades, why shouldn't we have been able to recommend ourselves for once? I think that one should try to use one's skills to the utmost, and arrange things so one can contribute as much as possible to social progress.

Am I making sense?

Menghong

She didn't write back to Su Menghong. She didn't know how to answer her questions. She simply felt that no matter what Menghong did, she was always so self-assured. But she also thought that if everyone behaved like Menghong, wouldn't that mean chaos? Who'd become a nurse? Who'd clean these bandages and test tubes?

Five years later, when Su Menghong returned to Hospital 547 as a bona fide army surgeon, she was still a nurse in the second surgical section.

That Su Menghong, she was an ambitious one. Last year, she'd enrolled for the postgraduate entrance examinations. It was all above board this time, and she didn't get anyone to write a recommendation letter for her. She was only seven points short. Lots of people felt sorry for her, but she said, 'It's better that I didn't make it; next year I'll pass with a score high enough to study in Beijing.' Now Menghong had gotten herself loaned out to teach technical foreign languages at some place in town. Yamei said she'd fixed it up herself for sure, because she wanted time to study for the exams.

There were lots of stories about Menghong's personal life too. Some said her old boyfriend had dumped her, others said she'd made up her mind to be celibate, and still others said she got on much too well with Doctor Lou, who was divorced. Qiao Xiaoyu didn't believe any of it. She knew Menghong had been in love, but that was long ago, probably when she had just enlisted and before she went to study. She'd asked Menghong what she planned to do about it, but she just smiled and said, 'Women, we keep hoping, but all we ever get is disappointment. Maybe I don't want to be disappointed again, so that's why I don't hold out any hope anymore.' Listen to her! She sounded like she was writing poetry. But what Menghong said somehow saddened her. She'd always thought Menghong's soul was bright as a sunbeam, clear as a cloudless sky. She hadn't thought she had bottled up suffering and dark shadows too.

'Xiaoyu—come on, let's eat. The canteen's got fried fish today.' Su Menghong had brought back the food and put out four or five bowls of it. She returned so soon she must have jumped the line. That's just the way she was, always in a hurry and convinced she was in the right. At eighteen she had been as mature as someone ten years her senior, but ten years later she was still as youthful as an eighteen-year-old.

'I'm not hungry,' she answered flatly. She wasn't sure whether she should forgive Menghong again the next time she caused a tragedy in her life.

'How can you not eat? You're on night duty, aren't you?' Menghong knew everything.

She didn't say anything or even move.

Menghong sat down next to her, 'Not feeling well?' She felt her forehead.

Xiaoyu ducked away from Menghong's hand, turning her back on Menghong to face the room.

After a moment's silence, a pair of hands landed on her shoulders, stubborn and full of feeling.

'I still haven't asked why you came back so soon. Did you have a fight? Did Tu Jianli mistreat you?' Intimately, naturally, she brushed a lock of Qiao Xiaoyu's hair from her forehead and tucked it behind her ear. Firm and confident, her other hand held her bony shoulder so she couldn't turn away again.

She shook her head. Maybe it would have been better if they really had fought, or if he'd mistreated her; at least that way she'd know why. But now she didn't know anything and she couldn't say anything, but her skull felt pressed between two bricks, as if just a little more pressure would split it open. She didn't want to cry, but the tears flowed silently down her cheeks.

'Are you in a bad mood, then? Got your period?' Menghong took out a handkerchief and wiped her tears, still gazing calmly at her. Only she had that look; seeing it was like drinking a warm cup of tea on a cold and cloudy day. The walls Qiao Xiaoyu had put up to keep her out the last few days came tumbling down so easily, and even her resentment turned into regret. Just like back then, when even though it was obvious she had helped Menghong to mop the floor, she felt as though Menghong had helped her.

She smiled awkwardly, and felt a little better inside. She stopped Menghong from wiping her tears, but she wasn't ready to get up. She hoped she could stay like this with Menghong for awhile, that she might rest under Menghong's sincere gaze a bit longer. Her mind was blank; it was like before, when they were all young. She was filled with sisterly affection. She hadn't been this close with a friend for a long time. At some point everyone had become busy with their own lives, and the times when they opened up to each other had become less and less frequent, until even their feelings for each other had waned. How much better if it could always have been like when they first enlisted.

'Doctor Su, are you coming or not? Hurry up!' Someone yelled from outside. Su Menghong jumped up from the bed and pushed the window open to shout back that she was on her way.

'Xiaoyu, I've got to go. There's a hospital jeep going into town, and I want to get a ride back with them because I've got classes this evening.' Menghong was gathering her things up as she spoke. She was always in such a rush.

Menghong picked up her backpack and sat down on the bed again. 'Xiaoyu, life is tough. There are lots of obstacles you cannot foresee and you have to deal with them all by yourself. That makes it even more important to be good to yourself and not to get down on yourself. Think about all the things you still want to do, all the roads you still want to explore.' No one could resist sincere advice and encouragement like that. She nodded earnestly, and took Menghong's hand. She wanted to tell Menghong, tell her about what was happening between herself and her husband Tu Jianli, about the request to turn down her job transfer, and lots more. But she couldn't get anything out.

'Xiaoyu, if you want to get something that is truly all your own, you'll have to pay a heavy price, and that's especially true of love. Often you give a lot more than you get back. You'll never get from someone else as much as you give, so you have to value what you already have. That's the price we have to pay.' Menghong smiled as she took her hand away. On the way out the door, she looked back and asked, 'Why don't you ask for a leave and not go on night duty?' Xiaoyu shook her head. If she didn't go on night duty, what would she do in the evening? All alone in the room, would she be able to sleep?

Menghong gave a last charming smile, said 'Bye-bye,' and left, closing the door behind her. She hadn't even had time to eat before she left. How wonderful to be like her! She bubbled unstoppably like a brook that had just thawed in the springtime, full of confidence and vigor, able to put anything behind her.

There was the sound of a motor starting down below. Xiaoyu got up and ran over to the window without even bothering to put her shoes on, pressing her face up against the glass. The roaring of the engine made the windowpane vibrate.

4

'Xiaoyu, his name's Tu Jianli. He's a friend of one of my old boyfriends. They're in the same troop,' Menghong had said seven or eight months ago, her arm around Xiaoyu's shoulder.

'Do you know him well, Menghong?'

'I haven't met him very often, but he seems a straightforward, hard-working guy.'

'What's he got to offer?' She was playing the same game as everyone else by now.

'He's a battalion-level cadre in the regimental administration. His family background is more or less the same as yours, I think. He's thirty years old, and when I ran into him on the street on home leave, he told me he was looking for a girlfriend who worked in an army hospital and asked me if I could help. I got a letter from him a few days ago, saying he'd be passing through on business. Do you want to meet him?'

'What do you think, Menghong?'

'You! You should meet more men, and besides, it's only a meeting, no strings attached.'

'Won't he look down on a woman like me?'

'Huh! Won't we Maidenhome girls look down on him? That's the question!'

'All right, Menghong.' She smiled, feeling more self-confident.

'I'll get in touch with him now, and I'll arrange a meeting when he gets here.' Menghong hopped down from the table, gave her a hug, and then set to work.

Qiao Xiaoyu, if you'd known then how it would turn out, would you have agreed to meet him?

Five days later, she got a letter from Menghong in town. She swapped days off with a colleague and then asked her section leaders for two days off to go into town because she had some things to take care of. She hadn't expected them to be so amenable; they agreed almost without asking. From the look in their eyes, it seemed they knew everything. Head down, she hurried out of the office; she really couldn't stand sympathetic—or perhaps they were pitying—eyes. She could imagine what they'd be saying once she closed the door.

She'd been going into town on the local bus for many years now, and it was still one of those Czech jobs with a red chassis and a yellow hood. Actually, the hospital had its own express bus in the mornings, but she hadn't taken it because she was afraid people would ask why she was going. She wasn't a good liar, so she preferred to walk twenty minutes and squeeze onto the local bus. She couldn't say what she was feeling right then, but it wasn't excitement or anticipation. It was as though she was on a mission she would be criticized for if she didn't complete, or as though she was doing someone else a favor, because it was someone else who had told her how to get there and what to do. She felt a bit ridiculous, and couldn't help feeling a little upset too.

'Thank you, dear. Come on, us girls can share a seat.' At the stop, she helped an old lady with a big basket of eggs onto the bus. Perhaps out of gratitude, the old lady started chatting away.

'How old are you, dear?'

'Twenty-nine.' She knew country folk were very particular about age, but she wasn't lying, she still had a few months before she turned thirty.

'You don't look it, you don't look it at all. Your face is so fresh. How many kids?'

She shook her head.

'Oh, family planning. On your way to see your husband?'

She didn't know whether to shake her head or nod, and she felt hot. She was probably blushing, too.

'Oh, I understand. You're going to see your boyfriend. It's all the same in the end. When I was your age, I'd already had my fifth. I've got a stack of grandsons now. My time's nearly up.' She let out a long sigh, and it was hard to tell if it was sadness or satisfaction. 'Is your boyfriend an officer, too?' The old lady wouldn't take her eyes off her. It was like an interrogation.

She actually nodded, acknowledging it.

'Good. I can tell from your ears that you're going to have a lucky life. Officers earn a lot, they don't have to spend money on clothes, and they're good people. How old is he?'

'Thirty.' Granny had told her she was lucky, too. Would this thirty-year-old man bring her luck?

'What's his name?'

'Tu.' Good heavens, what are you doing, you fool? She reproached herself.

'Oh, Tu. My second grandson may know him. My second son's in the army, too. He just got promoted last year. Let me say something personal, dear. You should get married. You can't afford to be too picky, and having children gets more difficult…'

The good-hearted old woman chattered on about all sorts of things. Qiao Xiaoyu didn't dare turn away from the window; she really didn't know what to say if the old woman asked anything more. However, their brief exchange had affected her quite strongly. It made it all seem real, although she hadn't even met him yet.

She remembered something from two years ago. She was twenty-seven that year, and at some point her marriage had become a major topic of conversation at 547.

One day, someone had come knocking at her door during lunchbreak. It was the fat matron from internal medicine. She was known throughout the hospital for her warm heart. Almost forty, she was so plump her feet nearly popped out of her shoes, but she still worked as hard as a young person.

'I've found a boyfriend for you,' the fat matron whispered to her as soon as she came in, even though there wasn't anyone else in the room. 'But first, I need a photo of you.' The fat matron flicked through all her snapshots starting from when she was a baby, grumbling that she hadn't had her photo taken often enough, and finally selected the most appealing two from her rather limited collection.

The fat matron bent over melodramatically and whispered in her ear again, 'He's a staff officer based in Tianjin troop, a distant relation of mine. He's a good man and he has a great future ahead of him.' The fat matron left his family name and address, and said not to be frightened when she got his letter.

'You just wait patiently. I'll have him write after he's looked at your photos.' The fat matron gave another jovial laugh and left.

Her mind was full of nothing else for a whole week. What did he look like? Was he tall? Was he nice? What was he like? She even thought about their future together, where they would settle down, and so on.

Two weeks passed and she hadn't received his letter, nor had the fat matron come to see her. Furthermore, she found out it wasn't as private as she had thought at all. Lots of people in the hospital seemed to know about it, and they even knew more than she did: 'Xiaoyu, have you had a letter from that staff officer of yours yet?', 'Xiaoyu, first you fall in love, then you meet, huh?' It went without saying that this was the result of the fat matron's loose tongue.

At first, the fat matron still gave her an embarrassed smile whenever she saw her. Later she became very cool, as though nothing had ever happened, and she didn't even return her photos to her.

I should go and ask her. There's nothing to be ashamed of. At least I should get my photos back. She felt it was a matter of self respect. That day, she saw the fat matron chatting with some nurses at the other end of the corridor. She headed straight for them, but the minute they saw her they all stopped talking, and even those with their backs to her turned to look at her.

Her resolve of the last few days evaporated into thin air. She slipped by as though she was on her way somewhere else without even a glance at the fat matron. What's the point of asking? If it's not because he thinks you're too old, then it must be because you're stuck in a remote mountain hospital— even if you changed careers, you'd never get a transfer to a city. The only thing you'd get from asking is having it said to your face. She rushed back to the dormitory, and once she was in her room she couldn't hold back the tears any longer. She pulled open her drawer, and tore up his address. She thought about a lot of things: about the dozen or so years she'd been a soldier, about Maomao, about Ding Zhu, and that she'd never go looking for a boyfriend again. But she wasn't convinced; she wasn't ugly, she was such a hard worker, and she believed if she really did get married, she'd make a good wife. Even Menghong had said, 'If I were a man, I wouldn't take no for an answer. Xiaoyu, just ignore them; they don't understand a thing.'

How many guys had she met over the last few years? If they didn't like her, then she didn't like them. All her friends worried about her; even Lingling wrote letters urging her on and asking questions, as if she was in serious danger of becoming an 'old maid'.

'Xiaoyu, don't set your sights so high.' Even Commissar Lu said that when he saw her.

What could she say to these men? If the minute you meet someone, he says you must leave the place you've lived and worked in for over ten years, get out of uniform, abandon Maidenhome and go off with him, would you say yes? If he proposes before there are any feelings at all, could you accept? She didn't set her sights too high; she just wanted someone who could understand and respect her. It was all so difficult! She never expected it would be so simple with Tu Jianli. Maybe the old lady on the bus telling her fortune from her face had something to do with it.

When she got off the bus, she was surprised to find Menghong waiting for her at the stop, with a man beside her. That Menghong—she was always catching you off guard. She felt her face turning red. There was nothing she could do about it, it happened every time. She didn't dare look at him again, and only managed a few broken sentences with Menghong. But once she decided to throw caution to the wind and glance at him again she relaxed, because he was blushing too, even looking away. He feels the same as you do. She felt so much better she even managed to put her hand out first when Menghong did the introductions.

In the two days at Menghong's—no, to be accurate, in twenty-four hours—she met him three times. The first time was at the bus stop. From the moment she got off the bus, it was about twenty minutes in all. He said he had some business to do and he'd go on ahead. Menghong took him aside and said something to him that of course Xiaoyu wasn't meant to hear. As if waiting for their verdict, she stood under a tree about five meters away from the bus stop, watching. He wasn't what you'd call handsome, but he was in good shape. His complexion was ruddy and his hairline low, which made his forehead seem rather small. He'd had a shave and a haircut and put on a clean shirt before he came; the cuffs still held the crease from when it had been folded. She felt a tremor of excitement; he was sincere, he was taking it seriously. Maybe he didn't really have something to do, maybe it was just to find a way to talk it over with Menghong. That was one of the laws of matchmaking.

'What do you think?' Menghong ran over and asked once he'd gone.

'I don't know.' She blushed again, afraid Menghong could tell what she'd just been thinking.

'He wants to meet you in Jiexin Park this afternoon.' Menghong took her arm.

Her heart jumped for joy. She hadn't felt like this in a long time. Maybe it had something to do with being away from the hospital and all the brightly-dressed people on the streets.

It was summer, but in the hospital she hadn't noticed it was the season to wear pretty blouses already. It was the first time all year she'd been out in something other than her uniform. Look at Menghong—she was wearing a white silk blouse with a bow. It made that clean face of hers even more bright and youthful. She wasn't even wearing an undershirt, and the wind blew her blouse flat against her body, outlining her breasts quite clearly. For some reason Menghong could always get away with such things.

After they'd gone for lunch at a restaurant, Menghong went to class, telling her to be sure to take a nap before her date. 'You must make yourself maintain a positive attitude.'

She didn't sleep. She retrieved a blue, patterned, crêpe de Chine blouse with short sleeves from under Menghong's pillow. It was the first time she'd ever worn such a beautifully tailored piece of clothing. Facing the mirror, she was pleased to see that suddenly she was showing off her waist and bust, and that her bare arms were light-skinned, albeit a little flabby. Not bad at all. She smiled at the mirror contentedly.

After she'd washed her face, she picked up the Meijiajing brand perfume Menghong had left on the table and, after a moment's hesitation, whipped out the stopper and casually dabbed a drop here and there. She smiled wryly: want to make him like you, huh? She couldn't pretend that wasn't somewhere in the back of her mind. Picking up the mirror, she examined the twenty-nine-year-old face in it. 'You don't look it, you don't look it at all. Your face is so fresh!' Even though the goodhearted old lady on the bus had said that, she couldn't make drooping eyelids and evident crows feet disappear. Oh well, why not? In an effort to convince herself she fit the image, she dabbed on some more perfume.

They were both very punctual at Jiexin Park. They walked together and sat down together. At first, when people glanced at them or passed by, she felt jumpy, but before long a happy glow took over. You're out on a date, she told herself. His hand brushed against hers. She wasn't sure if it was intentional or not, but her heart skipped a beat. She was scared he might go too far, but she also wanted to get a little closer to him. She began to enjoy the admiring and friendly looks they were getting from passers-by.

They were together all afternoon. Conversation was hard going at first, and just when they were beginning to laugh freely, it was already time to go. He said he had to return to his company the next day. She didn't say anything about seeing him off, because she wasn't really sure what she wanted to do. She just felt that she was comfortable enough with him, that they had a lot in common.

'The first impression's very important. I think you should go and see him off.' That's what Menghong said after she'd heard all the details. Only then did Xiaoyu realize she'd forgotten to ask him which train he was taking, but she could vaguely remember him saying 'around nine o'clock'.

She got to the train station before it was even half-past seven. You're really stuck on him. How could he be here this early? But if she went back there'd be nothing to do, because Menghong had gone to class already. Sitting around on the bed by yourself fidgeting; you might as well wait here awhile. She stood beside a small kiosk opposite the station. An old man was laying out his wares in the empty space next to her. He was selling malted candies. She was going to move on, but stayed put. She pulled a couple of coins from her pocket; maybe a few candies would help kill the time. As she sucked on a piece, she remembered childhood pleasures. Back then, if she had five cents' worth of malted candies in her pocket, she felt rich as a princess all day long. She couldn't help smiling. Suddenly, someone was calling her name. Damn, it was him; he was early, too. She felt annoyed, although whether at him or herself she didn't know. Instinctively, she jumped away from the stall, then she slipped the candy from her mouth into her handkerchief, pretending to wipe her face. At least it hadn't stuck to her teeth. She knew this must have made her look taken by surprise, or at least awkward. She couldn't tell if he really hadn't noticed, or if he was just pretending.

Why are you so inhibited, even about a little thing like that? Afraid he'll look down on you? Or do you think it's conduct unbecoming an officer?

They met three times in all, and they weren't together for a total of more than five or six hours. Not even enough time for her to figure out whether she might fall in love with him or not. As far as she was concerned, love was no abstraction but something very specific, and that was what she wanted too. She felt tired and worn out. She needed to flop beneath a tree and catch her breath, needed something to hang on to. Oh, the endless road of life.

They started corresponding. They didn't go beyond what they'd already covered in those five or six hours of conversation; study, work, life and even the weather. They did go a little deeper into their expectations of a spouse and their ideas about marriage, their own strengths and weaknesses, their respective families...and that was about it, she thought. It was one letter every two weeks or so. His came punctually, and she answered promptly too. Finally, after six-and-a-half months, his letter came with a marriage certificate. This time, she didn't answer promptly. She waited two weeks—no, it was seventeen days.

'Don't rush it, Xiaoyu. I think the two of you should spend more time getting to know each other, and if you're still not a real couple after another six months, you'll know you're not really talking marriage.' Menghong came back specially from town to tell her this. 'I know he's a nice guy, but do you love him? Are you actually in love?'

She couldn't answer; she didn't know. She just felt time was passing by, and doing repetitive nursing work surrounded by mountains on all four sides was grinding her down. She waited for a wave of passion deep in her heart, but there was none, and maybe there never would be again.

'Xiaoyu!' Commissar Lu straightened up behind the little wattle fence around his house and called her. She wasn't sure exactly when he had started, maybe since he'd become a political commissar, but Commissar Lu maintained his little vegetable garden enthusiastically now. Any lunchbreak she passed this way she was sure to see him hard at work. Under the sun, his deeply lined brow would be dripping with shiny beads of sweat. He could barely keep himself going mentally or physically, let alone adapt to the demands of today's ideological work. But was he aware of this? Menghong said, 'He's done a lifetime of political work without even knowing his own mind.' Xiaoyu didn't agree, but she did feel Commissar Lu hadn't quite come up to scratch.

Still, Commissar Lu was as concerned about her as ever, as though she was his own daughter.

'Xiaoyu, you'll be thirty in three months, won't you? You should get married. The Party's checked him out for you already. He's outstanding in all work-related matters, enlisted in sixty-eight when he wasn't even sixteen, and joined the Party in seventy before he was even eighteen. He's got a future ahead of him. Put in a request for marriage leave quickly. I've already spoken to your section leaders.'

She wasn't sure what 'future' the commissar meant. Politics? Business? Life? He used to speak to her like this. Looking at Commissar Lu's full head of graying hair and his kind, concerned look, she checked her incorrect thoughts. He's still the old commander, he's looked after you all these years, he even remembers your birthday, and he's taken a lot of trouble over you. A wave of gratitude coursed through her, and she nodded to him.

She went and got a marriage certificate to match his, and took a westbound train to him.

Almost without thinking about it, she was a married woman with a husband. No more snide remarks behind her back now, and no more exaggerated expressions of concern. Now she too had the right to talk about all those unmarried girls, men, children, homes and all the topics only married women could discuss with each other at the hospital. She'd never have to worry about old ladies asking all sorts of questions on the bus again. She was still in uniform, but she was a real woman at last. She tried to make herself think like that, but it was no good; on the overnight journey on the train she wasn't filled with all the excited happiness she should have felt. Women singers crooned endlessly about love and emotions over the train's loudspeaker system, but it wasn't her husband she thought about; she thought more about them, about Maomao, about Ding Zhu, and all those years already past and gone.

5

And that was how she, Qiao Xiaoyu, went off after a man she had spent five hours with face to face and corresponded with for six months. Because he was her husband. She didn't know why, but she knew she had to have a husband, just like all other women. After getting off the train, she had an eight hour bus ride before she finally reached the place where Tu Jianli was stationed. She stayed in the guesthouse at first but, with the help of the leaders and comrades, they were married within three days.

It was only on her wedding night that she understood what a mistake she had made. They had never spent more than five minutes looking at each other the way that really lets you look into each other's souls, the way that tells you things that can't be expressed in words. Their most intimate moment before they were married was when he took her hand as they were crossing the road. She didn't know what she felt right then; a bit queasy, maybe. His hand was hot and sweaty. Maybe because she didn't respond right away, he dropped her hand the minute they were across the road. It was late at night, so he couldn't possibly have been afraid someone might see. Yes, they were both in their thirties now and they'd come together at this age to get married, so why expect adolescent passion?

Get closer to him, closer still. You're getting married tonight, you're a couple now. That's what she told herself.

Together, they fixed up the office that had been lent to them as a sort of bridal suite: 'Is the bed okay here?', 'Where should I put the apples and candies?' He asked for instructions and was terribly cautious about every little thing.

'Why don't you put on a new uniform?' she said. Just now, when he'd bent to sweep the floor, she'd noticed he was going prematurely gray. How come she hadn't noticed before? She smiled wryly to herself; we'll get to know each other bit by bit, I guess. She turned her head to glance at him; he was sitting on the bed changing his shoes. Suddenly, her heart skipped a beat and she found herself thinking 'Flat-footed?' before she even knew it. He was flat-footed. Maybe the thought had just popped into her head, but she felt a little short of breath, shocked, disgusted even. She hadn't thought she could be this way.

She rushed to the window and flung it open. 'Aren't you bothered by the cold?' he asked. She didn't answer, she couldn't answer. She needed open space, the sky and a biting cold wind. You shouldn't be like this, it's not his fault at all. 'Prematurely gray', 'flat-footed'—it's not as though he's deceived you. He always exaggerated his shortcomings in his letters, but he didn't see these things as shortcomings he had to tell you about. Besides, even if he had, what could you do about it? Would you have based your decision on those things? No, it's all just because you don't know each other very well yet. Good heavens! With one last deep breath of the air outside, she closed the window and turned around. She didn't dare go on looking out the window, ignoring the fact that he was waiting for her. What would he think if he knew? Maybe every woman needs a period of adjustment when she gets married. Besides, mightn't you have some off-putting physical features of your own? One of your ears is bigger than the other; Maomao used to make fun of you for it when you were kids, although he was just teasing.

She flashed a smile at him, and although it was forced, it was apologetic. He smiled, too, but she didn't understand why.

After all the guests had gone that evening, she burst out crying, unstoppably, in torrents, heartbroken.

'What's the matter? What on earth is it?' He asked rather anxiously, as though maybe he'd done something wrong.

She didn't know. Perhaps it was nothing at all; perhaps it was everything.

He sat down on the chair in front of her, and after staring at her blankly for awhile, said, 'Maybe we should just call the whole thing off.'

She looked up at him, unable to tell whether the smile on his face was meant to mollify her or was a bitter comment on his own fate. His lips were cracked and dry. There's nothing more to be said. He's like you, he needs a home to return to. Neither of them had been looking for love, and neither had known how things would turn out. She didn't say anything. That evening, it was she who unrolled the quilt and got into bed first.

Maybe it was because they had such similar backgrounds and characters that there was nothing more to say to each other or wonder about each other. Or maybe it was because they were past the age when one is curious, and had reached a time when the windows of the heart close. Either way, they had pitifully little to say to each other and, as though they had reached an unspoken agreement, neither disturbed the other. The room was only fourteen meters square, but they each went about their business, quiet as quiet could be. They seemed very close, so close that there was nothing more to know about one another. At the same time, they were so far apart they would never touch the depths of each other's souls as long as they lived.

At meal times, he brought food back from the canteen. If there was any housework to do, sweeping, or dishes to wash, they'd compete to get to it first. After three days' honeymoon leave, he went back to work. She didn't know what to do with her remaining two weeks. Their so-called bridal suite consisted only of a double bed (made up of two singles pushed together), a table, and a few chairs, and none of it actually belonged to them. If she wanted to fix the room up, there was nothing to fix up. It was cold outside and because the base was so out of the way, there was nowhere to go, nothing to do. Her mood was as cold as the weather, and she didn't have the heart to read novels, never mind professional books. A dozen pages and she'd realize she hadn't retained a thing; she'd even forgotten what the book was about. And although it was a big room and no one disturbed her day after day, somehow she felt there was nowhere to stand or sit. When she picked up the sweater she was knitting for him, if she didn't drop a needle, then she dropped a stitch. It made her mad enough to pull the whole thing apart.

Evening was when they had the most time together, but he often brought work home from the office. Did he really have to work nights to keep up? Still, it was better that way; what would they do if he was free? How much could there be to say? He felt the same, for sure. She knew it.

Sometimes, after dinner, he took her out for a stroll and a chat, but it was all empty talk about the weather, local lore, or jokes about what had happened at work. Humor wasn't his strong suit, however, and the laughter she managed out of politeness rang hollow and flat. Shortcomings can become lovable in someone you're close to, but the smallest thing can put you right off a stranger. I guess that's what they'd call a philosophy of life, she thought.

God! He was going through papers again. He never told her what these important documents were, and she never asked. Could there be anything sadder than this? She had no desire to understand him, to get closer to him, to become truly intimate with him, or even to make him like her, and this man was her husband.

She flipped through the song book with the red plastic cover that she took everywhere with her. Page one: 'Xiaoyu, I wish you every happiness'. Page two: 'The Sun is Gold in Beijing'. Page twenty: 'Katyusha'. Page twenty-five: 'Where Do the Frogs in the River Come from?'. Page one hundred: 'Our Lives Are Full of Sunlight'. She went through one page after another. She realized that over the years, all her feelings, yearnings, desires and rushing emotions had been poured into this book. So many beautiful hopes and dreams, and so many waves of intense, heart-rending emotions had all been buried here. She came to the crumpled note written in ballpoint pen; it was the one and only thing Ding Zhu had given her, and all these years she had treated it like a song lyric.

Someone was standing behind her. It was him, and she didn't know how long he'd been there. He was fighting to keep his breathing even. She'd never felt like this before, and she wasn't sure what to do. Maybe then, at that very moment, if she had shut her eyes and leaned back a little, that man behind her would have held her gently, softly caressing her head and her face, giving her all his expectations, longings, losses and hopes. But she didn't. She realized her feelings for the man behind her weren't even as strong as for the book she was holding. She closed it and stood up, turning to look at him. His tender, expectant gaze froze, and turned in an instant to betrayal and hurt. He blushed and smiled awkwardly.

The moment to touch souls had passed them by, and they closed the windows of their hearts again.

That night she couldn't sleep. Did she regret her callous behavior just now? Who knows? But she was waiting; if he would only call out 'Xiaoyu' softly, she would cuddle up to him at once, tell him everything, and ask everything of him. But he didn't; right through to dawn he didn't call her. She knew he hadn't slept, either. Just like all the other comrades, he never addressed her directly by her given name. What was he thinking? About another woman? No, that was impossible; his background was too similar to her own. So why couldn't they talk it through? Why did they both have to guard their emotions so stubbornly, each watching the other so carefully? She'd so wanted someone to go through this world with hand in hand, facing every difficulty and enjoying every happiness together. But is what you have now the love you've longed for ever since you were a child? She didn't want to think about it.

Early the next morning before he left for work, he asked if there was anything the matter, and she said she wanted to go back, back to Hospital 547. Why didn't he seemed surprised, or even try to dissuade her? He just said they'd discuss it when he got home from work. 'Get some rest now, you didn't sleep well last night.' He knew everything. But what use was resting? As though that was what she needed!

She left, leaving a note.

6

Finally, she had reappeared in Maidenhome a married woman; a fulfilled woman. This morning's awards had taken place immediately afterwards.

She'd never felt this lonely before. It was even more unbearable than her loneliness as a single woman in Maidenhome. She took out the transfer request; she had thought about it more times than she could count today, and more timidly each time. Would the leaders approve it? And what if they did? Where will you go? Back home, or to him?

Her head was a lot clearer once she got out of bed. The sounds of laughter, singing, and horsing around floated up from the first floor. Somebody was making a terrible racket playing that leaky old accordion off-key.

It was after eight, and the supper Menghong had brought was stone cold by now. There had been a little hot plate in room 307 once, but it had been confiscated after Commissar Lu had cut the electricity to the outlets in all the rooms in Maidenhome. When the meeting broke up that morning, he had asked her over to dinner, saying his family was making dumplings. Nurse Chen had asked her over for spring rolls, too. It was the first day of spring, and everyone was making their best dishes, but she didn't take up either invitation. Think about it; what happy family wants a guest tonight? Even a best friend would be superfluous at a time like this. She was past the age for eating melon seeds and candies with a bunch of young girls, hanging their arms around each others' necks and singing.

She picked up the man's sweater she'd been knitting for six months but still hadn't finished from the head of the bed, then put it back down after a few stitches. She flicked through her song book again.

Someone knocked on the door. She was a bit irked that they would not leave her alone even for a few minutes. She kept quiet and ignored it. Whoever it was didn't give up, but called right out. Was it Yamei?! Had she quarreled with 'idiot' again? She opened the door. Yamei stood there smiling, her hair full of plastic curlers and carrying a lunchbox.

'Xiaoyu, you haven't eaten yet, have you? Great! Try some of these! I came by awhile back and saw the light was off so I thought you were probably getting some sleep before night duty and went back. We made these fresh specially for you,' Yamei jabbered away. Probably because she'd just climbed the stairs, she looked tired; her face was flushed and shiny, her brows and the corners of her eyes yanked up tight by the rollers.

'Come on, try them, try them.' Still standing in the doorway, Yamei opened the lunchbox and picked a spring roll out with her fingers, stuffing it in her mouth. 'It's got three different fillings, including shrimp.' They always ate the best. 'We're the only family making spring rolls on our floor. What do they know? Eating dumplings on the first day of spring! What's so great about them?' If you don't flatter her about their cooking, she'll never go away.

'Delicious! Your idiot really knows how to cook!' she enthused.

'Xiaoyu, let me have a look at the award you got today,' Yamei said, shoving the lunchbox into her hands and bending over to pull the cardboard suitcase out from under the bed by herself. She knew it was sure to be in there.

It had never occurred to her that Yamei would look at her third class merit award like that. Was it admiration? Envy? Or ridicule? Maybe all three. Probably to pre-empt Yamei's sharp tongue, she hurriedly said, 'Actually, I don't deserve it at all.'

'Stop it, Xiaoyu. You think it's all in a day's work, but it's fifteen whole years since we enlisted and came to this godforsaken place. Menghong said in the canteen today they should have given you a first class award. Who's been keeping the place going all these years? That's what she said. Who's taken all those thousands of day and night shifts? Qiao Xiaoyu, right? She even said that if she was head of the hospital, she would have given me a third class award, too. She's okay, that Menghong.' Yamei gave a sharp little laugh, a bit dismissive, but openly smug all the same.

Yamei left, her curlers bobbing along with her steps. That woman, she'd never get rid of her bad habits! Still, why should she? That was who she was; gossiping about you in the morning, then sweet as can be in the evening. Someone like that isn't worth getting too worked up about.

She got ready for night duty. Like the hundreds, even thousands of times before, she washed her face, dabbed on some face cream and combed her hair just before she left. It was important to give the nurse she took over from confidence in her and the patients the feeling that they could rely on her.

'Xiaoyu.' In the distance, she made out Commissar Lu smoking a cigarette under the light at the end of the path. She had thought she could slip by because it was dark and the old guy's eyes weren't too good, but he'd caught her. 'Night duty?' the Commissar asked. He knows I'm on duty, so he must be waiting for me.

'Uh-huh,' she didn't say anything, just nodded and kept walking. It's bound to be the same old thing; be modest and prudent, pride comes before a fall, keep working hard, and all that. This Political Commissar really fit the bill! Right now, perhaps for the first time ever, she didn't want to listen to anything he had to say.

'Xiaoyu.' He was still following her, panting up the steps. She slowed down. Grateful but embarrassed, he gave a little laugh. He didn't speak right away, but like her, watched his shadow stretch and shorten under the street lights.

'Xiaoyu.' This was the third time he had addressed her by name already.

What is the matter with him tonight? Does he know about the transfer request in my pocket? She felt a sudden twinge of anxiety.

'Xiaoyu, I've watched you girls grow up.' The usual opening remark, but she had not foreseen what followed. 'I'm old now, and I may retire soon. I've worked in this mountain hospital for thirty-odd years, and I've had my successes and my failures. I know many people curse me behind my back, hate me, and even long for the day I leave.' The Commissar paused for a moment, laughed wryly, and then continued, 'The senior officers who attended our ceremony this morning asked me whether I wanted to transfer to a unit in the rear. I won't do it. I said I wasn't going anywhere. If I cannot go on being Political Commissar, I'll plant crops or become a janitor, and when I die I want to be buried at the foot of the mountain behind Maidenhome. Thirty years! Human beings are sentimental creatures! Look, I even organized people to fire the bricks in this wall around the hospital!'

If someone you had considered your commander for years suddenly opened up his heart to you, you'd be thrown for a moment too.

'Xiaoyu, it's always been my greatest wish to see you all study well, work well, and avoid any trouble in your personal lives. That's what I wanted, but I'm not sure if I've been a help or a hindrance all these years. Xiaoyu, I know something must be wrong for you to have come back to the hospital so soon. Maybe I really am getting too old to keep up anymore or else people today are different, but after doing this work for decades, all of a sudden I feel out of touch. I keep thinking there's something I haven't said to you girls, as if I've left something out. But right now I can't figure out what it is. No wonder you all resent me.' Commissar Lu gave a great sigh, and shook his head very deliberately. Maybe he felt wronged. Maybe he was passing judgment on himself.

Xiaoyu suddenly brightened up. In his vague way, the Commissar had almost touched on what was worrying her. His words lightened her load, even moved her.

'No, Commissar, I don't resent you. I don't resent anyone, I...' She stopped and turned to look at the old, gray-haired Commissar following by her side. How should she put it?

'Xiaoyu, will you hear me out?'

What was the matter with him today? He almost sounded like he was begging her a favor.

'Xiaoyu, I think we should ask Tu to come and stay at our hospital for a few days. When people spend more time together, get to know each other better, feelings are bound to grow between them. Married people need mutual understanding. I want to tell him all about you. I've written him a letter.'

'Huh?!' Commissar, Commissar! She was overcome with emotion.

When Lu Zengxiang finished speaking, he was like a little boy who'd done something naughty. He couldn't look her in the eye, and turned away into the shadows beyond the street light.

'Commissar, I must go on duty. Take care and turn in early.' She had to get away or she would cry. She wanted to cry, not out of gratitude, and not because she felt bad, but as if she had something to be happy about. Future generations of girls in Maidenhome are sure to do better than me, she thought.

As she entered the wards the smell of lysol in the air perked her up immediately like a tonic. It was strange; she'd worked in the hospital for a dozen or so years, but the more familiar she was with these smells, the more they had that effect.

Maybe it was the smell of lysol that did it. Or the sound of the girls messing around. Or Menghong's bustling, or Yamei's spring rolls, or Commissar Lu's kind eyes. Because of all these things, she still hadn't handed in her transfer request. All that wondering what she should do and who she should hand it to was only an excuse she'd found for her hesitation. A place you've lived in for a long time is like someone you know well—once you become attached, even shortcomings become lovable. Could you really leave this place?

As for the transfer request, maybe it was all just a fantasy, a way of letting off steam under pressure, not for real at all. Or maybe she was placing too much emphasis on the ups and downs of her personal life? Has Maidenhome ever done you wrong? From fifteen to thirty, you've gone from a teenage girl to a Party member, from a girl who passed out at the sight of blood to a matron in surgery. Everything you are is right here, where they took you in and gave you everything. Your hopes and your dreams, your youth and your maturity—when you stop and think about it, you didn't even start your periods before you came to 547. She had felt too embarrassed to write and tell her mother. Her roommate Lingling and the other girls had had to help her.

Was there anywhere in all 547 she hadn't left her mark? A single ward, corridor floor or window she hadn't cleaned? Every test tube, bedpan, and urinal that was her job to wash and sterilize was done perfectly, and the entire military area knew it. Wasn't that her joy in life? 'Life may be tough, but you mustn't doubt your own worth.' She couldn't recall exactly when Menghong had told her this, but she was sure it was Menghong. Oh Menghong! If only she and Commissar Lu could be one person!

Yes, there are so many people here who will never forget you. If you do leave, they will be disappointed if they come back and cannot find you. They'll be as upset as you were that year when you couldn't find Maomao, or when you couldn't find Ding Zhu. Where else could you be treated like this and have such complete security?

There were two letters waiting for her on the table in the ward, one from Tu Jianli and one from Lingling. She opened Lingling's first, because it was her habit to leave important things to last.

Over the last few years, she and Lingling had become diligent correspondents; she had nearly as many letters from her as from everyone else put together. Lingling did not seem to have made any more close friends since leaving Maiden-home to get married, and so she wrote to her about every little thing. That's women for you; they cannot do without friends. Lingling never wrote to Menghong, but she never failed to ask about her in every letter, writing, 'Menghong is a real heroine.'

Tu Jianli's letter didn't come as much of a surprise. He couldn't blame her in a letter. But why didn't he blame her, call her names, even accuse her? Surely she was in the wrong, leaving that way without even saying goodbye? His handwriting on the envelope was as calm and clear as ever, like a stream never stirred by waves.

> Xiaoyu
> After you left, I did a lot of thinking. I thought about you, and I thought about myself. All those papers are still piled up on the table, but they've lost all significance now. Actually, I never really read a word of them while you were here, either. Are you laughing at me? I'm so stupid.

Suddenly, her eyes filled with tears, tears of joy and of sorrow. She read the first few lines over again, and then it continued like this:

> I must take most of the blame for what happened be-tween us. I really mean it. Now I'm leaving it up to you. I'm willing to accept any decision you make or action you take, so long as it is sincere and the result of careful consideration. I won't put any obstacles in your way at all, and I'll do my very best to help you sort our situation out.
> Still, I do hope that you will give me another chance and let us start over. I think we would have a good fu-ture together, and that we really can work things out.
> Anxiously waiting your reply,

> Tu Jianli

After doing the ward rounds, she read his letter again. Was he really ready for any decision she might make? Even leaving him? 'Actually, I never really read a word of them while you were here, either. Are you laughing at me? I'm so stupid.' For some reason she suddenly remembered the dazed, hurt look in his eyes that evening. Can I really let him go? The Commissar's right; why don't I invite him here?

For the first time in her fifteen years at 547, she broke hospital regulations by doing something personal while on duty; writing back to her husband, her new husband. She didn't answer the questions in his letter, but just wrote that she hoped he'd be able to visit as soon as possible, taking his annual leave early and spending lunar New Year and the Lantern Festival here.

She was convinced that here, in Maidenhome, she would be able to renew her relationship with her husband, that they would really get to know each other. Here you're young, attractive and self-assured. He's bound to fall in love with you.

In the morning, she handed over her duty record and walked out of the wards. It was a little chilly outside, but the air was so fresh it nearly took your breath away. She half ran to hand the letter to the person on duty in the mailroom at the gate so it would make the first mail truck. On the way back, she bumped into Ding Zhu. He'd come out to do his morning exercises, and he was carrying a book. He started over to talk to her, but she just smiled and waved. She didn't want to hold him up. Then she rushed straight back to Maidenhome. She didn't need anyone right now, not even Commissar Lu or Menghong; she wanted to figure out how to handle her affairs alone.

She needed to go into Maidenhome and pull herself together a bit. Then, after breakfast, as soon as she got to work, she'd hand her request in to the Party committee; not the transfer request, of course, but a request to borrow a room. She would fix it up properly, like a home. Then she'd write to Menghong in town, and ask her to buy her a paraffin stove. She was sure Tu Jianli would arrive within a week. She knew him.

The girls were all up. The metal wires sticking out of the red eaves on Maidenhome's little porch had already been claimed by the girls who got up early. The corridors, the washrooms and the toilets bubbled with laughter, singing and squabbling.

'Get your washbasin and toothpaste out of here, quick—I want to dump this water out!'

'Are you going to shit or piss? If you're taking a shit, let me go first. I'm going to be quicker than you.'

Nothing had been done about the shortage of toilets and washroom space in Maidenhome for years. Wait until summer and it'll get even noisier!

Going into room 307, she got a roll of toilet paper from under her pillow, picked up her washbasin and squeezed toothpaste onto her brush. She did that every morning; Menghong called it her 'morning trilogy'. She walked out of her room, and into the melody of Maidenhome's morning symphony.

Maidenhome, always so young and beautiful, so mysterious and deep. This was strength; a strength that could overcome everything, endure anything. It was a foundation, too; the foundation of her fulfillment.

translated by Chris Berry

Indica, Indica

The room is like a wok turned upside down, dark and close. The darkness has spread to your eyes; open or shut, they can't see a thing. Everyone on the kang* is sound asleep, and there is nothing but snoring, deep and ragged, high and thin, like the bubbling of a boiling kettle. When you're sure no one knows your eyes are open, you just stare into the darkness all night long.

You don't dare turn over; it is as if a rope binds you to everyone on the kang and any small movement will yank them all awake. Even your man—you don't even dare pull the tip of your braid out from under Eldest's shoulder. You are lying so close you can smell the warm air rising from his thick chest. It hits your face in gusts, now faint, now pungent, like the odor of drying mushrooms.

You are afraid those asleep will awaken, and even more afraid those awake will know you are awake too. The old woman at the end of the kang has coughed for the seventh time, muffling her mouth with the quilt. Two bodies away from you lies Two, who hasn't snored or turned over once. 'Two, isn't your neck sore? Turn over, go to sleep!' you plead in your heart. Let this long, dark night belong to you alone. Let your soft body regain a little strength, let your burdened heart find a little ease. Let the stifling, oppressive air in the room escape through the window seams, the door cracks. That hand, not big really, but broad and

* Brick platform bed heated from beneath.

hard, moved to the other side when Eldest turned over. But you still feel something tangible and real on your smooth, tiny breast. And your tight, tight underbelly.

Are you willing to go away with Uncle, your parents asked you! That day, a man came to the house. He didn't look much younger than Pa. Pa had you call him Uncle. Right away, Ma calls you into the kitchen, says that man lives in the northeast, he's rich, a good man. You don't know why Ma didn't call in Big Sister. There are four girls in your family; Little Brother didn't come till fifth. You are the second oldest, and because you are not as resourceful as the oldest and not as exacting as the youngest and not nearly as good-looking as the third, you have always been the most obedient. You know that if you assent to Ma, she will praise you for being sensible. She will smile, and she rarely smiles.

You remember clearly that first thing the next morning Ma gave you a really truly brand new pink guazi,* a pair of green nylon socks and a new pair of black cotton velour shoes. The shoes had white plastic soles and looked dazzling on, even if they were a bit too big. That morning, Pa said Second Oldest doesn't have to go to the fields today, she can do whatever she wants at home. Your two younger sisters eye you with envy. One says how pretty your clothes are. The other, how pretty your shoes are. In all those years, this is the first time you've received such regard at home, and you are right proud.

At noon, Uncle comes. Takes you. When you leave home you aren't sad and don't cry. Even though you'd planned to weep and wail like the others when that day came for you. You are just a little edgy in your excitement. Only that night, when you board the train with Uncle, and watch the trees and mountains flying past outside, do you realize the significance of leaving home this time. But what you wonder about most is whether your place in the bamboo bed you shared with Big Sister will be given to Third Sister. She'd been clamoring for ages to leave your parents' big bed and squeeze into the little bed you and Big Sister shared. When you think of these things your nose starts to prickle, and you quickly copy Uncle by curling up in the aisle and very soon are fast asleep.

After three days and four nights on train, truck and tractor, you are finally led by Uncle through the sturdy wooden door.

* Shirt with mandarin collar and frog clasps over the collarbone and down the side.

You've been hankering to arrive soon, for you truly no longer have the energy to keep up with Uncle. To get you onto the truck piled high with burlap bundles, he had to pull you up with a tug that made your arms pop and even now you don't dare swing them back. But you didn't dare tell him. Mountain kids aren't worth that much, and have all sorts of ailments that come and go. Also, it was lucky for you Uncle handled everything on the trip, or you wouldn't have known where to catch the train or get anything to eat. It was a chance for a silly girl like you to see the wide world, a chance that no one else in your village, not to mention Ma and Pa, would probably ever have.

Uncle leads you over to a couple in their fifties, pats your shoulder and says simply, these are your parents-in-law, be good now. And leaves. When they go to see him off, you just stand there in the middle of the room, eyeing the tempting clouds of steam rising from the wok on the stove against the wall, the lid of which is bigger than the millstone in your village.

'Daughter-in-law, come here!' comes the voice of an old woman from the inner room. You don't know whom she is calling; when you look around, there is no one else in the room. Then—you have no idea where from—a little person appears, so black from head to toe that, aside from the whites of his eyes, the only white is from two trails of snot. Snot nudges your arm, looks up at you and says, 'She's calling you, Daughter-in-law.' You glance at him in confusion; you want to tell him you aren't called Daughter-in-law. But you don't, because you are afraid the old woman will hear you and think you are contradicting her. 'She's calling you, Daughter-in-law,' Snot says again (only because the name is new to him), wrinkles up his nose at you and, quick as lightning, sniffles up those two trails of snot, which resemble thick boiled bean-starch noodles. All you hear is the gulp.

'Daughter-in-law, you're Daughter-in-law!' Snot reels to the floor with a scream. In no time, a dirty ankle appears on either side of his waist. The feet are stuck inside a pair of yellowed tennis shoes too big for the skinny legs. Straddled by Shoes, Snot howls in protest, and the two make ready to tear into each other. You quickly enter the inner room to dodge them.

They really are rich. A big kang, big enough to cover the whole world, stretches from the east wall to the west, taking up four-fifths of the room. The kang is covered with colorful paper, a big sheet of uncut candy wrapper. Maybe because it is so big and colorful, you don't know which way to look.

'Daughter-in-law, have a seat.' The old woman is sitting in the far back corner of the kang. You don't know whether to sit or not. Before your butt touches the edge of the kang, a young man comes in the door.

'Grandma, I'm home.' Maybe it is his red sweatshirt that makes his neck seem so white, so white you can see the veins. He bends over and pats the scufflers rolling into the doorway and says simply, 'Cut it out.' And sure enough they get up and leave the room. When he straightens up and sees you sitting on the edge of the kang, his neck reddens, yet he still says something loud and bold. You don't hear it; you are too nervous. You jump to your feet, but he has already turned and gone. So dumb one measly line is beyond you, you scold yourself.

Even by suppertime you haven't figured out just how many people are in the family. Grandma and Father-in-law are sitting cross-legged on the kang. They've given you one side of the kang table; Mother-in-law is at the other with the bowls and spoons. Children are inside, out in the yard, leaning in the doors and windows, eating from their own bowls in their own little worlds. You just stare into the bowl in your hands; you don't dare lift your head, never mind chopstick any food from the little table. You know how clumsy you are in front of strangers. The only aluminum spoon on the small table is not being used by the youngest person in the family at all, but by the eldest. The old woman is using it like a symbol of power to spoon up pieces of onion omelette from the coarse earthenware bowl, calling to everyone in the family. She is like a mother hen meting out food to her chicks, which include Mother- and Father-in-law, in their fifties.

'Daughter-in-law.' This time you know it's you she's calling, and you do as Father-in-law did and hold out your bowl. 'Eldest,' she says next, and this terrifies you more than when she called you. 'I don't want any,' abruptly comes a faint voice through the window. You brave up and glance over to see a squatting back with broad, square shoulders. He wasn't the one in the red sweatshirt, you think. The old woman puts Eldest's eggs in your bowl. Everyone in the room is watching, and this makes you very uncomfortable.

'My brother sure knows how to look after his wife.' Two walks in and the old woman calls him over. The red sweatshirt sets off his sweat-beaded brow. Your face burns and has got to be red. You are both afraid and happy, because of what Two said, and for Eldest's eggs.

After supper, Mother-in-law has Four wash the dishes. That was Shoes. I should be doing it, you think, and say, but everyone ignores you—they are all busy rolling cigarettes as if nothing could be more pressing. The tobacco is kept in a bamboo basket that is put on the kang and pulled back and forth as if greased. They use little papers in the basket to roll the crumbled tobacco into horn-shaped cigarettes. Even Five—Snot—leaning next to Grandma is rolling up faster than the old woman herself. In no time the room is so thick with smoke you can barely open your eyes.

That night, you are put between Mother-in-law and the old woman, and go to bed very early. The warm kang is big enough for everyone's fatigue after a long day. You are asleep as soon as your head hits the pillow, and have no idea where the others sleep. When you open your eyes the next morning, only you and Five are left on the kang. A shaft of dusty sunlight brazenly swims between you. You don't know how long Five has been awake; he is staring at you spellbound with yellowed eyes, and grinning, baring two yellowed little canines. Embarrassed, you sit up and dress quickly, whereupon Mother-in-law yanks open the door curtain and bustles into the room, folds up Five's quilt and slaps him on the butt. The child jumps up with a yelp and quickly covers his privates with his hands. Heavens, he isn't wearing a thing. You smile at him, remembering how, dressing your little brother back home, you always called him Spigot.

When, after washing and combing, you come out of the inner room, Mother-in-law hands you a bowl of congee. Your chopsticks find a hard boiled egg inside, big and white and slippery, which you nearly drop on the floor. Before you finish your congee, Mother-in-law hands you thirty yuan.

'Go have a look around the commune; buy whatever you like.'

'No thanks.' You have never held so much money.

'Take it. Just have a look around. Take the big dyke; it's just twenty-some li.'* You continue to resist, but Mother-in-law says, 'If we weren't so busy in the fields I'd have Eldest

* A Chinese unit of distance, about one-third of a mile.

take you.' At that you quickly take the money. Mother-in-law's hand is coarse and warm. Just outside the door you are stopped by: 'Don't forget to buy two catties of soy paste; we're having cold noodles for supper tonight.' Mother-in-law hands you a small crock. Your heart is eased considerably by such trust.

Early May is when the pagoda trees bloom. Blossoms of white mist and radiant yellow that block out sun and sky turn a two-dozen-li-long dyke into a flowering arbor. A light breeze blows over the fields, bearing the damp, sweet fragrance of the trees. Suddenly you're short of breath. Heavens, what is it?! *Indica*, it's got to be! You've never seen them, but at first sight, at your very first sight of these flowers so purple they set the heart a quiver, you know they're indica. Don't panic, calm down, look around. The horn-shaped flowers are blooming beneath every pagoda tree. Your heart swells with the thrill of your discovery; you can feel your thin chest about to burst. The flowers you've been looking for and singing about for ten years are like what you'd imagined, and yet not. The purple is deeper, the petals thicker, the stamen more erect.

The year you were eight, a girl about your age called Lili came to the village. She was the granddaughter of Wineshop Granny Wang, come to spend summer vacation. Many many times, coming home from grazing the water buffalo on the mountain, you saw Lili skipping a length of fine elastic in Granny Wang's little bamboo-fenced yard. She sang a ditty as she skipped. You watched entranced outside the fence. Lili jumped so beautifully, her little round white legs deftly kicking and twisting back and forth, lifting her pretty dress like a big butterfly fluttering its wings.

'I'll teach you to jump, okay?' Lili called warmly out to you each and every time, but you always reddened and refused. It wasn't that you didn't want to or that you didn't know how. When you were grazing the water buffalo you took the rope used for bundling grasses and put it on the ground and practiced jumping, and you kicked and twisted just like Lili. But you couldn't jump rope with Lili. You didn't have a flowered dress like hers—you didn't even have shoes. Your black black bare feet, and even your calves, were covered with mud from tending the water buffalo. You buried your feet in the grass—despite the burrs—till they hurt.

Indica, Indica,
Not afraid of wind,
Not afraid of rain.
We work all day and
Have something to say:
Please bloom now!

You learned the song and would stand in the grass outside the bamboo fence helping Lili sing. Over and over and over again. You were very happy. Later, Lili left, but before she did she gave the jump rope to you so you could learn it. She said, wait till next summer vacation and I'll be back and jump with you. She never came back, and you never jumped it, but you always remembered that ditty. Whether grazing the water buffalo or cutting grasses, you never tired of it; you sang it over and over again, to the mountains, to the trees, to all the flowers. There were no indica in your village, but you knew one day you'd find them. And now, no, right before your very eyes, these purple flowers are blooming so exuberantly at you, as if they know the girl before them, now 'Daughter-in-law', has sung for them for so long.

You count them as you walk along. You lose track but keep counting; at any rate you don't miss a single one, you don't leave a single one out.

The commune streets really are busy, with everything under the sun for sale. Street vendors are shouting high and low, beating little brass gongs, shaking rattle drums, doing everything possible to hawk their wares. When you notice the oil cakes frying to a yellow turn in the wok, your mouth starts to water. You hesitate before the smoky wok. Back home, Pa always said once you break a ten it's worthless. Don't break a ten for an oil cake; go and have a look around first. You make the effort and swallow that saliva. You walk past stall after stall, wanting everything, buying nothing. Better get the soy paste for Mother-in-law first, for you feel only then are you doing right by her.

There are hardly any customers in the State grocery. A few bored clerks are sitting huddled together watching the doorway; any customer at all is likely to become the focus of their conversation. A curly-haired clerk gets up and greets you warmly, ladles out your soy paste and asks where you are from.

'Chen'gecun Brigade, over by the big dyke.' You are quite willing to tell Curly everything you know because you'll be seeing each other often from now on.

'I asked whereabouts are you from,' Curly says again, really wanting to know.

'Hunan, far away', you answer, shaking your head, as if the place were no longer your own.

'Oh, I know, you're the daughter-in-law they bought down there, aren't you?' Curly brightens as if she's eaten a sour apricot, and her glad smile nearly splits her fat face. 'Am I right? Who's your husband's family? What...'

You want nothing more than to throw the crock of soy paste into that fat face. But you don't. You flee the shop and turn onto the busiest street, where you let out a deep breath. Looking back, you vow never to set foot in that shop again.

An old man with a red nose is shouting 'river shrimp for sale' and taking nips from a liquor flask—a shout, a nip—and then popping tiny gray shrimp into his mouth, cracking and crunching as if eating peanuts. The mouthful of saliva you'd swallowed comes rushing back. Go and get a yellow oil cake, you think. This time it isn't because the bill has been broken, but because you want to let everybody see, let Curly see—you are sure that fat face is hiding somewhere, staring at you—that you aren't a bought daughter-in-law, you are one of them, and you can buy whatever you like to eat on this street the same as they can.

'Damn!' comes a sudden screech like scratched glass from up ahead. All you see is a woman running like crazy through the narrow, crowded street. You jump aside and nearly knock the tray of oil cakes to the ground.

'You keep on running and I'll beat you to death, you little glutton!' The shout is a man's, the voice deep and resonant. Before you can figure out what is going on, the man and the woman are grappling right in front of you. The woman is big and tall, and the half of a red, cooked crab she is holding waves back and forth in the air with her flailing arm. Her hair tie has flown off somewhere, and her sweaty hair covers half her face so you can't really tell what she looks like. The man is dark and thin and not very tall, but he's strong; the veins on the hand clutching the woman are straining through the skin.

'I will eat it!' The woman keeps shouting, pushing the man off balance with all her might. 'I will! You never give me any of the money we earn. I'm damn unlucky to have married you...' The crowd roars with laughter. She has upped him one, and his seething face is as red as a cock's comb. Having gained temporary advantage and lowered her guard, the woman just stands there starting in on the crab again. Much to everyone's surprise, the man picks up a little stool beside him and hurls it at her without a thought. It hits her on the leg and she screams and staggers a couple of steps towards you (standing to one side scared out of your wits), as if asking you to steady her. You don't know whether to help her or duck out of the way. But before you can react, the crock of soy paste has hit the ground with the woman.

The crock smashes. The soy paste rapidly forms a puddle that looks, upon cold and level inspection, like watery shit. No sooner has the man grabbed the woman than they are rolling together in the puddle of soy paste. The onlookers form a tight circle around them. No one pays any attention to you or the soy paste on the ground.

With empty hands and an empty belly, you walk along the dyke, looking at all the indica still unabashed and in full bloom, and your heart is very heavy.

Another chime of the clock, four-thirty. Grandma at the end of the kang hasn't muffled a cough in the quilt for a good while; Two, three bodies away, seems to have turned over. They're all asleep now, and at long last no one is watching you or mulling things over as you are.

'I should get up and get to work,' you think. It seems this is the only way to lighten the guilt you feel. You gently extricate your braid from beneath Eldest's shoulder, but don't dare dress on the kang, for waking any one of them would amount to waking them all. The moon has escaped the dark clouds and shines into the room, casting shadows of the book-sized window lattice onto the faces and bodies on the kang, making them seem strange and distorted. Not daring a second look, you tiptoe into the outer room, clutching your clothes to your chest.

You yank on the five-watt bulb and see that the big beancake Mother-in-law had put in the big iron pot to soak last night has swelled to a pale yellow. Half of it is submerged, and half floats above the surface of the water. It takes nearly all your strength to lift it from the big pot. Whatever you do, you can't drop it, for that would awaken those in the inner room. Come what may, you dig your ten fingers into the surface of the beancake and hold it tight, till the spaces beneath your fingernails ache to the quick.

As Eldest did, you sit on a little stool. You brace the beancake upright between your heels and take the two-handled knife in your hands. Throwing your strength into it, you start shaving off pieces of beancake like wood chips. You don't know if it's because the beancake hasn't finished soaking, but inside it really is harder than wood, and after just a few chips, your collarbone aches so badly you give up. How did Eldest make it look as easy as slicing beancurd yesterday?

Eldest—you can't help remembering what happened last night, and that real, tangible thing presses down on your chest again... If you'd stopped trusting Eldest the way you did the night before last, if Two had stopped smiling at you as he had the day before, maybe you wouldn't have agreed to go on sleeping at the far end of the kang.

The day before yesterday, when you were walking back from the commune and had just reached the dyke, you saw a spot of red swaying in the distance. It's Two. When he smiles, his dry lips stretch white.

'Big Brother told me to come and meet you.' Without addressing you by name, he says, 'Where's your stuff?'

'The crock broke.' Your voice is tiny, and you work to keep it from trembling.

'What about the other stuff?'

You say nothing.

'Boy, you're really stupid. If you didn't buy anything you'll just have to give the money back to Ma.' He's already on your side. Your mouth is smiling, but your eyes well up with tears. He pretends not to notice, and walks back ahead of you.

Mother-in-law doesn't say anything about the broken crock, and she doesn't ask for her change. That day, she had moved your bedding to the far end of the kang. You notice— the only new bedding in the house. You are glad to obey Mother-in-law; since breaking the crock you haven't had a chance to make it up to her. Besides, you are happy to sleep at the far end. Back home, with your big sister, you were the one against the far wall. The mat near the wall had hidden all sorts of good things of yours—little mud people, a pair of burgundy cotton socks, things girls use when they become women—things you were too embarrassed to show even your mother. And an elastic jump rope, the one Lili gave you, which you gave to Third Sister when you left. Ma wouldn't let you take it with you; she was afraid they would laugh.

Everyone beds down except Eldest, who went out—you aren't sure when. Actually, he hasn't been inside since supper. Right up to the time when Father-in-law smokes his last puff and goes to bed for the night, he still hasn't returned. Mother-in-law has left a space between you and Five, but it doesn't have a quilt. This makes you somewhat apprehensive. But everyone acts as if no one has noticed, and you don't dare ask a thing.

Only when everyone on the kang is snoring and you too seem to have drifted off briefly do you hear someone tiptoe into the room. It is Eldest. He doesn't turn on the light. He feels around for his place, takes off his shoes, climbs onto the kang, and promptly curls up between you and Five, without even taking off his clothes. You can tell he is fighting to hold his breath, as if afraid of startling someone.

When you opened your eyes the next day—yesterday morning—Eldest was already in the outer room cutting pig feed.

'Let me,' you hurry out and say softly. You feel it is your job.

'You're not strong enough.' Eldest doesn't even lift his head to speak. He isn't at all full of smiles like Two. You feel something like regret.

After breakfast, Father-in-law gives you a hoe too. You go down to the fields with the men. You don't mind hoeing. You work with Eldest and Two, each of you taking a row. Father-in-law is off somewhere else. Eldest can really work, the hoe in his hands like a razor, quick and true, and before long he's put quite a distance between himself and you. But each time you work forward, you notice a good bit of your row has already been hoed clean. At first you think you have jumped rows, but you quickly realize that Eldest has been helping you. That way you can keep up with Two, and you like working with him. He tells you about things in the village, and often makes you laugh.

At first you are too embarrassed to laugh aloud, and make a point to keep your mouth closed and swallow the sound of your laughter. But later you forget and double over at the waist in gales. After all, you are a girl who loves to laugh. And Two seems happy to see you laughing; otherwise, why would he keep going on and on!

Mother-in-law brings lunch—onion cakes and pea soup. She sits to one side watching everyone eat, giving more to whoever has finished, just like at home.

As she is giving you more soup, she suddenly says, 'Daughter-in-law, later our house will belong to you and Eldest. When Two, Four and Five get married they'll have to build homes of their own.' You are embarrassed, and wonder why Mother-in-law said that. You look over at Eldest—his face is buried in his bowl. You look at Two—he is smiling, but there is something weird about his smile.

It is quite hot at noon so, following everyone else's example, you take off your overshirt, toss it to the side of the field and follow Eldest and Two back to the rows. You don't know why, but Two isn't as talkative as he was before lunch. You really want to explain, to tell him you'll still be living together, that nobody needs to go off and build a new house. But you don't know whether you should say that, or how. You find yourself somewhat irritated. Probably because you aren't paying attention and hit something hard in the field, the head of your hoe flies off, the handle still in your hand. Two turns around as if he's been expecting it and parts his dry lips into a grin again, a drink of mineral water to your heart. As if by magic, he comes up with a rock from somewhere and has you steady the handle at the bottom so he can pound from the top. You don't know why he pauses in mid-air with the rock, his eyes trained on your neck and his nostrils reddening. You think some strange bug is crawling on you and quickly lower your head. Heavens, it's because your shirt is too big and unbuttoned at the collar and you are leaning forward. Viewed from above, your breasts, not big but full nonetheless, are completely exposed. Everything, from the beads of sweat to your pink, pink nipples, is in plain sight. Flustered, you clamp your collar to your chest with both hands, not daring another glance at Two. My god, oh my god, you cry desperately in your heart, but when you lift your head Two has already fixed the hoe and gone off to work far away from you. He could work as quickly as Eldest all along. He'll ignore me from now on, you think, and your sad heart trembles.

At night, when everyone else is smoking, you take the opportunity to fill a basin of water from the crock and duck behind the wood pile in the yard to sponge off beneath your undershirt with a wet cloth. This is your bath. You hastily put on a clean undershirt. What happened in the field today left you unable to swallow supper; every pair of eyes in the family makes you flustered and confused. You long for night, the sooner to burrow into your quilt. Only when every eye is closed will your heart find ease. When you go inside, you see that Four and Five have been bedded down by Mother-in-law. The adults suddenly stop talking; whatever they've been talking about, no one is willing to catch anyone else's eye. Have they been talking about Eldest? His hand holding the cigarette is trembling. Tonight, no one goes out, not even Eldest or Two. As if they have been ordered to stay home.

When you lie down on the kang, you feel all the aches and pains brought on by a day's work, but you aren't tired. Four and Five start squabbling again, but a couple of slaps from Mother-in-law stops them; they don't dare move again and before long are snoring evenly. Two is different from usual tonight; instead of lying down with a book, unwilling to turn off the light despite Mother-in-law's repeated urgings, he shuts his eyes tight as soon as he is under his quilt. Sometime after nine Father-in-law beds down in his clothes, but Eldest is still squatting in the yard fiddling with something. You don't know why, but you sense that everyone on the kang except Four and Five is awake, but no one is making a sound, as if they are all waiting for something. What? Are they waiting for Eldest?

You don't know how much more time has passed, just that your eyelids have stopped obeying your will to keep them open, when you hear Eldest feeling his way through the darkness to the edge of the kang beside you, where he sits down and takes off his clothes, very gently, very slowly. But what happens next you never could have imagined in a million years—he tears back your quilt and jumps right in. Your whole body, including the back of your tongue, instantly hardens to stone. But you don't dare make a sound; all you can do is feign sleep, and use your body to hold down the edge of the quilt between you and the wall, as if that could keep you safe.

Has it been half an hour? The clock hasn't chimed at all; it seems a hundred years have passed, and then some. Your whole body is numb, particularly the lower half, which feels as if it is being pricked by countless tiny needles, and your chest is so tight you can't breathe. Eldest hasn't moved a muscle either; his arm against your back is as stiff as a two-by-four. Has he fallen asleep? Counting your lucky stars, you let out a breath and extricate the edge of the quilt stuck beneath you and move slightly to readjust the part of you that has fallen asleep. As if receiving some sort of signal, the moment you move, that strong, hard thing darts straight inside your under-shirt and lands on your chest. There is no stopping it. It is Eldest's hand, rough and hot, rubbing your smooth, small yet full breasts. You hear a sudden urgency in his breathing and somehow your stiff body softens, as if boneless, as if it does not belong to you...

You don't have the strength to push his hand away; you don't have the strength to escape; you don't have the strength to stop whatever Eldest wants to do. But you have the strength to sense this deathly still room, the sound of every heart beating on the big, long kang...Oh god, a searing pain below the waist, like being shoved into an icy river on a scorching summer day. Your whole body is bathed in cold sweat. You can't tell if the sweat is yours or his. Your whole body is like a piece of cloth, torn to shreds, floating away.

A sharp pain nearly makes you cry out. When you lift your hand you see bright red blood surging from the split nail of your middle finger and dripping onto the beancake, mottled yellow and white. You put your finger in your mouth and taste a fishy saltiness and for a moment cannot tell whether you are tasting blood or beancake. You swallow it. This is what you did back home; Ma said if you swallow your blood it can become your own again.

You are crying, and your tears silently yet uncontrollably run down your cheeks, along your nose, to your mouth. These are not tears of fright or pain, but tears that come from your sense of being all alone with no one to help you, no one to tell. Let them flow—you don't use your hand or sleeve to wipe them away, but let them flow to your lips and open your mouth and take them with your tongue. You lean against the wall behind you and savor the throbbing pain in your finger-tip, the tears running down your cheeks and their taste on the tip of your tongue. Still so stupid, you think slowly.

You don't know how much time has passed when you suddenly notice Grandma standing before you. And Father-in-law, Mother-in-law and Two. What's going on? You desperately want to know what exactly has happened, why everyone is surrounding you like this, their eyes so anxious and uneasy. Oh, that red-black face, that thick, short hair, those squat hands hanging from the sleeves. When you see Eldest standing behind

Grandma, it all comes back to you. You bury your face in your lap. If Grandma hadn't kicked everyone out and taken your arm and cajoled you, you never would have lifted your head.

You don't go down to the fields; the old woman won't let you. She shoos everyone eating breakfast off to the cooking area in the outer room. Including Four and Five about to leave for school. And she bandages your finger for you. Two borrowed some iodine from the neighbors. Eldest, you discover, is long gone, without having eaten even a bite of congee. Gone to the fields, shouldering his hoe.

The old woman settles you onto the kang for some sleep and has Mother-in-law red-boil two big chicken eggs and put them beside you on the kang. Except for you, and the old woman sitting on the kang weaving a basket, the house is empty. Even Mother-in-law has been sent off by the old woman to do something, you don't know what. You really can't sleep, so you clamber down from the kang and go out to the yard to feed the chickens. Grandma doesn't stop you, but you can feel her watching you through the window over the kang. The little yard is warm in the sun and the chicks, delirious with joy over the feed your hand lets fall, bump and roll into each other all over the ground.

'Comrade, may I come in?' someone asks. You lift your head—it's a girl student in her twenties with a big portfolio on her back. 'I've come to draw from life and got thirsty passing here,' the girl student adds with confidence and ease. You don't know what 'draw from life' means but you know she wants a drink of water. When you take her inside she makes herself right at home; without waiting to be asked she plops her butt down on the kang and greets the old woman.

'How many in your family, Grandma?' the girl student asks to be polite as she drinks.

'Eight, four grandsons,' Grandma says with smiling eyes.

'Where do you come in the family?' The girl student turns to you.

'I...' You don't know how to answer.

'She's the wife of my eldest grandson,' Grandma interjects.

'How old are you?'

'Seventeen.'

'Hahaha,' the girl student laughs as if she's heard something amusing. 'I'm all of twenty-seven and no one's wanted me yet!' She speaks frankly, without a hint of mocking you.

'Got your own place yet?' She cranes her neck towards the doorway as she asks. 'Then where do you live?' For aside from the outer room where the cooking is done there are no others. 'Here?!' Turning around, the girl student is amazed. You nod your head, admitting this fact to her without the slightest evasion, yet you feel neither meek nor shy. You even want to tell her that because Eldest is the oldest grandson, the oldest son, this house is his and yours. You won't have to move out. But when Two, Four and Five take wives they'll have to go off and build houses elsewhere. But you say nothing; you just think it. You're afraid she'll keep asking questions. She might ask how many years you'll have to wait before Five moves out. By that time your son will probably be...Ai, anyway, people like her are always so good at asking questions. And you've never liked answering them.

When the girl student is ready to go, Grandma has you see her off. Actually, she's letting you go off to collect yourself. You quietly pick up the eggs by your pillow.

'Are you used to it? Are you homesick?' See, sure enough, she asks another question, furrowing her brow, staring at you intently, as if she knows what you are thinking better than you do.

You don't answer her, but point to the flowers beneath the pagoda trees on the dyke, the indica so purple they set the heart a quiver, and tell her: 'Those are indica.' You think, I wonder if she knows that ditty.

The girl student goes off, still waving to you from the distance. You don't go back to the house. The indica on the dyke in unabashed full bloom in the sunlight fill your heart with a purple glow. The path off the dyke leads to your family's fields. Maybe you should give the eggs to Eldest; how can he do a morning's work on an empty stomach? Didn't Ma always give Pa two eggs as he went off to work in the fields? But you and Eldest won't be as poor as they, and when you have a child you won't send him or her off to graze the water buffalo!

'Indica, indica, not afraid of wind, not afraid of rain.' You sing that ditty once more, convinced no one can sing it as beautifully as you.

translated by Cathy Silber

Killing Mom

I killed my mother.

The mother who bore me and raised me, the mother who fed me every day, took me to the bathhouse every week, and got me out of bed every morning—that's the mother I killed.

Now I feel great, carefree as a goldfish just swimming around. Looking out the window, I see the poplar just outside with only a few leaves left; yellow and brittle, they sway though there's no wind, back and forth, back and forth, no doubt trying to figure out how the world so noisy just a moment ago so suddenly fell this still.

So silent, so still. Never in my life have I been this still, not even in my mother's belly. No matter how hard those few leaves sway, they don't make a sound. Not like in summer, when they forever rustled and whispered, wind or no wind. Anyway, I love hearing that sound and I love watching them. Starting with spring: first they kick up a skyfull of cottony fluff, which flies up my nose on my way to and from school, comforting me and making me uncomfortable at the same time. Then on the branches slender oily leaves appear, giving off a sweet smell. Next, before you've had time to understand what has happened so far, they're already lush green, blocking out the sky, shading the ground. Then it's like it is now. No matter when, I love them with all my heart. Whenever I'm the only one home, I watch them. I watch them with all my might, every minute, every second, I watch them and in watching them I forget myself. I forget to practice the piano, forget to do my homework, even forget to pee. Right up until my mom's shout and slap land. More than once I've heard her scream: I'll board up that window if it's the last thing I do. My mom has always been one to do what she says. This is the only exception, and the reason is very simple. If she boards up the window we'd have to turn the lights on in the daytime too, and she'd never run up the electric bill like that.

If the blood from my mom's neck hadn't flowed to my heels, if this blood hadn't soaked through my cotton shoes, if my toes didn't feel so sticky squishy in my shoes every time I moved, I'd go on watching and thinking. Quick, go and get the grownups! Maybe there's someone home next door. I think this, but don't move. My thoughts are absolutely powerless to direct my actions. This is a serious problem I noticed a long time ago.

I don't want anybody in here right now, jabbering, shouting, shrieking—what for? It was hard enough getting this place quiet. Wait awhile. Wait till the grownups come on their own. It won't be long. The walls in this building are full of cracks. Sometimes when the nice man upstairs mops his floor, the water soaks through our ceiling, and when my mom notices she whizzes up the stairs like a rocket to yell at him. Ha, ha, the nice man upstairs will never mop his floor again. My mom can sure scream; no synthesizer could beat her. Sharp and bright, like scratching glass, her voice can bore through several layers of cement straight into your ears. In our whole building, upstairs and down, there is no one who is not afraid of my mom.

Wait and see. It won't be long before her blood seeps through the ceiling of the people downstairs, just like the water from upstairs, winding like a worm. No, more like a snake, a long, long snake. I've never seen a real, live snake, but I've dreamed of one a few times. Only what seeped down from upstairs was water, and water is clear—when it dries you can't see a thing. My mom's blood is red and sticky, and when it dries I guarantee nothing will get it out, not even a pickaxe, unless the nice man who builds houses tears this building down and puts up a new one. But I hope the new one won't have these winding cracks.

Actually, I didn't mean to really kill my mom, I just wanted to kill her voice. When she is yelling and I'm scurrying away like a mouse I get this idea that I could go into her throat to see just what kind of a world it is in there that can produce such bloodcurdling sounds. I've always wondered if there wasn't some kind of electrical appliance installed down there. Have you ever heard the cry of a vampire on a starless, moonless night? You might not know what I'm talking about, because my good friend Xiao Min says there's no such thing as ghosts, only fairies and Snow White. Oh yeah, there's a garbage dump by our building that I'm afraid to walk by. Not because of the funny smell, but because some nights two stray cats fight there. They roll together and howl. They don't want to bite each other to death, they want to rip each other's skin off.

Mom's blood is still gurgling out. To tell the truth, I swear I never knew one person could have so much blood. The blood is flowing straight into the onions, which seem to revive instantly. The wilted greens are snapping to attention.

My dad bought the onions on his way home from work at lunchtime, a big bunch of them. When I got home from school for lunch, my mom and dad were fighting about them. My mom said my dad was really stupid; this bunch of onions you bought looks okay from the outside but undo it and look inside and they're skinny and small and covered with mud to boot. My dad said he wasn't stupid at all, because he hadn't spent a cent on the onions, he'd traded ration tickets for them. But my mom said ration tickets are money. My mom has said that before, because I have a pretty little plastic chair that she got for me with ration tickets. I still haven't figured out the logic behind this, because if ration tickets are money, then why have ration tickets at all? Wouldn't it be simpler if they were both made into money or both made into ration tickets? Sometimes grownups like to think they're so smart, but they make something this simple so complicated it makes your head spin.

It was fun standing there listening to them fight. I didn't find it surprising at all, because it's like I heard them fighting before school was even out—I've got ESP. My mom and dad looked over at me, but didn't miss a beat. My dad pointed at the onions and said to my mom, you undid them so you can tie them back up. My mom said fuck off, I couldn't care less. My dad said then why did you go and undo them? My mom said because I'm the boss and I felt like it. (My mom always calls herself the boss. I remember my teacher said fathers are the boss but when I told Mom this she still went right on calling herself the boss.) My dad said, are you going to tie them up or not? Because if you don't I certainly won't. My mom said, if you don't you'll never hear the end of it! That's how my mom and dad fought, all the way from buying the onions to tying them up. Finally, I just couldn't keep from laughing, laughing out loud till my whole body shook like I had malaria. My number was up. Go wash your hands! My mom trained her voice on me again, just like a machine gun suddenly shifting direction. Served me right. As my mom spoke, she lifted her foot and kicked the splayed bunch of onions to kingdom come. That's how my house became the house of onions. Onions everywhere—sitting, standing, lying down, all over the floor, big and small, young and old, black and white, yellow and green, like one big happy family, Grandpa and Grandma, Mommy and Daddy, and grandsons and grand-daughters. So scared I peed my pants, I grabbed the soap and ran into the washroom. When I say peed my pants, it's not just a figure of speech. Whenever I'm excited or upset, I can't keep from wetting myself a little, so the crotch of my pants is often damp.

During lunch, my mom and dad talked about other stuff, as if the onions all over the floor had nothing to do with them. My mom shoved half the big plate of soy beef into my bowl, not taking a single piece of it for herself, yet saying, eat up now, eat as much as you can.

Because I have always eaten too much chocolate ever since I was little, my teeth are bad, and besides the beef was tough. Before I'd chewed two mouthfuls, it had lodged itself between my teeth as if racing to occupy some strategic stronghold, turning my mouth into a bulging jumble. Yet I kept stuffing soy beef into my mouth for all I was worth. Because if I didn't, Mom would do it for me. She smiled at me, her lips closed tight.

After lunch, Mom washes the dishes and Dad naps in the armchair, his face red and bright in the sunlight. I sit at the table rummaging through the school books in my satchel. Actually, Dad and I are both faking it—he isn't asleep and I don't feel like reading. I am figuring out how to escape so I can go to school and play hacky-sack. I made plans with Xiao Min and those guys earlier, and if I don't go they'll be one short. I don't know what my dad is thinking, probably close to what I am, though he wants to play cards, not hacky-sack. My mom is making quite a racket washing the chopsticks and bowls, as if determined to scrape off a layer of skin.

It's five after one, and it takes eight minutes to get to school, five if I start running at the door. This means that if I leave right now, I could have twenty minutes to play with Xiao Min and those guys before class. My heart is nearly shouting out loud over this plan of mine.

Cong Jie, where are you going? A bolt from the blue. I always wonder whether my mom really has grown eyes in the back of her head. I know what will happen if I pretend I didn't hear, but I move towards the stair without looking back. You come back here! Come back! The words barely out of her mouth, my mom has caught me, and with a hand still greasy and smelling of food from washing the dishes she grabs my collar and drags me inside like a stray chicken.

Teacher told us to come back to school early! Teacher told us to come back to school early! I know Mom knows I'm lying, yet I keep on telling this lie. You little cunt, lying to the boss. Mom pushes me staggering into the room and I land on a grandfather onion. The smell of onions fills the room. Teacher did so tell us to come back early! I stand my ground. You little motherfucker, you lie one more time and I'll kill you! I don't pay twenty-five yuan a month for piano lessons so you can go out and play! Mom's got her hands on her hips. I've only got fifteen minutes I say. You still have to practice, or else read your music, she says. I stay standing there on the onion. Though I know what the next episode will be, I just stand there. Sure enough, a big bang in the back of my head—Mom's slap has landed. When I still don't move, another bang. I still don't move, not that I don't want to, but I just don't. Not for any particular reason either, my mind is just blank. I have been like this for years.

Mom throws kicking in with the slaps and pushes me to the piano as I fight to regain my original position. Her slapping starts up again, her mouth still screaming—but of course she has never stopped screaming. The components in her throat are turned on full blast, spitting strings of speech more rapid than machine gun fire. My hair stands on end, and the crotch of my pants is wet again. Maybe because ever since I was little my mother always gave me haircuts so short they couldn't be shorter, I've always had great hair. Black and stiff and healthy, when the hairs stand up they pierce my scalp like needles. I suddenly screw up my face, cover my head, and start screaming for dear life, stop hitting me, stop hitting me, you're beating me to death, stop hitting me! Actually, I've never felt any pain when Mom beats me, I just hear the sound. This is nothing—if you don't mind me I'll kill you, she says. I start running around the room, but she shows no sign of flagging. At the smell of victory she'll move in for the kill. I am running, dodging onion after onion, squealing myself hoarse like a hog before slaughter. Actually, I just hear bang upon bang; I don't feel a thing.

My dad's still napping like the dead. You could drop an atom bomb on him right now and he wouldn't look at us or say a word. Yet I am convinced that the sound of our screaming would wake even the dead. But do you know what it would mean if a live person intervened at this point? My mother would, without a moment's hesitation, turn her eight thousand watt voice on you and blare you to death. So you who are alive are really much better off pretending to be dead. Our neighbors have met this fate so many times by now that no one will come. Still, I keep on screaming and jumping all over the room, as if my mom and I were part of a major competition, each desperate to win, braying like donkeys. Right up until my dad says, it's almost one-thirty, Cong Jie will be late for school. Only then do I make my escape. You know without even having to think about it that my father is now taking over for me, right up till he goes back to work at two.

The devil only knows what evil possessed my mother to make me take piano lessons. One day when I was six, she came to get me at kindergarten looking prettier than I had ever seen her. Her face glowed, her eyes glowed, even the sound of her voice glowed. She said, Jie, would you like to be a pianist? I said yes. I had seen lady pianists on TV. They had long, long hair and wore long dresses like fairies and I wanted to be like that more than anything. But Mom always cut my hair short as boar bristle, too short for a bow. Now, all of a sudden everything would be fine. I could grow my hair out, and Mom would never again snip snip snip with her big iron shears at my scalp. When we got home that day, she carried me up the stairs, my arms around her neck, smelling the pomade in her hair.

I had no idea I would hate the piano so much. I began hating it from the very first moment I touched that white keyboard. From then on, every time I opened the lid I felt the piano was a huge mouth filled with enormous teeth about to eat me up. I didn't set out to make Mom mad, I just utterly lacked ability when it came to the piano. From the day I started kindergarten, the singing and dancing of my little classmates never had anything to do with me. One time when our class put on the dance 'Little Kitten Goes Fishing', Teacher had me be the butterfly. Rehearsals went pretty well but the first thing that happened the day of the performance was me taking a big fall, and the second thing was peeing a big wet spot on the butterfly's skirt.

It's been nearly four years since I started the piano and I've never even played a triplet right. At first I always played them as dotted notes, and later, after my teacher's repeated corrections and my mother's forking over yet another hundred yuan, I finally showed a knack for playing them syncopated. I know my piano teacher gave up all hope for me a long time ago. She keeps teaching me because, one, she can't resist Mom's compliments each time she brings me for a lesson, and two, because she needs the money. Think about it: at twenty-five yuan for four hours a month, if she teaches four students sixteen hours a month she makes more than a regular salary. Nonetheless, I have deep sympathy for her, because this one hour a week is pure torture for her. My mother is the only person on earth convinced I'll be Chopin reincarnate. Even though one time she called him Hopkins.

Actually, I'm not completely untalented. What I like best is making paper flowers, doing handicrafts, making little people out of modeling clay, that sort of thing. Teacher Li in kindergarten said my paper flowers looked just like real ones. Every time we did crafts, she always gave me more colored paper than the other children, and she always made a point of sticking my paper flowers on a big white sheet of paper for all the children and parents to see. Teacher Li even gave them a name, 'Bouquets'. Teacher Li said this was art too. It was the proudest moment of my life. I've never been that happy since leaving kindergarten.

At home, Mom won't even let me touch the scissors to make any more flowers. I used to try making some more anyway. Not only did she yell and hit me and rip my work to shreds, the last time she even ripped my 'Bouquets' right off the wall. By the time I lunged for it like a wolf protecting her young, it was already too late. Mom waved it around in the air a few times, crumpled it up, flung it to the floor and stomped on it with all her might. Go ahead and make more of these stupid things, go ahead! she shouted as she stomped. I just stood there watching my 'Bouquets' being stomped to smithereens by Mom's black leather pumps. Judgment Day had arrived. It seems like it was from then on that my mind lost the power to direct my actions.

Actually, I didn't mean to really, truly kill my mother. What would I want to kill my mom for—no one in the world loves me more than she does. I can't even count all the things she does for me in a day. She buys treats for me, makes me new clothes, sometimes even helps me with my homework. She empties my potty first thing every morning, and props my feet on her chest to cut my toenails.

My mom has a pair of very sharp scissors. Never mind how heavy they are when you pick them up, I guarantee you they're sharper than my dad's razor. My mom often cuts my toenails with those big scissors. Whether I want them cut or not, no matter how I try to escape, all she has to do is prop my foot against her chest and my heart is in my throat. Because the slightest struggle on my part and she'd snip my toes right off, sending them rolling all over the floor like broad beans. So the moment her scissors touch my toe, all I feel is an icy instant when my toenail is nearly yanked out at the root. A couple of times I couldn't even go to gym class the next day—my toes hurt so much every time I jumped, it was like walking on coals. I truly cannot fathom why my mom loves cutting my toenails so much; it seems to have become an addiction with her. She checks my feet from time to time, and if the toenails haven't grown enough for her to cut them again, she sighs with great disappointment, shakes her head, and then clips her own. I've noticed that she cuts her own toenails just as ruthlessly, down to the red tender quick that hurts so much even she grimaces. When Mom finishes cutting my toenails, she calls to me sweetly, Jie, come here, let Mommy kiss you. At times like this I really want to cry.

I really didn't mean to kill my mother, I just wanted to stop her from making noise, that noise that can penetrate layers of cement walls, that can bore into my every hair, my every pore. If my mom would merely beat me, she could beat me any way she likes—up and down, side to side, jumping, sleeping—just as long as she doesn't make noise. Or take what she wants to yell at me and write it on the walls, the floor, or hang it from the sky—this I could take. I've dreamed more than once how wonderful it would be if she were mute. Then she would be the dearest, the most lovable, the best best best best mother in the whole wide world. Why can't my mom be mute?

Mom's blood is making bubbles as it flows. I think as long as no one disturbs her this blood will flow a lifetime. The onions are lapping it up. The old onions have turned young again and the baby onions have grown up, all of them growing, out of control. The onions that haven't eaten my mother's blood are crowding desperately forward. Little onions become big onions, big onions become bigger onions—now my mom can't yell at my dad for not getting his money's worth. These onions are growing so fast it's enough to blow your mind. They are moaning, as if unable to bear this boundless joy, yet they desperately press on, turning themselves into mighty things like stalks of ivory, jabbing and poking at me. One is about to bump the tip of my nose.

When I made it back to school after lunch, our math teacher had already begun passing out exams; only then did I remember today was the midterm. The teacher didn't ask why I was late, she just told me to hurry up and take my seat. I like this math teacher very much; she looks a little bit like Teacher Li from kindergarten. She wears white glasses, and her voice is like a brook, so gentle it just flows right into your heart. Our math teacher is giving instructions as she passes out the test, probably things like write neatly, don't rush, and when you're finished check your work. I'm just guessing here, for I haven't actually heard a word she said. Or, to be exact, it's not that I didn't hear what she said, just that I didn't hear the content, only the sound of her voice.

Oddly enough, I'm not a bit nervous when I get my test, not like other tests, when, the moment the teacher starts passing them out, my heart starts drumming in my chest, beating so hard my mind swells and my head spins and my stomach does flipflops right up until I turn my paper in. This is because my eyes are on the move from the moment I get a test. I don't know where I got this bad habit. It doesn't even matter whether I know the answer or not; I always have to see it on somebody else's paper before I'll write it down.

The test today is very easy, the problems printed neatly and clearly. As I look them over, my heart is not drumming, but so calm I'm shocked. I even wonder if something's the matter with me to feel that every problem is so laughably simple. Reading through them, I'd be laughing out loud if I didn't control myself. I take out a pencil, prop my chin on my other hand to create the appearance of deep thought, and fiercely guard my paper with my arm, as if afraid somebody will copy from me. When the teacher walks by I give her a smile brimming with confidence, and she gives me an approving nod. Then with redoubled energy I cast my eyes skyward, thinking so hard my brains nearly leak out. When my eyeballs ache from so much darting back and forth, I strike a pose one hundred and ten percent earnest and bend over my desk to write, my hand moving so fast I cannot control it. I scribble and figure madly, like a great scientist, thinking this is the way Einstein did it, so why not? No one could possibly know the joy of victory swelling in my heart. My classmates look ridiculous sitting there agonizing—and what for? Even using their erasers, stupid pigs, all of them.

As far as I can remember, the math tests I have passed amount to less than twenty percent of the ones I've failed, but I've never been ashamed of this. One time the teacher kept me after school to help me when I was supposed to be at my piano lesson and my mother came charging in and got into a big fight with her. My mom said, this isn't part of your job, what's the big idea driving my Cong Jie this way, my Cong Jie is studying piano, her grades don't matter so much, but if you interfere with her piano and she doesn't become a pianist, you'll never live it down. My teacher couldn't say a word, she just stood there trembling. Another time, it was finals last semester, when I got a 37 in math, my mom and dad winded themselves beating me when I got home. But before I retook the test, my mom took three boxes of aphrodisiac to my math teacher. According to my mother's sources, my math teacher was looking for a man, and women looking for a man like aphrodisiac the best. As it turned out, my math teacher really did give me a 67, and I moved up to third grade without a hitch. Is my mom good to me, or what?

I am very smart—I wait to turn in my test until a whole crowd of my classmates is up there turning in theirs. This way my test will end up in the middle of the pile, and I know that by the time my teacher discovers the hieroglyphics and oracle bone inscriptions scrawled all over it, I'll be long gone. There's no way she can find me. Ha! Victory!

I make a break for it and run home as fast as I can. You know what treasure is waiting for me there? It's a secret I've been keeping all day long, but I'll tell you anyway: it's the scissors. That heavenly gleaming pair of scissors. I happened to notice last night after my mom cut my toenails she got distracted by something and set them on top of the wardrobe, forgetting to lock them in the drawer the way she always does. And she forgot all about it right up to lunch today. She didn't even remember when I glanced over at the wardrobe during lunch.

Mom forbids me to touch the scissors. At first it was to keep me from making paper flowers or doing crafts, and then because she was afraid I would maul my hands on purpose to get out of playing the piano. Once when I'd snuck the scissors I decided to cut off my left index finger so I'd never have to play the piano again. But because I was a chicken—or, more to the point, afraid of pain—I scared myself to tears as soon as I'd broken the skin. With blood spurting like a geyser, I panicked and grabbed my mom's pillow cover to stop the flow. It soaked through instantly. Afraid Mom would find out, I stuffed the pillow cover way inside the wardrobe, where it promptly stained several articles of clothing. My mom cracked the whole case in under a minute. She's a female Sherlock Holmes. I don't even need to tell you what kind of a beating I got that time. She screamed herself hoarse, and spent the next day in bed with a fever. All she did was moan, she couldn't even swallow water. From then on, she guarded those scissors with her life, always locking them in the drawer where we keep our money. They say that lock was my grandmother's, trusty as a lock can be or something like that. Don't even think about trying to get past it, not even if you turned into Houdini himself. One time I crawled under the table and tried getting my hand in through a crack in the bottom of the drawer, but I didn't get the scissors, and I nearly got my hand stuck in there for good. When I crawled out from under the table, I bumped my head so hard I got a knot the size of a superball that throbbed with pain for days and days every time I blinked.

I don't hate my mother at all. You know, that day she climbed out of bed moaning and groaning with a bad sore throat, she went right out and bought me the prettiest red coat. She said it was pure wool, very expensive. When I wore it to school, even the math teacher looking for a man just up and died with envy. Actually, it's all very simple: as long as I play the piano like a good girl and stop having so many wicked ideas, my mom would even bring me home a pet tiger if I wanted one. *I'll play the piano like a good girl and never make Mom mad again.* You could wrap all the times I've made this resolution, out loud and in my heart, several times around the globe. I have made this vow more times than all the sutras a monk chants in a lifetime. But it's no use, no use at all. I have done this so often, vowing with all my heart as I sit at the piano staring at the music, unable to bring myself to touch my fingers to the keys. Is there anyone out there who can help me explain just what the devil is going on with me?

If somebody could only make my mom understand that her Cong Jie is just not the stuff of which pianists are made, that her Cong Jie and music were simply not fated to belong together in this lifetime. If only my mother could understand this simple truth, I would play a hundred hours non-stop for her, never mind tiring myself to death, never mind spreading my ten fingers split into twenty. But at the thought of spending the rest of my life with this piano, my eyes go blank and the base of my tongue turns numb, not to mention my fingers.

I rush in the door and without even stopping to take off my satchel climb up on a chair to get to the scissors on top of the wardrobe. The instant my fingers touch the icy iron I nearly reel off the chair with excitement. Like a stray cat crazed with hunger snatching a fresh fish, or a starving rat stealing a piece of bread.

The world is so wonderful. I sit at the table, my heart as calm as a little white rabbit after a good night's sleep, my hands deft as two larks. I cut and snip away without a thought in my head. It's just a pity I don't have any colored paper like in kindergarten, but the sheets of my piano music aren't bad— they're big and thick. Exotic flowers bloom in my hands, blossom upon blossom; string upon string of magnificent butterflies open their wings and take flight; row upon row of happy little people bound forth... I am so happy, so calm, with just those few poplar leaves watching me silently outside the window, swaying for me. I have a whole world here, a world so wondrous, so glorious, so magnificent. Straight to the devil with all of you, Étude No. 9, Czerny, Beyer, math tests! My heart is filled with happiness and love, the brilliance of spring, a murmuring stream, Snow White, and a beautiful garden as far as the eye can see.

Yikes! As I live and breathe, those footsteps I hear are my mom's. She's home from work. My mom often comes home early to supervise my practicing. I ought to hide all this stuff this instant, right now. There's not a moment to lose. I think this. I order myself to do this. But it's no use. My hands are still flying along. It's not so much that my hands are bewitched so I can't stop them, rather, these scissors are scissors from hell, their flashing silver blades prancing like demons in my hands.

Cong Jie, open the door, my mom calls. I don't move and I don't make a sound. Cong Jie, I know you're in there! Hurry up, open the door! She starts pounding on the door, though actually the key's right there in her pocket. But she loves to bang on the door like this, like she just loves to hear the noise. I still don't make a sound, nor do I stop my hands. I know in my heart more clearly than anyone what will become of this, yet I still don't make a sound, or open the door. Now she's opened the door herself with her key. All of a sudden, my world disappears, just like that, gone forever. Swallowed up in the huge waves of my mother's voice.

All my flowers, my butterflies, my little people, have scattered, swept up by the typhoon winds of my mom's voice. I don't hear a word of whatever she's shouting and screaming, yet every one of the one hundred thousand hairs on my head and the million tiny hairs all over my body are standing straight up from sheer force of the vibrations, quivering, piercing my whole body like needles.

I really didn't mean to kill my mom as I raised in the air before me the scissors still clasped in both hands to keep her away, not to ward off her blows but to stop her voice, which had already left me unable to breathe. If I didn't stop it I would suffocate. Waving the scissors in both hands, I raised my arms towards her. I hear her shouting you're going to kill me, you're going to kill me, quick put those scissors down for your mother! Not only do I fail to stop, I leap forward, no, I positively fly into the air with all four limbs flapping. And so the scissors in that instant jab into my mom's throat, and so she collapses to the floor with one last gulp, and her blood begins to flow. To tell the truth, I was very disappointed in my mom's last sound, not at all of her caliber, neither very loud nor tragically impressive, more like an old mother goose. Only when she fell could I open my mouth, my nostrils, all the pores of my body, and take a deep breath. One second longer and I'd have suffocated for sure.

My mom's blood is flowing into a puddle. Enormous brilliant red flowers are blossoming forth from the base of her neck.

And I feel fine now, thinking how quiet it is. Though I no longer feel like cutting more flowers. I am quietly sitting here. I am not afraid, not afraid of anything. The onions on the floor are still growing at full speed, and I know beyond all doubt that by the time my father and the grownups discover all this, I will be long since covered by onions, along with my mother, grown into onions. All they'll need to do is clear out these onions they've never seen before. On top of which, naturally, many exotic flowers are blooming.

translated by Cathy Silber

The Other Woman

1

There was a notice on the blackboard outside the theater offices:

> 8:00 a.m.: Discussion of Comrade Wang Keke's play, *The Chair*.
> Place: The Big Room.

Close by was another notice saying:

> Deep fried fish will be selling at two yuan a kilo in the canteen this lunchtime.

I felt like a fish about to hit the pan myself, poised between life and death.

The so-called Big Room was the largest room in the theater besides the rehearsal room, and it was a mess, piled with costume trunks, props and I-don't-know-what from every dynasty. When I saw my scripts printed at last and stacked ready on a big wooden trunk, a feeling I can't put into words came over me.

I didn't hear the theater head calling me over to the padded chair next to him, but headed straight for the big wooden trunk, as though the scripts had grown arms and legs and were dragging me over. Just one short, deep breath and I could smell their inky scent. It made me feel warm and secure. It was their breath.

People filed in, the early arrivals taking the best seats, or failing that, the best positions. They were all big shots in the theater, or at least they thought they were. Little Bull arrived. He was the actor everyone thought had the greatest future. A drama school graduate, he was a handsome guy with straight eyebrows so thick they almost grew together. To show off his muscles, he liked to wear tight T-shirts in all sorts of colors. Little Bull and I were in the same graduating class, and later we were assigned, one after the other, to work in this theater.* He insisted he'd acted in a sketch I'd written in college, and that we'd danced together at a student get-together back then. He said I was very slim at the time, but I'll be damned if I can remember ever being slim. Still, it didn't matter whether what he said was true; in our two or three years at the theater, he had always been my best friend. He was the most ardent supporter and devout worshipper of every play I'd written, even those last two things, which had been killed at birth.

For my plays, Little Bull could argue himself red in the face, neck bulging, haranguing people till he was fit to burst, and utterly regardless of whether he got the original meaning of the work mixed up or not. Nevertheless, he was the one I wanted there the most, because as long as he was around I couldn't feel isolated.

As soon as he saw me, Little Bull grinned and made his way past several other people over to me. He parked his butt on the other end of the big wooden trunk, stretching his long, thick legs out in from of him. No matter what the season, he always wore those springy-soled sneakers with lots of white stripes, as though ready to go rock climbing at the drop of a hat.

The theater head said a few opening words, much the same as he'd said the last few times, then the discussions warmed up pretty quickly. That's the good thing about actors—they aren't stage shy and when they get talking they sound good regardless of whether they are making sense. They especially like new words. I don't know who it was, but recently someone had imported the catchwords *ego* and *superego*, and so many people embellished their speeches with them I didn't know whether to laugh or cry.

The doorway lit up; it was Meilun. She was wearing a bright yellow dress of the type most popular on the streets that year. I don't know why, but that color always reminds me of the

---

* Under the traditional socialist system, upon completing education, young Chinese do not go out and look for jobs, but rather are assigned work.

big mango Chairman Mao gave the worker's propaganda team years ago.* Meilun was twenty-three. I don't know what dance troupe she came from. The way she told it, she couldn't dance anymore after she'd had a knee injury for two weeks, but I think it was because she was overweight and no male dancer could lift her or, at least, if he did he'd be completely winded. I have no idea which leader it was who loved talent so much he thought a pretty face was all one needed to act. God knows why, but whenever I saw her, my gums ached. Whenever that girl showed her face, in a meeting or backstage, she was always clutching a big, thick, hardback book to her chest. If it wasn't *An Anthology of William Shakespeare's Plays* then it was *A Collection of Essays by Stanislavsky*. I knew what that smile she gave me meant; she wanted to sit next to Little Bull. I smiled right back, just as sweet, but I didn't move my butt to make room.

An exchange of fire broke out again between Lin Mo, an actor in his early forties, and Lao Xie, another playwright in the theater. It was the old problem of whether the play should be called *The Chair* or not.

'Why does it have to be called *The Chair?*' said Lao Xie. 'I can't believe modernists have to use cold words totally unconnected with the plot for the names of their works. If that's the way it is, why not go the whole way and call it *Wood*, *Furniture*, or *Primeval Forest?*' Lao Xie was a writer not a talker, and even these few words stretched his long, thin neck another inch.

'You're still a playwright, aren't you? With those ideas of yours, you wouldn't get any takers even if we were street hawkers. You don't even understand what symbolism is! No wonder you haven't turned out any plays for so long!' Lin Mo trashed Lao Xie, then expressed his own opinion:

'The word "chair" is meaningless, but its meaninglessness is its meaning. That's just the sort of atmosphere that Comrade Wang Keke wants to create. She's using the chair to symbolize all the things that are locked down in the human world. People can think of it as the office, the classroom, or the home, and even extend it to include traditional morality and common

* Chairman Mao's gift of a mango to young revolutionaries in the south of China during the Cultural Revolution acquired mythic proportions and was circulated as evidence of his concern, thoughtfulness and generosity at the time, although its comic dimension is not lost on Chinese people today.

prejudice! And people live in this reality that is at once complex and simple. Everybody tries to get away from it, but in the end they still have to sit in the chair—to sit in grim reality!'

Lin Mo was an effective speaker, his well-modulated voice rising and falling. He'd got it all from me just yesterday, but hearing it from his mouth, even I found it most profound. I watched Lao Xie's long, thin neck reddening and bulging, and although I knew he hadn't understood a word, Lin Mo's beautiful speech alone had shaken him up. Lao Xie's Adam's apple bobbed as he swallowed once more, but there wasn't another peep out of him. Poor Lao Xie never got the upper hand in an argument, although it never kept him from having a go. Meilun twisted her shimmering yellow body about, flashing her smile this way and batting her eyelashes that, as if to make sure everyone got a fair go.

I listened attentively to each of the impassioned speakers. For me and my script, they offered up their most brilliant thoughts. I nodded sincerely to each one, telling them I understood their opinions completely. At the end of each speech, I smiled modestly and looked grateful. Even though I couldn't remember anything anyone said, every word had an effect. Deep inside, I began to wonder if I hadn't become a complete hypocrite, despite being so damned sincere about everything.

At New Year, which was also the time the school children had their winter holiday, they lost touch with each other. She didn't remember who it was who cut off contact first.

Later, he said that New Year was the most boring he'd ever spent. Terribly boring. But still, there was an incredible amount of socializing, what with inviting people over and being invited over. Relatives came, and he had to go with his wife to the movies and to buy things for the kids. His daughter ate too much, her stomach hurt and she had to go to the hospital. This, that, and the other—a whole heap of things.

Afterwards, it was he who contacted her again first. He said it was because he missed her so much.

Keke, Keke, he called into the phone. He pronounced 'ke' like 'ko', so that, if heard all of a sudden, it sounded like he was talking about a coffee bean or a cocoa bean. He said it again; he'd missed her so much. She believed him; his voice on the phone was full of ardor and hope.

—It's me. Did you recognize my voice? he said. Did you?

—Uh huh.

—*What have you been up to? What are you doing right now?*

—*Why ask? You haven't bothered about me for ages. You've got a wife and children.*

—*I miss you. I've missed you. I miss you so much!*

—*...*

—*Don't you believe me?*

—*...*

—*When can I see you?*

—*I'm busy. Very busy. Terribly busy. I may be getting married soon.*

—*I'm coming to see you!*

—*Don't.*

—*Why? Keke, why? What's wrong?*

—*I don't want you to. I'm not up to it.*

—*I'm coming to see you, he said again. I'm coming to see you.*

—*Don't. Don't you dare. I won't be home. Even if you do come, you'll be wasting your time.*

Later he came anyway and she was home. She knew he'd come, and he knew she'd wait for him.

—*Haven't we been apart long enough? he asked.*

The discussion got tangled up again in the issue of whether the main character was good or bad. People find things that are commonplace in real life impossible to understand when they appear in plays. They brought up one 'why' after another, and from one 'why', another 'why' was born, from which yet another 'why' was born, like sons and grandsons. They forced me to become a granny of 'whys', until finally even I couldn't tell which were my own sons.

'What do you say, Wang Keke? You're the playwright; you tell us.'

What was I supposed to say? All I could do was smile like a damned fool. Little Bull's got what it takes, though. He got up and started waving his arms about for me, hands slicing through the air like wild daggers. Even existentialism got into the act, and Sartre and Camus became his buddies. Whatever and whichever; all sorts of things I'd never even thought of when I was writing the play.

'Existentialism is the French modernism. It was invented by Sartre.' Meilun interrupted with some unneeded help, speaking as though existentialism was a thing like a steam engine or a rockethead. Her voice was sharp and grating, vibrating at high frequency like a summer cicada tucked away in a leaf. My gums started to ache again. Little Bull didn't even glance at her, making it clear Meilun's helping hand had nothing to do with him. How on earth could I explain my ideas, which were so simple they couldn't be made simpler? Should I just explain that all the many complexities in life are man-made?

Everyone wanted to sound better than the last person, and as they argued back and forth, I felt I was like a thoroughly worm-eaten book. I could only treat the arguments as nothing to do with me, or that play of mine would never be done with rewrites as long as I lived. A stupid smile was the best approach. I gathered the stack of plays up tight in my arms, holding my chin against the black words which were giving off their inky smell, and begged for less loneliness in the midst of all the righteous racket.

I don't know who, but someone surprised us all by letting out a crisp, clear fart, making everyone burst out laughing, and helping to put a full stop on Little Bull and Director Zhao's debate. I grabbed Little Bull to make him sit down, and also to thank him.

Bang! Bang! Two hand claps; the theater head's unmistakable signal for everyone to quiet down. The theater head, hard-working, competent, liked and respected, finally stuck his enormous face out from a fog of smoke.

'Everybody's been very enthusiastic. You've all spoken very well. The opinions expressed have all been excellent. That's what teamwork's all about!'

I thought that if everyone else had done very well, that meant I had to be in the wrong.

I never expected him to go on and say, 'We don't have anything playing right now. Comrade Wang Keke has rewritten this play seven or eight times; she's worked very hard. The basic material is very good. If people still have constructive criticisms or suggestions to offer, they can do so during rehearsals. Progress comes through experimentation! Good, that's settled then. The theater leaders will meet tomorrow. Keke, you come along too. The day after that, the cast and director will be announced. Now let's all express our appreciation of Comrade Wang Keke's hard work!'

The theater head was very good at being a leader, and the pit-a-pat of applause started. I went on gripping the pile of scripts tightly, flashing a stupid smile at everyone, but inside I was flustered and apprehensive. What was he doing, turning my play into the single sweet potato that sees everyone through a famine?

'Congratulations, Comrade Wang Keke!' Lin Mo raised his voice as he came across to me, extending his right hand warmly but ostentatiously, and then grasping mine with both of his. I knew he'd already begun angling for a part, but I enjoyed his behavior nevertheless, because in public like this it gratified my vanity. I shook eight or nine hands, male and female, all sorts, some coarse and some smooth, but even if people acted the shadows there could only be six roles in the whole play. Meilun danced her way over to me too. I didn't shake her hand, but I patted her on the shoulder, and said her yellow dress was pretty and that she was slimmer than ever. Her eyelashes started batting about again, and her carriage suddenly suggested an immense fragility, as though she lacked even the strength to truss a chicken. This was all for the benefit of Little Bull, who stood beside me. He stayed there, making it clear his relationship with me was closest of all, that no matter how much you shook hands with me it was no use, that the leading role was, of course, his.

I got home before dinner. As soon as I got in the door, my cute but selfish niece threw herself into my arms. 'Auntie! Auntie!' she kept yelling. Her next move was to rummage through my purse. I was just the same when I was her age.

The first thing Mom said when she saw me was, 'What? Killed again?' The whole family knew my play had been discussed for the eighth time that day.

'Comrade Wang Keke's masterpiece was passed to the sound of prolonged applause,' I announced with a flourish.

'Really?' Mom ran into the room, shouting and flapping her hands like moth's wings. 'Old man! Old man! It passed! Keke's play!' That was Mom's problem; she always made a mountain out of a molehill. However, I also heard a clucking noise like an old goose makes. It came from my old dad's throat. He shuffled over to me, the backs of his slippers trodden down.

'My daughter,' he said. 'My girl!' He embraced me, and kissed my forehead. My niece was so mad she screamed with jealousy.

Dad poured out a glass of wine for me at the dinner table, and uncorked his mouth too. 'That year I went down south with the People's Liberation Army, I wrote a play in a single night once. It was performed the next day. Our commander said it was good, and it wasn't rewritten.' He proudly shook his head, not a single black hair left, making sure I knew I wasn't as good as he when he was young. There was no way for me to explain today's dramatic concepts and forms to him, and he didn't have the faintest understanding of what I wrote. All I could do was nod and show immense interest in what he said. Old people can also be vain sometimes, and their vanity needs to be satisfied too.

'Did anyone call?' I asked Mom. She said no, not even Nan Huang. She also asked why Nan Huang hadn't come by today.

'I've split up with him.' My family still didn't know about our last words. 'Really,' I said. But seeing my parents' shocked expressions, I winked and laughed; I was only joking. I didn't want to cause a big fuss over this. I couldn't deal with it. I couldn't explain.

There was a pink poster stuck up at the entrance to the school's third canteen:

By special arrangement, the famous poet, author and feature writer Tain Xinpeng is coming to our department to discuss the relationship between the eighties and plurality in the arts. Everyone is welcome to attend, bring along questions and join in the discussion.

Time: 2 p.m.
Place: Physics Department Lecture Hall.
Sponsor: Physics Department Student Association.

—Hey! It's that guy of yours again!
The dark girl behind her nudged her and yelled. Everyone turned to look at her.
—Of course! What's so strange about that?
Holding her lunch box steady, she denied nothing. She recognized Nan Huang's handsome brush-written characters, and believed in his abilities even more. Meeting all the gazes surrounding her, she felt very pleased with herself. Nan Huang could always secretly satisfy her vanity.
—You going? the dark girl asked.
—Of course. Need you ask? She stuffed the last piece of beef into her mouth, though she'd meant to throw it away, and chewed noisily.
—I'll go too, then.
The dark girl was her good friend, but their classmates all called her a hanger-on. That was because the dark girl followed her absolutely

everywhere. Sometimes when she saw her with Nan Huang, she even tried a few flirtatious words too. Recently, the dark girl had seen a guy in the Physics Department she wanted to date, and she was pestering her to go and get Nan Huang to help.

—Get Nan Huang to talk to him, the dark girl pleaded. Please, Keke. It was as though her entire fate was in Nan Huang's hands.

—You'd best go talk to him yourself. Really. Be brave, she advised the dark girl, trying to pep her up a bit. That way you can make him see you really mean it. Don't be embarrassed. I only got Nan Huang when I finally took the initiative, didn't I? If I hadn't, I'm so ugly who knows when I would have had a chance? In the animal world, it's quite normal for the female to chase the male, so why must human beings be so false?

Finally convinced, the dark girl blushed and bounded off full of confidence.

—You're great, Nan Huang said. You're great. You have all the makings of a real con artist.

In the Physics Department lecture hall, Nan Huang had long since reserved a good seat for her with his handkerchief.

The writer entered to enthusiastic applause. He was so famous, so very famous. Even before she'd started college, she'd already copied lots of his poems into her notebook. Over the last couple of years, his feature articles had been just fantastic! Bold, meaningful, sincere. His writing was charismatic, talented, witty.

The writer was of medium height, with a big head and cropped black hair. Each hair stuck straight up like a needle, like wheat stubble that had just been cut, still not bowed or burned. He was wearing a pair of ordinary white-framed glasses of the sort popular in the sixties. They made his eyes, which weren't really large, look incredibly deep and full of life's vicissitudes. Of all his features, his nose was especially prominent. It was not only big, but also a bit crooked, as if it had gotten bent out of shape because he'd been thinking too much. Still, it gave his whole face a lively look too. His mouth was rather attractive, rather distinctive, rather you-know-what. His hands, with which he gesticulated, were quite rough, not like a writer's hands but more like a blacksmith's.

—I never thought you'd look like that, she said later when they knew each other. You're not a bit like I thought you'd be.

—What did you think I'd be like?

—I thought you'd be tall and thin for sure, with your hair long and brushed back.

—That's Mayakovsky, he said. Not me.

When the writer spoke, there were frequent bursts of applause, mixed with high-pitched cheers from the girls. He wasn't a particularly good speaker, and his slightly accented voice stammered at times. Still, his keen mind, original expressions, pointed words and sometimes rather coarse descriptions really made people listen.

She hung onto his every word, feeling tremendously excited. Quite a lot of students stood up to ask questions or hand over written ones, all of which he answered very frankly, winning even more enthusiastic applause. She'd meant to ask a question herself. She'd thought of it while chewing on her beef in the canteen, but she gave up on it now. Those notions of hers were so unworthy of mention in his presence, so feeble and immature, so laughable. She was pleased she hadn't gone through with it and made a fool of herself.

Supporting her elbows on her notebook, she propped her chin in her hands and stared at him fixedly. She felt wisdom like black lightning shining from his eyes, and spreading quickly above her head. His words could stimulate so many wild, galloping imaginings in her mind. Oh, she really admired him.

The session came to an end, and the students all gathered around for autographs. Some had the writer's own books, and some just had their notebooks. She didn't have anything, but she didn't want to lose this opportunity. Maybe she would only see him this once in her whole lifetime, she thought, so she ripped a page out of the dark girl's notebook. She didn't dare force her way to the front straight away because she was afraid people would laugh. She waited until nearly everyone else had finished before handing him the piece of paper.

The writer was really nice not to refuse her an autograph because her piece of paper was so crude. He put his foot on a chair and, using his knee as a table, carefully signed his name. His handwriting was dashing, as though it had swept onto the paper rather than been written.

—What's your name? the writer asked as he was signing.

—Wang Keke, she said hurriedly. I'm called Wang Keke.

The writer raised his head to look at her. She was nervous he might be thinking the piece of paper was too frivolous, too disrespectful. But the writer just shot her a smile, a natural friendly smile, a very infectious smile. She couldn't help grinning a little too, feeling grateful towards him. A long time afterwards, she asked him what he was thinking at that time.

—I was very moved when I saw that piece of paper, he said.

—What else?

—I also had a premonition, he said, a very powerful premonition.

'Keke, go and keep your father company,' Mom said as she came in. 'Don't go mooning around in your room all by yourself the minute you get home.' Mom looked in the mirror as she talked to me. She wasn't getting any younger but she still loved bright clothes, and just after dinner she'd changed again, into a silk blouse I'd never seen before.

Dad had already set the go board up in the lounge. As always, he gave me a four piece advantage. He said this was something I really didn't have any talent for. I said that when Nan Huang and I played checkers, I never lost.

'Well, then, either he lets you win, or he's even more hopeless than you are.'

I made the same mistakes I'd made a hundred times before. Dad told me in exasperation I was beyond hope as he helped me move the black pieces I'd put in the wrong places to the right places. Looking at his head, which was much neater now it was half bald, I suddenly felt sad. How had he spent his life? Dad had been married twice and Mom was his second wife, but he never said anything about the past, and no matter what angles I tried I never got anywhere. I found out about it when I overheard Mom and Dad arguing when I was little. Mom said, 'Don't think I don't know about the other woman before me!' She might have been quite right, but so what if she knew? Dad was still your husband, wasn't he? Surely he'd love you forever?

The phone rang. It was ten sharp. I knew who it was. I leaped up to answer it before Mom could. Insisting on getting to the bottom of things was one of her habits. I didn't know if I was scared of getting that call or if I was longing for it. I'd warned him before not to phone me at home.

Only when I heard his voice did I realize how much I wanted to see him, and how much I had to say to him. Everything I did was for him. I felt a warm wave spread from my stomach through my whole body, but all I could say was 'Tomorrow, okay? Tomorrow.'

By the time I got back to Dad, I didn't want to play anymore. I seemed to start every move wrong, so Dad had to guide me every step of the way. In the end, he was playing against himself. I felt I'd really let him down, but there was nothing I could do about it. I was no longer my own person.

2

Probably because I had almost no choice over what I read when I was small, or else I don't know why, I'm easily influenced in all sorts of ways by all sorts of books to the point where I actually *want* to be influenced. Almost from the first time I held a book I could read, every character that could attract me inspired new interests in me. A picture book about Ulanova made me believe my future was as a beautifully poised ballet queen able to point her toes behind her till they touched the back of her head. I became obsessed, turning somersaults on a pile of sand, and I got my brother to tie a rope around my waist and dangle me from the balcony while I made dancing movements, imitating Ulanova's soaring poses in the picture book. I really believed that this was how you trained to be a ballet dancer.

Later, the magic of *Madame Curie* took hold. That frail Polish girl made me dream of becoming a scientist. I even prayed that there might still be several undiscovered elements waiting for me to grow up. I made myself love being scientific, even though I wasn't cut out for it at all. Often, I got so muddled my mind was like a pot of paste, but I pressed on from morning to night. I stuck the formulas I had no way of understanding all over the head of my bed, the corners of my desk and the walls, until for a long time, no matter whom I saw, I wanted to figure out some body measurement or other with those formulas. Even now, when I'm on the bus, I still have to try my damnedest to calculate how many panes of glass there are in the tall buildings on either side of the road, often until my head swims. I can't remember what character in what book it was that finally saved me from my madness.

To cut the story short, when I read *Jane Eyre*, I hoped to become a woman like her; self-possessed, self-confident and self-respecting, good-natured and virtuous. But after seeing *Carmen*, I was drawn to her passionate and joyous character, and decided I was really cut out to be a romantic lotus-eater. As I kept chopping and changing, Mom delivered the verdict to me—I wouldn't achieve anything or get anything my whole life through!

'Nan Huang, let's call it quits', I said. He was sitting on that single bed of mine, reading. Two days ago, we'd decided that if we got married we'd put a double in its place.

'Let's split up and call it quits!' I was sitting at the desk, chewing the pencil in my hand into a rotten stump of wood.

Nan Huang looked up at me and then blankly went on reading his book. It was the fifth time I'd brought it up in the last two months, second only to the number of times my play had been discussed at the theater, but we were still sitting together like this again.

Twice I'd changed my mind the minute the words left my mouth, twice he'd come to see me again, and each time we went back to the way we'd been before without saying a thing. The last time had been a week ago, when I went to his office to see him. Though he looked furious, he seemed well prepared for my arrival.

'Don't make a fuss, Keke,' he said. 'No more crazy stuff.' He didn't say how he'd got along since we'd split up, but he looked perfectly fine.

Nan Huang still thought I was just acting up, and that made me mad.

'Hey! I've come to talk to you!'

My stronger tone made him look up again.

'What are you doing here again?' he asked, eyeing me calmly, as if I was the boy who cried wolf. I was so angry I almost jumped up, but I immediately recognized my fury as a sign that I might well lose control again. I flared my nostrils and breathed in deeply.

'Nan Huang, let's call it quits, let's just break up and forget it!'

He didn't say a thing this time, and his gaze, still calm and level, made it impossible for me to tell what he was thinking. I was determined to make him understand that I wasn't kidding this time. This time, there really was a wolf. This time I had thought things through, and I wouldn't change my mind, I wouldn't turn around and come looking for him again. The die was cast.

'Nan Huang, I've thought about it for a long time. We're not meant for each other.'

'Why?'

'When we're together we just get on well, but there's no passion.'

'What about *then*?' he asked, and I knew he meant the time at university when I'd chased him.

'Then, I didn't understand,' I said honestly. 'I didn't know what love was then. I was blind then.'

'So, you understand now? Go on, tell me.'

'I don't know how to put it,' I hedged. 'But I know it's not us.'

'You set your sights too high; you ask for too much. Keke, I can't satisfy you.' He didn't sound sarcastic at all.

'Nan Huang, you're better than me. You're better educated, more intelligent, more honorable. You're better looking, and you've got a better heart too.'

'I'm more honest emotionally than you too!' he said, his eyes misting at last.

My mind went blank for a second, and my heart started beating wildly, as if a tank had just driven over it. Maybe he'd worked it out long ago, but just hadn't said anything. Why had he never said, never asked? If he had, I wouldn't have strung him along this far.

'Nan Huang...'

'There's always someone phoning you, and always at the same time of day.' He didn't let his tears of humiliation flow. He'd said that once before, but I'd lied and said it was a colleague calling. I still thought he'd believed me, but apparently I'd overestimated my abilities. 'The minute you pick up the phone you get all worked up, and you go on talking and talking. Tell me, is it him that excites you?'

I gave way. No matter what he said now, I'd give way to it all.

'If that's the way it is, why have you gone on with me, deceiving me? That's shameful and disgusting, isn't it?'

My shame went far beyond that.

'Two days ago, didn't you say you wanted to be good to me, so I wouldn't leave you? Then, then you wanted me to stay the night with you. You said we were going to be married soon anyway. What's the real story?'

He stared hard at me, as though I had another face behind my face.

'Fortunately, I left.' He added that line to show how noble and virtuous he was.

Nan Huang, oh, Nan Huang, how could I explain to you? I was full of passionate dreams about you once too. When we were apart, just like any other good girl, I read your letters and your name a dozen times, a hundred times. For a long time now, I'd cheated you and been sweet to you, even tried to seduce you, all in the vain hope that I could build a wall with your virtue and your love, a wall between me and that man. But it was impossible, he was unstoppable. Everything I had for you, all my vows and dreams, became just like a kite with a broken string when he arrived, crashing to the ground despite all my efforts.

Have I caught the sun? she asked. Ugly or not, right now I really have turned to Koko.

He held her tight around the waist with one arm, and skimmed his spare hand over her forehead beneath her bangs. She was certain she looked awful right then, her forehead dark and shiny, oily from any angle. Just like a greasy doughnut.

Koko is the color of the sun, he said. Koko is the sun bean, you're the daughter of the sun.

He bent to kiss her, as though he really wanted to turn her into a sun bean and eat her.

I didn't say anything at all to Nan Huang. I couldn't get the words out, I couldn't explain. I just felt terribly tired. I wanted to sleep.

The public phone in the corridor rang again. Ten o'clock. It was him. I never would have thought I could have hated the sound of that ring as much as I hated it then. If I'd had the energy to leave the room, I'm sure I would have thrown myself on it and smashed it to pieces.

I don't know whether it was the ringing phone that made Nan Huang shut up. We just sat there, listening to it angrily calling and then eventually giving up.

—I've had enough! I don't want anything to do with you anymore!

—What is it now? You're always chopping and changing.

—I just don't want anything to do with you anymore.

—I really can't think that I've done anything major, or is it that I've just forgotten? Give me a hint, he pleaded. Give me a hint, okay, Koko?

She laughed at the silliness of what he had said. Sometimes he was quite stupid. But inside she was worried: is he really confused, or is he just putting on an act?

They'd talked about the marriage issue several times before. She'd said she never wanted to get married. Especially recently, she'd become less and less interested. He'd warned her solemnly that she'd regret it.

—For a woman not to marry goes against people's expectations, they won't be able to accept it.

They'd never managed to talk their way to a conclusion on this issue,
but she'd realized she was already deeply in love with him.
—I don't want to go on living, really, she'd raged the last time. I'll
just die and be done with it.
—Are you crazy? You nutcase!
His eyes wide with shock, he twisted her wrist around behind her
back, as though she were about to go kill herself right then.
—Never go having crazy ideas like that again!
He said that again, a long time afterwards. She laughed and said she
wouldn't.
After hanging up, she didn't keep their date. There was no contact
between them for a long time. During that period, she and Nan Huang
split up five times.

I was so tired I couldn't keep my eyes open. My mind was
so overloaded it had short-circuited. All my odd thoughts
were like sodden bread, mushed together, unable to separate
themselves out. After I don't know how much time, Nan
Huang finally said, 'Get some rest. I'll go. Aren't they going
to discuss your script again tomorrow? I hope it goes well.'
    I leaned back in the chair, eyes closed, and nodded my head.
He got up, but then stopped by my side again. 'Keke, just one
more thing. Vanity could destroy everything you have, your
whole life. Do what you think's best.' He was worried about me.
    I couldn't hold back any longer, and the tears came flooding
out. I opened my eyes, and grabbed one of his hands with both
of mine. I lifted my head to look at him. I understood—it was
all over. Everything was really finished. Even if I kneeled down
and begged him now, he wouldn't want me. I'd already lost him
completely.
    I lowered my head and rested my forehead on the back of
his hand. In no time, it was smeared with my tears. He wanted
to pull it away, but I wouldn't let go for the life of me. He
had to use his other hand to pull a handkerchief from his
pocket and pass it to me. I took it, but I didn't use it to wipe
my face. Instead I grabbed him around the waist. Nan Huang
stroked my head with both his hands, saying 'Okay, okay,
don't cry, you'll be all right in a couple of days.'
    I really couldn't take him talking like that. I shook my head
and stamped my feet, grabbing his jacket and saying, 'Really,
what am I? What sort of thing am I?' I was all choked up. 'What
the hell am I? Don't say anything. Don't bother about me

anymore, don't comfort me. Why are you being so good to me? Really, even if I come begging to you again, just ignore me...'

I let myself wipe my tears across his front. In the end, he started crying too. 'We can still be friends, Keke, we can still be friends.'

I understood that this was truly the death sentence on our relationship, but I still clung to a glimmer of hope and even asked, 'Let's still go to the movies together, okay?'

'Okay.'

'When you've got another girlfriend, still come and see me, okay?'

'Okay.'

We both knew these were empty words. Suddenly I thought of something from our past and said, 'Nan Huang, you've forgotten, but once you came to see me. It was winter. I said I still hadn't had breakfast, and you went and bought me two blocks of ice cream. Almost crying with rage, I threw them out the window. And you said, Keke, isn't that your favorite food?'

'I haven't forgotten,' he said, smiling.

Then we thought of some other funny things from the past. And after that, I fell asleep. I slept like the dead, not a single dream all night, and I don't know what time Nan Huang left. That's how it all ended. Simple and easy, right?

What is happiness? Is it love? Does it only exist in the embrace of a man and a woman? Of course not. That's a kind of thrill, a fever, sometimes almost a painful struggle.

—It gets into your blood, he said. It gives you a fearlessness about everything.

She stared at him without blinking so as to understand more deeply.

—The key is the process, not the goal, he added, putting his rough hand on top of hers, trying to communicate something to her.

3

The theater head brought Meilun back to rehearsal. Her eyes were still red and swollen like clam shells, but the look in them was completely different; it was imperious and even a bit couldn't-care-less. She had the theater head backing her now. Firing Meilun from the female lead had been my suggestion to the director. In fact, Zhao had had the same idea long ago, but he worried how she'd take it and so he had hesitated. When I suggested it, he jumped at the idea. I never thought that only half an hour later sobbing Meilun would be back so full of herself. What could I do? Even if I insisted, it wouldn't do any good, and Zhao had compromised already. All I could do was watch as Meilun turned the female lead I'd created on paper, part likeable and part hateful, into a twittering cicada.

My gums began to ache again. Forget it. Let her do her worst. Even Little Bull, my faithful supporter and the male lead, did nothing but smile and stay on the sidelines, his long legs stretched out in front of him. It seems no man's against getting closer to a girl with a pretty face, a well-developed body and, moreover, the ability to bat her eyelashes like a cartoon character. If I'd said anymore, even Little Bull would have thought I was envious of her over-ripe good looks, never mind others. Well, I guess no one wants to back a loser.

Keke, my dearest Keke,

You can't imagine how it feels to get a letter from you at a time like this. I had almost lost hope, but now it's all right, what can I say? Words like sunshine and the spring wind pale into insignificance beside you.

My 'Reports From Home' was written with the tears I cried when I saw for myself how the people back home were suffering, but it has brought me greater disaster than you can possibly imagine. I guess I brought it upon myself. I was prepared for it, but the cold reception I've had on this trip back is something I'll never forget. The provincial Party committee has made it quite clear I'm their least welcome guest. They even told me their guesthouses and hotels were all full, forcing me to stay in this private inn.

The place is filthy. I got food poisoning the day after I arrived. Between throwing up and the runs, I've spent the rest of the time in bed. Without your letter, I'm afraid I wouldn't even have had the strength to lift my pen. Almost none of my old friends have come to see me, but I haven't told them I'm here, either. Human relationships are so undependable, but it's too early to tell you that yet. You were born with a silver spoon in your mouth. Still, I don't blame them. I know there are people watching me, people from the provincial authorities.

I hear they have already criticized the old school friend who gave me so much material last time by name, and that he may still be punished. When I'd just arrived this time, I even tried to phone a few old friends, but the most they said was to go back to Beijing. Keke, it's not that I don't want to leave this damned lonely place and come back to you. Keke, only now do I realize how much I need you. I need that clever little head of yours, I need your endless chatter, and I need those moist lips of yours. I need you! I need all of you! But I can't come back, Keke. I have to stick it out, and even push on further, into the mountains, to my old home. I'll go tomorrow!

Keke, my dear little Keke, do you still remember a story I told you once? It was a myth Plato recorded. Long, long ago, human beings were animals with four arms and four legs. They walked sideways like crabs, and nothing could block their progress. They were incredibly strong and fearless, masters of their own fates. This made the gods angry, so they sent a spirit to divide them in two. Then human beings became like us today, with two arms and two legs, and only one heart. They were terribly lonely. But after losing their other half, each human being did everything to find it—their other half. Those who succeeded became strong and fearless again. This strength was love. Those who tried and tried but failed were sad and alone all their lives.

Keke, my dear little Keke, shall I tell you? You are my other half. I've found my other half. I'm strong and fearless now. Having you, my inspiration flows like a rushing spring, and I'm full of confidence for the future.

Your other half.

She could recite his letter from start to finish without missing a single word. Even with her eyes closed, she could see how each word was written.

Mom's call got put through to the rehearsal room and interrupted my argument with Zhao, the director. It was just too weird! Zhao had supported me all the way through the writing of the play, but now he wouldn't let me have my way at all. He said the lead characters' dialogue wasn't dynamically philosophical enough, and he even found me a book called *Sayings of the World Famous*. My God! he thought life should be a book!

Mom said today was my niece's fourth birthday. She wanted me to go back for dinner, and she told me specially not to forget to buy a present. When had I ever gone home without something for her? I spent a third of my wages on that kid. Because my brother and his wife didn't get on and she went back to her mother's every chance she got, everybody doted on my niece and spoiled her so rotten this three-to-four-year old knew she was a key member of the family. She knew how to wrap people around her little finger. I'd advised my brother to divorce and get it over with countless times, but as soon as he thought of her, he was overcome with indecision.

By the time I finished talking to Mom on the phone, I wasn't in the mood to argue with the director anymore. I just kept agreeing to go home and think it over again, and then I slipped away. As the day wore on, my saliva turned to glue. Like hell I'll think it over again!

Outside the room, waves of hot air rose under the fierce sun. I felt a bit dizzy, and as I went downstairs my foot hovered dangerously in mid-air. Fortunately, Little Bull came up behind me and caught me.

'What's the matter, Keke?'

'These heels are too high.'

'You're exhausted, aren't you? Keke, why don't I get leave and take you home?' His voice was gentle.

'Don't bother. How come you seem to have something on your mind?'

'It's...nothing.' There was a false nonchalance in the way he dragged it out.

He had been a bit upset the last few days, and even in rehearsal he didn't spark the way he usually did, like an alarm clock that ran eight hours fast in every twenty-four. He had taken to sitting alone, staring into space like a sick chicken. I took his arm.

'Little Bull, you mustn't give up. If you do, I'll give way completely.'

I tightened my grip. He smiled knowingly and puffed his chest out, rippling those muscles of his. Little Bull was still Little Bull! I left, doing my best to make my step lighter and more graceful. I knew he was still staring after me. And I knew there was another pair of eyes staring at the two of us from the rehearsal room. Oh, Meilun, you silly girl! If you knew what I've been feeling, you could sleep at least an extra half hour every day.

I wandered along Wangfujing Street,* going through almost every store without finding a suitable gift for my niece. I remembered last year it was Nan Huang who'd come with me. We wanted everything we saw, and in the end we returned the little piano and exchanged it for a little train. We spent nearly all the money in both our pockets. Later, it was Mom who helped us out with that month's food bills.

When Nan Huang had assembled the train for the kid, she cried out, 'Little train! Little train! I want to ride the little train!' It really was too small, and she couldn't get on it. She got so upset she cried and screamed until Nan Huang and I carried her to the playground the next day and spent five bucks giving her ten rides on the electric train. By now, my niece had long since 'repaired' the little train to smithereens, and it didn't have a single wheel left. The wheel-less carriages and engine lay quietly on the windowsill in the hall, pieces of junk we didn't want to throw away but which had no more use. Nan Huang had said he'd get the spare parts and repair it. Now no one would ever bother about it again.

Suddenly I had a premonition, a very strong one: if you lose that guy, you've still got Nan Huang, but once you lose Nan Huang, you've lost everything.

He came; one dusk in early summer, he came to the place they always met. She was leaning back against the battered old bench, waiting for him. He was a bit late, but she wasn't angry. She was past the age when the slightest thing made her pout.

He was wearing a polo shirt. According to traditional Chinese taste, it was a bit trendy for someone of his age, but as a lover, he looked full of life, like a copse of trees in the wind, and so it didn't matter.

If she'd seen him like this before, she would have become as spirited as he was. Today, she didn't know why, but she felt faintly unhappy. Her breathing was labored, as though she had a cold. She got out her handkerchief and delicately tried to clear her nose, although it couldn't possibly be made any clearer than it already was.

—Why do we have to sit here? he asked.

He spread his arms, as though asking her, but also as though he couldn't stop himself from embracing her. She drew back.

---

* Beijing's main shopping street.

—*Let's go, he said. Why should we stay here?*

It was she who had insisted on meeting there. She knew as soon as they were in her room, she wouldn't get a chance to speak. He wouldn't leave her alone, and he wouldn't let her discuss anything seriously. She wanted to tell him the result of her last talk with Nan Huang, and she wanted to make him remember what he'd said before. However, the moment she saw him she knew her efforts would be in vain. He just wouldn't listen.

—*Let's go, Keke. We'll go to your place.*

—*No, I want to talk to you.*

—*We can talk at your place, too. Why do we have to sit here? We haven't seen each other for a long time, have we?*

—*I've been so busy with my play.*

—*And I haven't disturbed you at all. Didn't you say to meet today when you phoned yesterday?*

—*I wanted to talk to you about something.*

—*We can talk at your place, too. Why do we have to sit here?*

She had no choice but to go along with him. He was so stubborn. She couldn't talk him out of it. If he wanted to do something, he had to do it, that was the sort of guy he was. She was always reduced to this when she was actually with him. She had to go along with him. He put his arm around her waist, self-assured and carefree, as if the whole world was his. His arm was warm and strong, and it seemed she could sleep if only she could lie on it. He was always so stubborn.

Stubbornness is my wealth. He'd said that once.

He held her like that as they walked, sending his strength and warmth into her heart, making her feel she was rich, too.

—*Nan Huang and I are through, she said, following him when he went to buy an ice cream.*

His eyebrows jumped, which she felt was irresponsible and at least a little too lighthearted. She felt he wasn't taking her seriously. She wished she hadn't mentioned it in the midst of all these people, and her spirits fell fast.

—*Don't look so miserable, I love you.*

As soon as they entered the room, he held her close, as though the word love could hold up the sky. She didn't like it, and she resisted, biting her lips tight and ducking away. It was no use; he kissed her, kissed her face, her eyes, her neck. Whispering sweet nothings, he nibbled her ears. His blacksmith's hands held her tight, and gently moved over her.

—*I love you, Keke, don't be like this, he said. Don't you feel my love?* He went on and on. *Come on, come on, don't push me away.*

She picked up his passion so quickly she hated herself but at the same time let herself relax, accepting his kisses, his everything. The bastard, he'd *been prepared for this, it was what he'd come for. He'd even brought one of those little whatsits because he was afraid something might happen, afraid she might get pregnant. He wasn't the devil-may-care type at all.*

She fell into an ocean; unburdened of her will and her conscience for the first time, she got a taste of what it was like to fall into a boundless ocean. She bit the pillow, bit his shoulder, his arm, using them to stop her mouth. She let out a great, silent cry. She wanted to scream so much.

Two years after they met, she discovered for the first time, and for the first time she couldn't deny to herself, that, in the midst of her confusion about him and her struggle to restrain herself, and in the midst of his attraction to her, it was all because of this, and all because she needed this, too.

At ten o'clock, he left. She didn't get up to see him out. She couldn't get a word out, and he didn't ask anything, either. It seemed he'd forgotten what she'd told him completely.

—I'll be off, he said, and tilted his chin in her direction, as though seeking her opinion.

She didn't say a thing, but just lay on the bed like a languid cat. She watched him put on that red and blue striped polo shirt. He looked back with a meaningful smile, and then hurriedly kissed her on the forehead. However, she felt he was already just performing a duty. She didn't say what she thought. He left and the door slammed shut.

When she got up early the next morning, she discovered a purplish mark on her left breast. She thought it strange she hadn't felt any pain the night before.

You can do it, he'd said. You can do it, and I taught you.

4

Lin Mo and I were kidding around at a big, round table in the theater canteen.

'Keke, you're so busy you even spend all your evenings in the rehearsal room. Doesn't Nan Huang mind?'

'No, we've split up.'

'Why? Nan Huang's so good, it must be your fault.'

What's the real reason? What on earth happened? Why do that? They demanded to know, and they even helped me with a few suggestions. Was it mutual incompatibility? Did he have someone else? Only Little Bull said nothing. He just glanced at me, and then buried his face back in his rice bowl like a thief.

'He's too stupid,' I joked. It was all I could manage. 'We went up into the hills together once. It was very windy that day. We were sitting together watching the waves, when suddenly he said someone was drowning. I said there wasn't anyone, but he insisted there was and dived in before I could stop him. However, he's a lousy swimmer. His record is twenty-five meters across a pool, and even then he swallows a few mouthfuls. He disappeared the minute he hit the water.'

'Then what?' Meilun screwed her eyes up, as if scared to look. It was moments like this she was at her cutest.

'Then a surfer saved him and brought him up still clutching the rind from half a watermelon to his chest.'

Everyone laughed. Meilun cried, 'You're making it up! You're making it up!'

'Really, I had to look after him for three whole days because of that watermelon. His temperature went up to forty-one degrees, and blisters came up around his mouth, like a toad's skin.'

Lin Mo laughed so hard he spat his food out, and Meilun drummed away on Little Bull's shoulder with her spoon. They were always fooling around, and no one looked twice, but this time something annoyed Little Bull.

'Dammit! Can't you hold still?' He jerked his shoulder away.

Meilun stuck her tongue out and then burst out laughing. They thought I was kidding. In fact, every word was true, except Nan Huang and I didn't go to the beach, but into the hills. And the hills weren't by the sea, but by a river. And it wasn't Nan Huang who got sick, but me. I turned around a tale nobody knew simply to poke fun at myself and to bury my most beautiful memories of Nan Huang even deeper. They belonged to me alone; they belonged to my soul.

That was one of our happiest times together. School was out for summer, and we rode our bikes into the hills to pick mushrooms. I am nearsighted but I don't like to wear glasses, so Nan Huang found nearly all the mushrooms. It was more than my pride could bear.

'Enough,' I said. 'I quit.'

Then Nan Huang strung the mushrooms on a long reed, and hung them around my neck, saying, 'Okay, okay, don't pout like a pig—you picked them all.'

The mushrooms smelled damp and fresh, and I was happy again.

'You! You're just like a little kid,' he said.

He never said 'I love you' or anything like that, not even in his letters. It used to make me really mad. When I asked him about it, he avoided the question, and if I pushed him, then he said, 'Why does it have to be said?'

Right, why did it have to be said? Because I needed it, I was that damned shallow!

When we got home that day, I was sick. I guess I caught a chill rescuing the melon from the river. I lay in bed and wouldn't let him leave.

'You,' he said. 'You! All for that rotten melon.'

He tugged my braid. Why was that all he did? I wasn't happy about it, but I couldn't say anything, so I just let him leave.

In the end, I blew up at Zhao, the director. It was in the rehearsal room when we were going through the last act, and right in front of all the actors. Zhao absolutely wouldn't agree to the clappers I had arranged to accompany the characters' interior monologues, and he went behind my back and had the stage designer fix a hidden device to a chair, so when the lead sat down on it for the last time, a cloud of white smoke came billowing out. That pushed me right over the edge. I lost my temper more violently than I ever knew I could, like a shrew on the wrong pills. I jumped up from the bench, and started to yell.

'This is absolutely idiotic! This is a play, understand? A play! It's not vaudeville, and it's certainly not a magic show. You've turned her into a fairy who appears out of the blue! If you think smoke can puff out the profound philosophy you're after, then go set up a kebab stall on the street! Why hang around here?'

I left everyone dumbstruck, wide-eyed and tongue-tied, even Little Bull. The director's face turned the color of pig's liver, and goose bumps as big as rice grains popped up on his neck and cheeks. His lips trembled as he struggled to speak.

'You, you, you...' He pointed at my head with his script, as though taking aim at a large nail with a hammer, ready to bring it thumping down at any moment.

'You, you're insulting me!' he said through clenched teeth. 'You bastard!' he rasped like a pair of bellows, only bellows would have made more noise than he did cursing me. Zhao was so mad the whole of his face was twitching about, including his ears.

'And you're an *old* bastard,' I said. Actually, I already knew what the upshot of this argument was likely to be. But I'd had enough. I'd held my tongue and my temper long enough, and since the argument had started, I was determined to see it through. I put on the voice I'd learned acting at college. It sounded superb, just like it was coming through a loudspeaker.

'Look at Little Miss Perfect!' Zhao had dropped his usual act too. 'What's so great about you? To tell you the truth, this play's no good at all! If it wasn't for me, it'd have gone into the trash can long ago!'

His behavior pushed down the last of my barriers. Reason told me this sort of argument wouldn't solve a thing, but my whole body pulsed with a lust for battle, and I could feel every hair on me standing on end. Who cares about him! I was sick to death of those prim and proper discussions run by the theater leaders, who were about as potent as a pack of court eunuchs!

'I don't need you to tell me whether the play's any good or not! And to tell you the truth, you should never have become director in the first place.'

'How can you be so rude?'

'I don't need you to worry about my manners, either! Save your energy to teach yourself!' I acted like a fishwife.

Honest to God, I'd never had such a fierce showdown before, let alone such a brilliant victory. Dammit, I was having a good time! Why hadn't I discovered this talent before? I'd calmed right down; I'd even forgotten what we had been arguing about. There was only one thought in my mind: 'Drive him crazy!'

But when it came down to it, I was still too green, so in the end Zhao bore off the fruits of victory.

'Just you wait! Just you wait and see!' Zhao's last words were menacing and fierce. 'Don't think no one knows about you. Just you wait!'

He flung the script in my face and stalked off. He gained the upper hand by breaking off first, and then he left, washing his hands of the whole thing.

The script had been torn in two. It slid from my forehead down my chest, and then fell on the floor like an old rag. Months of hard labor and yearned-for success destroyed just like that, and by my own hand. My fury had vanished just as quickly. After a short silence, the actors started chattering, and

I stood alone in the middle of the enormous rehearsal room like a beggar stripped of her clothes. I felt nothing except shame.

I vaguely remembered something Zhao had said to me long ago. 'Wang Keke, I saw you,' he'd said. 'Yesterday, when I was taking a walk in the park with my daughter, I saw you.' He was full of mystery when he spoke to me, and he got right up close. 'I followed you two for a stretch, but you were too preoccupied to even glance back and notice me.'

At the time, what he said upset me for awhile but then, because I got busy with the play, I forgot about it. Only today did I realize it had become his weapon, but I wasn't scared of anything.

He'd gone, and the play was done for. He'd drained me completely. I stood there stupefied and shaking. I believe that at that moment, a fly could have knocked me to the ground.

She wasn't one of those superwomen. More and more, she was discovering her own weak points. Even though she'd worshipped those women when she was little, she'd still turned into the sort that loses her bearings in the slightest emotional turbulence. When close friends asked what she most wanted at the moment, she always answered right back, Marriage! And she could picture it all in color.

—If we got married, it would be a national sensation! Do you believe me? he said. An alluring light shone from his smiling face.

—Is that so? That'd be good. I'd like that. I'm not afraid of anything.

—You want to be famous?

—Yes, she said. I'd love to be famous!

Catching her off guard, he pulled her into the shadow of the trees; any further and they'd be in the black darkness of the woods. He planted his lips on hers.

—You're so adorable. Keke, you're my dearest!

She'd always known she was his first love, the only woman he'd ever loved.

Nobody came near me; it was as though none of them knew me. Watching the actors, who'd already started gathering their things and putting their coats on ready to leave, tears of humiliation and despair spilled from my eyes.

'Keke, what's the matter?' Little Bull came up from behind. He spoke softly and put his right hand on my shoulder without any hesitation. I felt his fingers pressing on my shoulder blade.

'Come on, Keke. It's no big deal.' He squeezed my shoulder and raised his voice. 'Hold on, everyone. It doesn't matter who leaves; the show must go on. Provided Keke agrees, I'll take over rehearsals and pulling this whole thing together. Keke, do you agree?' He lowered his head to ask me.

I hadn't expected this at all. I nodded, leaned on his shoulder and started sobbing.

Little Bull, Little Bull, my most faithful friend, I will be grateful forever.

'Hurray!' The actors who hadn't left yet started cheering, because of Little Bull's gallantry, and even more because the play might still go on.

'Yes! It doesn't matter who leaves; the show must go on. We'll do even better! Let's drive that imperialist revisionist crazy!' Lin Mo, who had made to leave, took his chance to speak again. He and Zhao hadn't seen eye to eye for ages.

I smiled through my tears. Even Meilun ran over and took my hand, squealing in her cicada voice. Although my gums started aching again, I still felt I'd been unfair to her in the past.

I don't know when, but the rain had started bucketing down outside.

I didn't go to the canteen for dinner; I just dragged my exhausted body back to the dorm. Even as a child, I'd never bothered to avoid the rain, so I was soaked to the skin by the time I got to my room. I took off my coat, and without bothering to dry myself off, dropped sopping wet on the bed and lay there, staring up at the ceiling.

I felt the script Zhao had thrown must have raised a bump larger than my head itself. Why else would my one head feel as heavy as two?

The corridor outside was very quiet. Today was Saturday, and everyone who could had gone home. Nobody would come to see me this evening. I knew they wouldn't come; it was the weekend. I reached for a mirror from the bedside table to check if I really did have such a big bump. As it turned out, there wasn't a mark. Only my eyes, which weren't large in the first place, had swollen and closed to slits. They were just like peeled hard-boiled eggs with a line cut across them with a thread. And why did my nose have to join in the fun? It was much bigger than usual. It had turned into a bulb of garlic, and purple garlic at that. Even I couldn't stand such an ugly sight. No wonder Nan Huang said I was the ugliest woman in the world when I cried. I'd wanted to jump up and cut his throat when he'd said that before, because he never comforted me. But when it came back to me today, I felt different.

I remember during my second year our Chinese Department and the Physics Department organized an outing. I was thrilled, because by then I'd developed a secret crush on the chair of the Physics Department Students Association, and that was Nan Huang. The only problem was that students in our two departments didn't get many chances to meet.

I knew quite a few women were after him already; you could see that at the basketball court. Every time he scored, they screamed, panted and almost fainted with excitement.

On the day of the outing, I got up early and dressed to the nines, like one of those women stallholders in the Beijing alleys. I even borrowed a compact from the dark girl and, ignoring her protests, put on a thick layer. Then I gritted my teeth and squeezed my feet into a brand new pair of white high heels. I'd pestered Mom to buy them the Sunday before, and we'd struck a deal that I had to wait until I'd graduated and started work before I wore them. Now, I'd snuck them out of the house earlier.

The bus was full of happy singing. Much to my surprise, the pleasure spot we were headed for turned out to be a stream in a long, narrow gully strewn with rocks, and at least six miles long. God! That's twelve miles there and back, enough to kill me.

How could I even think of flirting now? Just keeping up with the others would take all the courage I'd set aside for the campaign. I loathed my white high heels. Because of them, my dreams shattered. I don't know how I hobbled after everyone to our destination. It was a miracle; I'd always been terrified of pain.

Sitting down at the head of the stream, I could barely breathe. My feet were numb, and the pain raced to my gullet as if it had grown legs, squeezing it small and flat.

I noticed the chair of the Students Association had already rested, and now he was bounding about on a slab of rock, passing around a canteen filled with spring water. He didn't bring me any.

Suddenly a black cloud appeared out of nowhere in the sunny blue sky. Someone spotted it and yelled, 'It's going to rain! Quick, run!' Everyone jumped up squealing, as though an imminent downpour was lots of fun. One of my heels had already started to wobble. The dark girl pulled me up with all her might and then, scared of being left behind, squeezed in with the pack.

When the rain began to fall, those few backs I could still make out vanished, as though they'd sprouted wings and flown away. The rain soon grew heavier, and several bolts of lightning flashed across the sky, followed by rolling thunder. Suddenly, a terrifying thought raced through my mind. I might be killed by lightning right here by this mountain stream. No one would find me; they wouldn't even hear my scream. I was very upset and wanted to cry. I staggered forward with the greatest of difficulty; now my checked wool skirt was soaked through, it was heavier than a dead pig. I was exhausted and desperate. Looking down the stream, I felt I'd never get out of there even if I walked for the rest of my life.

Much to my surprise, I saw someone, someone running in my direction. He was running very fast and got close very quickly, but then he stopped about ten meters away. Because the rain was so heavy, I couldn't make out his face. He'd come to get me? I struggled towards him. But he turned and ran off again. Then, after putting some distance between us, he turned back and stood there looking at me.

Something told me it was Nan Huang! I couldn't believe it, but I did my utmost to run towards him. It really was him! He was standing behind a curtain of rain grinning at me. But he didn't wait for me; when he saw I was getting close, he turned and ran again. Damn! I was in too much of a hurry, and tripped over a stone. My whole body shot forward, and I was winded.

He'd stopped again. My leg hurt so much I couldn't get up, and the blood trickled from my knee like a spider's thread. I just sat there in the mud. The wobbly heel had finally worked its way off completely, and just stood there in the mud looking at me. I was a mess.

Finally, he ran over. I clutched my knee and burst out crying. 'What are you crying for?' he snapped. 'What's to cry about?' He didn't know; I wasn't crying for myself, but because of him, because he'd come. Hearing him talk like that, I sobbed even more bitterly, as if he were the cause of all my woes.

Ignoring me, he glanced at my injury, and said, 'It's no big deal. Don't make a mountain out of a molehill. It'll be fine tomorrow.'

'It's broken,' I said.

He laughed, pulled a handkerchief out of his trouser pocket and tied it around the wound for me. His handkerchief was filthy, and I thought that maybe it was no big deal to start with, but it sure would be now; by tomorrow it would be infected and full of pus. Still, I kept quiet and let him bandage it up.

'How could you wear these shoes? Aren't they just asking for trouble?' He pulled them off, and my insteps were all swollen out of shape. 'Why make yourself suffer?' he said, massaging my insteps one after the other. Then he took off his tennis shoes. 'Put these on.' I neither protested nor politely declined, but obediently put the big, boat-like shoes on. They were so comfortable! Then he tied them up for me. 'Don't ever allow your vanity to put your life at risk again.'

But I did it all for you, didn't I? When I told him that later, he almost fell over laughing.

After he'd tied the laces, he asked me what to do about the white leather pumps. 'Forget them,' I said right back. He picked them up and fired them against the opposite slope like artillery shells. The white shoes flew in an arc through the rain like two white birds.

He took my hand, pulling me to my feet. 'Don't start crying again,' he said. 'Don't ever cry again. You look dreadful when you cry.' Then he gave my braid a little tug, and like a big brother taking his lost little sister home, held my hand all the way down. When we were almost there, he let go, making me feel embarrassed for an instant. I wanted to ask, would you be like this with the other girls? But I didn't dare—I was afraid of losing him.

That was already five years ago. I never would have thought it could still warm my heart.

A knock at the door interrupted my thoughts.

'It's Little Bull, Keke. I've come to talk about the play.'

'Tomorrow, Little Bull,' I called towards the door without getting up. 'Tomorrow. I've gone to bed already.' I didn't want him to see me in such a state, all unkempt, like Red Riding Hood's wolf-grandma.

'It's not even ten o'clock. Are you really ready to go to sleep?' asked Little Bull, unwilling to give in.

'That's okay. I can count sheep.'

Little Bull didn't say anything more, but I knew he stood there awhile before he left. I crawled out of bed. Perhaps he might call.

5

In the end, Mom sent my elder brother to come and get me. Since the evening of my niece's birthday, when Mom had yelled and driven me out, I hadn't been home for two weeks. That was the day Mom finally found out Nan Huang and I had split up, and the reason why. She started out tactfully enough, saying, 'Keke, we're not like that. One play passed and you don't want Nan Huang anymore. You think he doesn't understand you, he's not good enough for you.'

'Mom, what are you saying? You don't understand at all!'

'Oh, don't I? I do know when you set out after Nan Huang, you had me cook things you took to school and told him you'd made yourself! You were at school all day but couldn't speak your mind when you saw him, so you wrote love letters when you came home, and had me mail them for you. I haven't forgotten any of that!'

What Mom said made me feel terrible, but I didn't want to take it any further. I was afraid if it got out of hand, it would be hard to patch it up.

'Stop it, Mom. Don't wear yourself out with suspicion.' I made a funny face, acting like a spoiled kid. When I do that, Mom usually has to smile, or else she just gives me a slap and it's all over. I had no idea that this time it would push her right off the deep end.

'Tell me the truth!' Mom said. 'Today, you're going to honestly and truthfully tell the whole family if it isn't because of that man, that married man!'

I felt all the blood in my whole body rush to my face. My heart beat so hard I couldn't breath properly. 'It's nothing like that!' I denied it.

'Then why?' Mom started pushing me.

I kept my mouth shut tight.

'Tell your mother the truth!' Dad had been sitting on the sidelines, but he spoke now. 'Keke, do as you're told. Tell your mother the truth.'

I gritted my teeth and kept quiet. 'I can't admit it, I absolutely can't,' I thought.

He knew her body like the back of his own hand.

—If I said you were pretty, I'd be lying, he said. It just isn't so. However, you really are exciting!

—Are you hungry?

—Just looking at you's enough to satisfy my appetite, he said. You're so beautiful, you don't know how attractive you are.

He buried his face between her breasts, breathing deeply the fresh, moist scent of her body.

—I'm going crazy! Really. One look at you's enough to drive me crazy.

Wasn't it true? She wiped out those other women, wiped out everything he could remember about them. That was her power. He said there hadn't been anything like that between him and his wife for a long time. She put her hand on his head, pushing her fingers through his hair, which was thick, hard and short like wheat stubble.

'You can stop deceiving us now.' Mom whipped out a letter and showed it to me. I recognized the handwriting; I'd know it with my eyes closed. Mom had been through my things!

I didn't take the letter, but just turned and ran to my room. The middle drawer of my desk had been pried open. What a filthy insult! When I wanted a lock, Mom had been against it. She thought she'd given me life, so she had a right to my soul. 'Let her have a world of her own!' Dad had said. He stood by helping me put the lock on, passing the screws one by one. I'll never forget that.

Now, the little green padlock dangled dejectedly from the smashed bolt, like a corpse on a rope. Oddly enough, this sight calmed me down considerably.

Mom went on yelling, 'Shameless! You shameless thing! You can fool Nan Huang, but you can't fool me!' Mom started to sob as she yelled. Seeing I wasn't reacting, she turned on Dad: 'It's all because you spoiled her. You've let her have her own way since she was small, and now it's come to this! Now what do we do?'

Listening to Mom, you'd think I'd brought ten fatherless children home. It didn't matter! None of it mattered. Let her go through all my letters. Let her shout.

'That's enough. What good is shouting? Let Keke speak.' Dad worked on Mom.

'I won't listen. I want her out of my sight!' Mom had given her orders.

Could it really be that simple? Just like sending me to buy soy sauce? I sat on the bed a little longer, then started packing a few clothes. On my way through the living room, I said a few words to Dad. Then I went out the front door.

Walking down the street, I wept. Not because of Mom's crying and yelling, but because she had gone through that letter. An indescribable mood weighed down my heart. It was like loneliness, the loneliness of not having anyone to turn to or anyone to tell your troubles to. It was even more like terror, the terror of not knowing what the future held. I walked all the way back to the dorm, afraid to take a bus in case I saw someone. I felt any pair of eyes would be able to see right through me, to see that secret of mine that was already no secret.

I don't understand how I could have become such a woman, sometimes terrifyingly self-confident, sometimes peculiarly weak. I walked for forty minutes, and when I got back to the dorm it was after two in the morning.

—Is the editor-in-chief in?

Having found the huge office, she popped her head in and made a timid inquiry. The office was piled high with little mountains of newspapers, manuscripts and magazines. She was thrown by the confusion, and didn't know where to look at first.

—The editor-in-chief isn't in, he said. He's not here, but come in.

—No, she said. She'd worry if she gave the manuscript to anyone else. I'll go, she said.

—Come in, come in. He may be back any minute.

She hesitated, then went in. She recognized the man sitting at the desk. It was him. He'd lectured in the Philosophy Department last semester. The white piece of paper he'd autographed was still in her notebook. She'd thought she'd never see him again. It had never occurred to her he might work here; she only knew he was a famous writer.

She stood there, a little excited, not sure whether to tell him she'd heard him lecture. Looking at him, so full of passionate commitment, she felt ridiculous. Lots of people had heard him lecture, he wouldn't remember her, he'd think she was trying to flirt with him.

—Sit down, he said. There aren't any tigers in here, you know. Sit down. Why so far away? Come and sit over here.

He looked up, put the cap on his fountain pen, and pointed to a chair in front of his desk. She sat down. Somehow she felt scared to look at him, so she casually picked up a newspaper.

—Wang Keke, he said out of nowhere. Wang Keke. When he said 'Ke' he pronounced it 'Ko', a bit like coffee bean, or chocolate. She didn't correct him, just put her newspaper down and stared at him in amazement. He remembers my name, she thought. How could he remember my name?

I'm a lilac tree on a summer night
You're the wind rushing through the black night.
You're the wind rushing through the black night,
Knocking at my waiting heart.

God! That was her poem! A little poem of hers that had been published in the school journal, and he'd memorized it! This great writer she worshipped had memorized a pathetic little poem of hers. She didn't dare believe her own ears.

—That's my poem! she said, as though someone had stolen something of hers. He laughed. His laugh was very open. It filled the solemn room with a bright and spirited light.

That's how they started talking. He asked about her studies, and what else she'd written. She was only too happy to answer. He drove away her remaining inhibitions, as though shooing little flies.

He went on to talk about poetry, about Eliot, Neruda and Whitman. He also mentioned a Chilean woman poet she'd never heard of, insisting her style was very much like hers, and that the woman was an unrivaled genius. He wasn't lecturing her at all. He was so relaxed and open, as though they were old friends who had known each other for a very long time.

He was very respectful of her opinions, and even agreed with some of the objections she raised. He was so generous and affable, he didn't seem to know how compelling she found his words. She was so lucky, so much luckier than all the other students.

Only when the end of work bell rang did she realize she'd been sitting there almost two hours. Only later did she find out the editor-in-chief hadn't been in at all that day.

That evening, she wrote in her diary: I got to know him. We had a conversation, just the two of us. I'm so lucky. I'm sure God has sent him to help me. I must read all those books he talked about.

The next day was Sunday. She was singing like a bird helping Mom do the washing, when her brother said someone had come to see her.

—Oh, it's you!

She hadn't thought it might be him.

—I was passing by, so I thought I'd drop in, he said. It was on the way. I've brought you a couple of books.

—Oh, that's nice of you.

She'd never had a guest her family didn't already know, so she wasn't sure whether to invite him to come and sit in her room or not.

—You're busy, I'll be on my way. I was just passing by.

He was so sensitive. But this made her feel she wasn't being cordial enough. She took him to her room, and even got her brother to bring some apples. Apparently he could feel awkward in unfamiliar places too. He just sat there for a moment and then insisted he had to go. She felt warm inside.

—Well, let me see you off then, she said.

He neither agreed nor protested, but just looked at her with his unfathomably deep eyes, meeting hers. She was flustered for a moment, and then, avoiding his gaze, she picked up two apples cool as could be and led the way out.

Neither of them spoke for quite a stretch. Maybe to appear innocent and lively, or maybe to dispel the solemn atmosphere, she deliberately looked all about, sometimes kicking a stone or jumping forward two steps. In the end, she cracked a joke, but even she knew it fell flat. He managed a laugh, but not because of the joke, rather just to be nice. She was furious, both because of his laughter and because of her own stupidity and falseness.

—Don't go back, Keke. Keep me company a bit further.

He addressed her without using her last name for the first time, and he took her gently by the arm too.

—I wasn't passing by, Keke. I came specially to see you. Why are you staring? Don't you believe me? I don't know why, either, but I think it was to make sure you really do look the way you do and your voice really does sound the way it does. Because yesterday, after you'd gone, it all went straight out of my mind and, no matter how hard I tried, even till it hurt, I couldn't remember.

She laughed loud and happy. She thought that was how poets and artists were. It was such a little thing, but it was still worth trekking into the sun all this way.

His frankness made her open up a bit, and she started chatting with him about all sorts of things. Without even thinking, she followed him into the park by the road. When they sat down very close together on a bench, she suddenly felt it wasn't quite right and, embarrassed, she instinctively shifted away. He smiled understandingly.

—Do you have any children? she asked.

—Yes, a boy and a girl. I like my daughter, she hates me to leave her.

He didn't try to hide anything about his family.

—Is your wife nice? Where does she work?

This time he didn't answer right away. He looked down and ran his fingers through his hair. He didn't look at her. Apparently, she had offended him.

—Are you reminding me? he asked. *Reminding me, a man with a wife, that I shouldn't ask you to come and sit here with me, that I can't do that, is that it?*

My God! He always sees straight through me. He sees me clearer than I see myself.

She jumped up from the bench, wanting to avoid this x-ray vision of his.

—Hit the nail on the head, didn't I?

He grabbed her hand, grabbed hard, pulling roughly, his palm damp with cold sweat. He looked up at her and smiled, not an understanding smile now, but bitter and cruel. She went weak at the sight of it.

—Come on, you'd better sit down, he said. He didn't let go of her hand. *Let me tell you, I don't have a wife. I just have an old woman. I don't have a wife,* he said.

He let go of her hand. She had calmed down, and her gaze was steady again.

—Your marriage is unhappy, is that it? she asked quietly, and sat down beside him again.

It seemed he hadn't heard her question, or he didn't want to answer. He stared straight ahead, as though gazing at some very distant spot. She believed it was a painful, lonely world beyond her imagination.

She had uncovered his secret, and seen a lonely soul. She didn't know what to do. Comfort him, or just keep him company? I don't understand anything, I don't know anything. I'm almost twenty, and still so shallow…

He took her hand again. This time he held it gently in his palm, stroking it with his fingers. She didn't pull away. Maybe this way she could do a little to alleviate his suffering and anxiety, she thought.

—You're my little friend, he said. *Are you my little friend, Keke?*

She nodded, and all of a sudden felt very upset.

—Okay, Keke. Go back home. I've kept you too long.

—No, I'll sit with you awhile longer.

—That's okay. Go on now.

She went, and he stayed. She felt awful, as though she'd been mean to him or owed him something. She hadn't been able to help him at all. On her way, she worried how long he would sit there. Maybe she should go back?

Mom and Dad weren't home. They'd taken their grand-daughter out to play. I figured they had discussed it and agreed to let my elder brother launch the attack. They knew that sometimes I would talk to him about things I couldn't tell them. Sure enough, my brother brought something cold to drink, then planted himself in my room. It was as though I was a guest he had to keep company.

I waited for the family verdict.

'I've asked around.' After a silence, he decided to lay his cards on the table. 'He's got a family, he's got children and he's got a wife.'

He thought he was announcing something that had been kept secret from me. He thought I was being cheated.

'I know,' I said.

'You dumped Nan Huang for him. He's not worth it. You'll regret it.'

'Maybe I will!' That was the truth; I'd already realized that.

'Well, then, why do you want to go on with it?'

Why, why, why. Perhaps if I knew why, I'd be able to stop it.

'Keke, you mustn't trust him. He's conning you.'

'No, he isn't. He loves me.'

'Nan Huang loves you too, and you loved Nan Huang!'

'It's not the same.'

'What on earth do you love about him, a man almost twice your age? Is it because he's famous? Let me tell you, Nan Huang will be famous, too.'

There was nothing I could say. How could I explain? And if I did, could he understand? I could say his fame had stopped attracting me long ago, and now it was his great pain and sadness, that pain which gave him an iron soul, deep and profound. It was that suffering soul that was so compelling to me. As for Nan Huang, all he could do was hang mushrooms around my neck. I could not tell my brother all that. I love him, to the point where I worship his suffering. Would he think I'd lost my mind?

'He's got a wife, and he's got two children.' My brother pointed the cruel facts out to me again. 'Would he get a divorce for you?'

I couldn't deny I was already feeling less and less confident about this, but I knew my desire to marry him was much more pressing now than when he'd told me he'd get a divorce.

'I'm the only one he loves!' I declared to my brother, and to myself.

—*I don't want to hurt the children, and of course I feel sorry for their mother too, he said. But the one I feel sorriest for is my little daughter. She's as sensitive as me, but she's terribly dependent too, like her mother.*
—*I understand.*
She thought she had the strength to say this, and concealed her despair with a sympathetic look. But later she discovered she hadn't admitted her true feelings at all, and that she hadn't understood anything.
She didn't understand. He had declared his love to her, had pleaded for her love so ardently, and had told her with such conviction that he wanted to marry her. She had trusted him so implicitly she displayed total commitment. So why did he have to mention the burden of his family even more often?

'Keke, what exactly is your relationship with that man?' my brother asked nervously, having finally realized something.

'We're involved, and I've had an abortion.'

I made up the part about the abortion, just to get him back. Once I had been afraid I was pregnant. He had said, don't worry, Keke, don't worry. If you really are, just blame me, me alone. He said that for me he would willingly take responsibility for everything.

'That stinking bastard!' My brother sprang to his feet.

'No, he's not. He loves me. He didn't force me.'

'When did it begin?'

I didn't answer, because I didn't know when I should calculate from.

'Never mind, Keke, don't be afraid.' My brother got a grip on himself, and spoke urgently. 'Never mind, Keke, as long as the child wasn't born, neither of you owes the other anything. Keke, I won't tell anyone, not even Mom and Dad. Break it off with him, Keke.'

He thought that was the only reason I didn't want to leave the guy. I didn't want to talk to him about anything anymore, so I turned over on the bed, my face to the wall.

'You really are a fool!' My brother yelled and rushed out of the room.

I was a fool and it was all my own doing. But how could my brother know the problems he'd pointed out were all things I'd thought of and sweated over thousands of times? In an effort to escape that man, I'd held on to Nan Huang to the last, and taken advantage of his feelings for me. How could I not know Nan Huang was younger, better looking, more moral, and maybe had an even better future? However, when he appeared before me, all that crumbled to dust. He was a monster.

—*Keke, it's me. Do you know who it is?*
—*Who is it? Her heart began beating so loudly he must have heard it. She knew perfectly well it was him, but she asked anyway. She wished she hadn't told him her family's number. This was already the third time he had called since she'd come home on Saturday evening.*

Come and meet me, okay? Instead of answering her question, he asked her out again. Can you come out for awhile? I've got something to tell you. I'll be waiting at the usual place in an hour.

She knew where he meant; it was that park she'd gone into with him last week. They'd only been there once; how could it have become the usual place already? She was a bit scared, as if she knew what was going to happen. Don't go! She told herself. Don't go! She made herself dawdle over dinner, and even volunteered to help Mom with the dishes. An hour passed; could he still be there? Could he still be waiting, hoping she'd come? She couldn't start doing anything else; there was only one thing on her mind.

—*Mom, I'm going back to school.*
Mom wanted her to wait till morning. She hemmed and hawed, saying she was about to graduate, so there was a lot to do. Mom thought she really wanted to go find Nan Huang, so she didn't stop her.

—*You're hopeless, Mom said.*
She ran to the usual place. Just before she left, she remembered to bring the two books he'd lent her. That way I can just return them and end it, she thought. It'll save me a trip.

He really was still there, sitting on the bench. The dim rays from a street lamp in front of him shone down, illuminating his forehead. His hands were neatly arranged on his knees, and he stared straight ahead, like a grade school student concentrating on the teacher.

—*Hey, I'm here, she said as she walked up to him. What's up? He turned to look at her. His reactions were slow, as though he was so preoccupied by his own problems he hadn't recognized her for a moment.*

—*I've written a few poems, he said. It's all because I met you that I finally managed to write them.*

Without waiting for her to connect, he began reciting them, one after the other.

I neither see,
Nor listen,
But can never forget...

Each poem was very short, but brilliant and full of unexpected depths.
She'd never known anybody express such profound feelings with such simple
words.

You're a clear, dear stream,
I'm a rock in the water...

She was touched by the honest beauty he had created, and felt a large,
invisible force drawing her towards him. Forgetting why she'd come, she
moved closer without even thinking about it.

—*You're cold, Keke? Are you cold?* He asked with concern, taking her
hand in both of his. *How come your hand's so cold? Don't you like my*
poems?

She shook her head, silently looking at him. She didn't know why, but
all she wanted to do was weep. He put his arm around her shoulders, and
began to draw her close. In spite of herself, she didn't resist. She went with
the flow and leaned against him. Her legs were frozen in place, for fear of
interrupting his flow.

In a deep, husky voice, he told her his life story. He was a peasant's
son. He'd begged and labored in the fields, and in hard times he'd seen his
own little sister torn apart by mad dogs. Marrying his wife was part of a
deal he made with his parents that year in exchange for leaving their poor
mountain gully to become a miner...

She felt she'd simply dissolved and fallen, fallen into his well, his well
of pain.

—*Keke, let me kiss you, okay?*

His sudden demand reawakened her. She panicked, realizing she had
just forgotten herself. She shook her head vigorously, and struggled out of
his arms to stand up.

—*I've got a boyfriend,* she said. *I've got a boyfriend.*

As if mocking himself, he clutched his hands in front of his chest, then
put them back down.

—*Why don't I walk you home? It's getting late,* he said.

But he didn't walk her home. They started wandering this way and
that, up and down the paths in the park. He talked again about the piece
of reportage he'd just published, 'Report From Home'. It had created quite
a stir.

—They've reported me, he said.

The bosses in his old home province had already written a letter of accusation to the Standing Committee of the National People's Congress, saying it was all lies.

—Go and explain then, she urged.

—Explain? What's to explain? And who should I explain to?

Suddenly he was brandishing his fist under a big tree, as though he was going to punch her out. She was stunned; he'd never spoken to her like that before.

—Have you ever gone hungry?

Searching her memory, she shook her head, because she never had, and because she was ashamed.

—Do you know what it feels like?

—Sometimes, if I don't have time to eat in the mornings before class, my stomach starts rumbling before it's over.

—You've never gone hungry, you've never eaten moldy dried yams, he said, shaking his head. You don't know that the most terrible thing on earth is to go hungry. I'm telling you, I can't explain myself to anyone, I can't lower my head to anyone. I'm going back to my old home again, to walk all around the mountains there, and I'm going to spend my whole life shouting out on behalf of the starving people!

Wasn't he blowing it all out of proportion, putting on a bit of an act, exaggerating? That was what flashed through her mind. But when she saw his eyes glistening with tears in the moonlight, she reproached herself for being so hypocritical and shallow, where he was so deep, so experienced. She didn't know what it was to go hungry, she hadn't eaten moldy dried yams and she hadn't dug coal in the deep, deep mines. She couldn't produce deep thought and rich emotions like he could, she...

She didn't know how she ended up in his embrace. She just felt the power of his arms and lips, fervent as the flames of hunger. If she hadn't resisted in time, she'd have gone limp on top of him.

She'd never been held and kissed by a man like this before; it was as if she could hear her ribs and shoulder blades creaking. Her lips and tongue were being sucked and bitten desperately. She couldn't stop herself from beginning to moan.

—Oh, Keke, I've hurt you, haven't I? I'm sorry, Keke, I've hurt you.

As he muttered, he went on kissing and biting her neck, her ears, her hair, her shoulders, her eyes, her forehead. She felt her whole body begin to tremble as if a current was coursing through it. Without even knowing it, she moved closer, clutching her arms around his neck and desperately burying her head in his shoulder. As if by doing that she could avoid him.

—*Keke, don't be like that, Keke. I'm for real, can't you tell? Don't think anything else, he said. Tonight, there's just the two of us. Kiss me, okay? Kiss me, Keke, he said.*

She looked up and saw his eyes; his deep gaze seemed about to envelop her. She stood on tiptoe and kissed him lightly on the cheek.

—*Why be like that, Keke? He took her face in both hands as he asked, staring at her lips. Am I asking too much?*

He covered her face again. This time he kissed long and gentle, holding her spellbound, leaving an unforgettable impression. She felt his love. She couldn't stop herself from kissing him back. This actually made him weep. The tears ran into his mouth, and into hers too.

—*I love you, Keke. These last few days, my heart has ached at every thought of you, he said. If you hadn't come this evening, I would have waited all night. Do you believe me? Still, you did come. You're so good.*

She didn't say anything. She didn't want to say anything, and she didn't want to think, either. She just wanted to rest quietly against his chest, listening to the beat of his living, suffering heart.

Were it possible, she would have happily stayed like that for the rest of her life.

It was late, but I could just make out the sound of the family talking in the living room. I was sure it was my brother reporting his talk with me back to Mom and Dad. I heard Mom's high-pitched crying. She wasn't screaming or yelling anymore because she had given up already. All because of me, no one had felt like eating dinner.

After awhile, the light in the living room was still on, but nobody was talking anymore, so I tiptoed in. Dad was by himself, sitting smoking on the big sofa with his back to me. I knew he'd given it up years ago.

As I approached him, it occurred to me for the first time that Dad was haggard and skinny. Apart from that gigantic nose, which still flushed red, almost all of him was white and pallid.

'Dad,' I called out softly.

'Oh, you've got up, have you, Keke? Hungry, are you? Have some of these.' He opened the box on the side table. He had been waiting for me.

'Dad,' I said. I didn't eat, I just sat next to him on the rug and buried my face between his legs. Dad really was skinny. The bones in his legs were like two old wooden stakes, and they hurt my face.

'Keke.' Dad took my head in both his hands, smoothing my tousled hair. 'Keke, don't be sad. We won't say any more, we just want you to be happy!'

Happy! Where is happiness?

I cried again, my tears dripping onto his legs.

6

I really didn't know how to thank Little Bull. If he hadn't helped me in the rehearsal room, it would have been all over by now.

Zhao proved more resourceful than I had ever expected. While I was up all hours with the actors and discussing changes with Little Bull, he was making accusations left, right and center. It started in the theater, and went all the way up to the Arts Bureau of the Ministry of Culture. I don't know what he told them, but they sent a special investigation team.

First, I tried a round of argument on the investigators. I explained I hadn't the slightest personal prejudice against Zhao, that the conflict had arisen over purely artistic differences. However, I quickly discovered that was no use. Indeed, it could only be counter-productive, because the head of the team was an old school friend of Zhao's from 1958, and it was all too obvious I wasn't even born then.

Later, I started to feel I was partly to blame, that I should lay my cards on the table and have it out with Zhao. Maybe it was just a lack of understanding. However, Zhao had disappeared, announcing I'd got him so upset he'd developed a heart problem and was going to the hospital. I couldn't understand how a man so glowing with health, who'd argued so vigorously with me, even thrown a script in my face, could have heart disease. If that woman doctor in the hospital who'd diagnosed his illness wasn't his little sister, then she was his—well, I'd better not say.

The decision on the problem was an order to halt rehearsals and for Comrade Wang Keke to be suspended from her duties while she undertook self-criticism. What damned duties did I have? The notice was pasted on the blackboard by the entrance to the theater offices. By then, it was too late to accuse Zhao of abusing and hitting me. Even if I accused him of smashing a hole in my head, it would be no use.

The play was off. Only then did I understand the full import of Zhao's last words that day. 'You wait, Wang Keke!…You wait and see!' I also came to the sober realization that if I didn't give in, he could step up the torture a degree or two. Maybe he would push me beyond the pale into total disgrace, out of the theater forever. At the moment, Zhao was only thinking about his own damaged standing and he didn't care about me at all.

When I went back to my dorm room, my morale was greatly improved and I felt none of it mattered at all. I used a brush pen to write on a big sheet of white paper, 'This person is writing up a self-criticism; please do not disturb.' At the bottom of the page I drew an ugly old dog barking furiously. When I finished it even I had to laugh. I stuck the notice on the door and fell into a deep sleep on the bed. I was exhausted.

A dusk deep in autumn, overcast and cold. It had rained all day, and it was still dripping now.

They hadn't seen each other for more than six months, and he had just returned from another province. For the sequel to that reportage, he'd hiked around nearly every village in the mountains of his old home. He was swarthy and thin, and he'd even lost some hair. The eyes hiding behind his glasses were so bloodshot it seemed even a lifetime's sleep wouldn't make them better.

He sat waiting for her on the bench in the usual place, holding an umbrella. His off-white trench coat was soaked. When he looked up he seemed weighed down with worry, and apparently he didn't even have the strength to greet her. He just gazed fixedly at her, then gave her a forced grin.

He must have been through a lot, there's even more pressure on him, she thought.

—Why do we have to sit here? It's so cold. She made an effort to sound bright and lively. Come on, let's go to my place. I'll make you some coffee.

He was unresisting and followed her like an obedient child, but he would not talk. He just listened to her bubbling away about her own new worries since being assigned to the theater. Dancing about and gesticulating, she gave a highly exaggerated account of the people there. She wanted to cheer him up. However, he neither spoke nor laughed, but just turned his head occasionally to look at her. Furious, she stopped walking.

—We're not going! We're not going! Go away!

He stood still, looking at her.

—You wanna make me laugh? Okay, then. He really started to laugh. He laughed so hard he doubled over, even clutched his stomach. He laughed

so loud everyone turned to look, but he couldn't stop. As though it was catching, she started laughing like an idiot too.

They went on, their mood much improved, though they still said almost nothing to each other.

The last six months had gone well both for her and for Nan Huang, both of them graduating and getting the work assignments they wanted. But she had to admit that every time they looked ahead, sometimes even planning their little family, she couldn't stop herself from thinking of him. She was always wondering where he was and what he was doing. There had been no news of him since that letter. Was he still alive? He wasn't in prison, was he? Also—she didn't know since when exactly—but it wasn't his fame or even his genius that attracted her now, but what he'd been through and his suffering.

Entering her little dorm room and turning on the light, she asked if he was okay, but his face fell again and he didn't reply.

—Sit down. I'll make you some coffee.

—No, Keke. Come over here. At last, he spoke. Come over here, he said.

She went over, feeling a little panicky. Sure enough, he grabbed her by the shoulders and pulled her towards him, pressing his face down onto hers.

—No, don't be like that, she said.

She struggled free. He was taken by surprise, then his eyes dimmed. He avoided her gaze, sighed heavily, then sat dejected on the bed.

—Okay, then, he said. Okay.

She felt she was acting strangely all of a sudden, so she sat by him and cradled one of his arms in her hands.

—I've figured it all out. We won't be like that again. We'll be good friends, the best of friends. Okay? But we won't be like that again. I'll go make some coffee.

He didn't let her stand up, didn't let her leave. He held her tight with his surprising strength and ardor, and she tasted his overwhelmingly passionate kisses again.

She couldn't resist, couldn't control herself. Couldn't even deny she'd yearned for his burning kisses again. He really was too strong, too powerful! She felt the room beginning to spin. To stop herself from going limp, she grabbed his shoulders, but he pushed her away, caught her toppling body, and laid her flat on the bed. Alarmed, she wanted to escape, but it was too late, he was on top of her already.

—I won't hurt you, Keke, he said. I couldn't hurt you.

Gasping, he said this to her as he kissed her, bit her and pressed down on her, his mouth blocking hers. His hands went for her underwear.

She shook her head and pushed him away, thinking I'm not that sort of woman, I'm not that sort of woman. But her resistance was weak and half-hearted. He had already undone her buttons.

—Let me look at you, Keke. I'll just take a quick look, just a quick look. It's been six months. I've missed you so much I almost went crazy. Didn't you miss me? he asked. Let me look at you.

She let go. She trusted him so. She wondered, aren't I being too easy doing this, and at the same time she let him take off her clothes, all her clothes.

This was the first time she'd ever bared her young body in front of a man. She was so nervous her teeth chattered, and a feeling she'd never had before rose up through her from the soles of her feet. Both shamed and joyous, she didn't dare open her eyes to look at him.

—Oh, so beautiful! Keke, you're so beautiful!

He began to touch her. His hands slid all over her.

—So delicate, so white, just like carved ivory!

With his gentle stroking, she found her inner shame had already turned into an indescribable tumult; a terribly exciting and stifling tumult she'd never experienced before.

Her thoughts were all over the place. Between her mind and her body, she couldn't find a focal point, a point she might fix on. She'd been dismembered. She wanted to grab something that could prove her own existence.

But the last thing she expected her stretched out hand to connect with was another body. Opening her eyes, she was dumbfounded. This man before her, this man she revered and worshipped, had taken off all his clothes.

She suddenly felt disgusted; this naked man was strange and terrifying to her. She struggled with him on the bed, but knew it was too late. She had no energy, couldn't find her own strength; he'd already dismembered her. He was like a lion, and her resistance only increased his strength. She was exhausted, her mind a blank...

He penetrated her.

—What? It's your first time! I'm your first! I must be crazy, Keke, he said. I must be crazy. Don't blame me, I love you! I love you!

She wasn't resisting anymore. Let him do what he wanted. She was his to do with as he wanted, even though her tears were uncontrollable.

—You're crying, Keke. Didn't you want it? Don't cry, Keke. I'm a beast. But you don't understand, you still don't understand anything! I'm not totally to blame for this. You're too attractive, too sexy, you know? You're so sexy it's frightening.

He kissed away her tears with his tongue, holding her and rocking her. She just cried, hung on to his neck and cried. She was surprised, but she

didn't hate him terribly, and she didn't regret it. Still, she kept asking
herself; have I become a bad woman?

'Keke! Keke!'
    I could tell it was Little Bull outside the door.
    'Keke, don't count sheep. Hurry up and open the door!'
He was getting worried. 'Keke, if you don't open up, I'll go
and get help!'
    He made it sound like I'd swallowed a bottle of tranquilizers
or hung myself. There was nothing for it: I crawled out of bed
and opened the door. Little Bull's head appeared around it,
looking for all the world like an unripe cucumber. I gave him
a couple of grunts, then let him calm down. Seeing what a
mess I looked, he ventured to ask, 'What have you been
doing?'
    'Sleeping.'
    'Really?' Little Bull looked me in the eyes, like a suspicious
cop.
    'Really. I was sound asleep. Even if the sky had fallen in it
wouldn't have woken me. I slept away a whole week's sleep.'
    Once he heard me talking like this, he began to breathe
again. 'What shall we do, Keke?' he asked.
    'What do you mean, what shall we do?' For a moment I
didn't know what he was talking about.
    'What about you? What about the play? What about me?'
He already associated himself with my play. I was so moved I
wanted to kiss him.
    'I give in. We'll go on with the play somehow, with you
as director. It's all up to you, friend!' I half joked.
    Little Bull looked as though he'd been entrusted with a
great mission. He even stuck his hand out and shook mine
firmly. That was a bit much; it was as if I'd just spoken my last
words. But never mind, I was deeply grateful he'd come to
see me.
    We talked about what to do. He was like an army com-
mander devising strategies. We agreed that first I should soften
my stance towards the investigation team and the theater
leaders and then go with him to the Ministry of Culture to see
a vice-minister. If we went over everything from the start with
the vice-minister, maybe he'd be sympathetic and speak on
our behalf. I said so long as rehearsals could begin again,
nothing else mattered. I asked Little Bull how his connection

with the vice-minister was. Was it solid? Little Bull said the year he was in the graduation show in the drama academy's small auditorium, the vice-minister had been impressed by him. As Little Bull remembered it, the vice-minister had even patted him on the shoulder and invited him to come visit him at home.

'Did you go?' I asked anxiously.

'No, but I'm certain he'll remember me.' Little Bull was very confident of his own appeal.

I knew this business had already shaken up the Ministry of Culture so much no one could have remained ignorant of it. However, I decided to go and try all the same. By now, I didn't care if I didn't get anywhere or even if it blew up in my face. Just so long as rehearsals could begin again. My dreams were filled with longing for the moment of success. If the play was done for, I might be done for too. I'd get him to see my play.

Finally, nodding his head at me meaningfully, Little Bull left. He always overdid it a bit. Maybe that's an occupational hazard for stage actors. We agreed to muster at seven o'clock the next morning outside the theater.

He'd regained his strength quickly and was full of confidence again. The sequel to his 'Report From Home' had attracted the attention of the government, and apparently they were already preparing to send an investigation team to check into the situation.

—You gave me this strength, he said. Do you know that? You gave it to me. The folks back home will be grateful to me.

He took her lips and kissed her all over, as though sucking in the nectar of life. She felt his flaming passion. Every time he spoke, a hot wave surged through her.

—What did the people back home call you when you were little? she asked with a giggle. Yam? Eggplant? Oh, right! It was Potato! Potato! Yes, you really do look like a potato. Latin name, Solanum tuberosum. Or was it Dried Yam?

She burst out laughing. Laughed until she couldn't breathe properly. She turned over, and the laughter was muffled by the pillow. She lifted her legs and kicked away at the footboard.

He spanked her and shook her almost angrily to stop her.

—Hit me, she said. Go right ahead. You're still Potato. Even if you wanted to be Chocolate, you wouldn't stand a chance. He crawled over and buried his face in her hair, eagerly taking in its scent.

It was a sunny smell, he said. Keke, your hair has a sunny smell.
She was so young and vital. Could she ever become old? In his arms,
she could.

Early the next morning, and seven o'clock at last. I was just
hesitating about whether to get up or hang on in bed a bit
longer, when I heard Little Bull yelling my name from down
below. That Little Bull, he's only worried someone may not
know he's with me! He's announcing his loyalty to the
whole world. Never mind! In for a penny, in for a pound.
Besides, everybody's got an eye on me already. I pulled on
the red dress that showed my figure off best, and I didn't
forget to dab some perfume on as I left.

I followed Little Bull on my bike; chin up, chest out,
through the front gate. Meilun was sure to be leaning out of
the window looking.

After fifty minutes cycling, and then three hours waiting at
the Ministry of Culture, we finally got to meet with the
vice-minister a few minutes before lunch. In the end, it only
took five minutes and the problem was solved.

The big shot vice-minister said, 'I completely understand
the matter, okay? You don't need to say any more, okay? I
think the play rehearsals can continue, okay? When young
people fall down, they get right up again, okay? Put your
energy into trying to win an award, okay? However, the
investigation has to be done too, okay? Genuinely and sincerely apologize and say you're sorry to Director Zhao, okay?
It's not like the old days now, okay? If you put a mistake right,
you're still a good comrade, okay?'

I nodded away like a woodpecker. I didn't know I'd ever
fallen, but I stared at the vice-minister's big mouth like I was
listening to the Bible being read out. Even after we'd got on
our bikes and gone a fair way, my ears were still ringing with
those okays, and I just could not shake them out.

At lunchtime, I invited Little Bull to a Western-style restaurant. We bought a bottle of beer and a pack of cigarettes. We
shouted and laughed over our victory and toasted the vice-
minister's approval, almost breaking the restaurant glasses.

Little Bull did a perfect imitation of the vice-minister.
'Fallen down, okay! Get right up again, okay! Young people,
okay! Put your energy into it, okay! Put a mistake right, okay!
Good comrades, okay!'

I laughed till my stomach hurt.

After we'd eaten, somehow we were still hungry, so we went to a grocery. We got out all our money. It was about sixty or seventy yuan altogether, and we spent the lot on food. Four bags of powdered milk, two pounds of chocolate, ten cans of various things, one heap of fruit, and four big watermelons. There was still some left. Little Bull wouldn't stand for that, so just to be different, he went out to the street stalls and picked some martial arts novels and romances. One was called *Water Dragon, Fire Phoenix*, another *Legend of the Sword*, and there was one even sillier, called *Who Does She Love?* Our bicycles draped with enough goods to open an exhibition, we rushed to the hospital where Zhao was.

When we turned up at Zhao's sickbed dripping with sweat and gifts, he was telling his fortune with a pack of cards. I figured he was chanting incantations to make sure my play was absolutely done for. When he saw us, he was scared at first, but quickly regained his composure.

Carrying our gifts, we stood by Zhao's bed. Unfazed by the surprised looks from the other patients, I sincerely criticized myself right in front of him.

'Director Zhao, I was wrong. I'm young, and I don't know much. I don't know my own limitations, and a sensible man like you really shouldn't take it to heart. If you've really been so upset it's damaged your health, that's a loss to the theater and to the revolution. I've already handed in a self-criticism to the theater Party Committee, asking the administration to punish me, but not demote me this time. The head of the theater will probably send someone with the self-criticism for you to read, so I…'

I went on and on, terribly emotional, until I even moved myself with my own sincerity. Everyone else was hanging on every word. They must have thought my crimes against Zhao were punishable by hanging at the very least.

Zhao was so magnanimous. He waved his hand at me palm inwards, as if brushing away cigarette ash. This gesture suggested he hadn't been upset at all, that he'd never taken what I'd done to heart.

It was as though Little Bull and I had been rescued from the electric chair. We put our things down, then panicked and fled.

I didn't feel the least bit humiliated. On the contrary, I was as happy as could be. As soon as I was out of the hospital gate,

I leaped on my bike. On the road, Little Bull watched my crazy movements with the amused tolerance of someone much older. Really, I wanted to turn the bloody bike upside down and ride it or, if that was impossible, pedal it with my hands. I completely forgot I didn't have any money to buy food for the rest of the month. Other people go broke at the end of the month, but I'm always broke halfway through.

7

They'd eaten out together many times before, and though the food was nothing special, at least it was a bit better than what the canteen had to offer. She didn't want him to spend too much, so sometimes she paid; she did everything to make her relationship with him equal. No matter where or when they ate, she was always ravenous. That seemed to make him happy; he kept putting more food into her bowl, even giving her some of the rice in his.

—When other girls eat out with their lovers, they act more refined. How come you're so hungry? Just like a little she-wolf!

She knew this was a compliment. He'd said she was the most open, the most natural, the most incapable-of-faking-it girl he'd ever seen.

Today, she couldn't swallow a mouthful. Just looking at the beautiful red and green food glistening with sauce was enough; she didn't want to touch it.

She couldn't remember how many times they had argued during the last few months. Although every disagreement ended with him overcoming her with ardent kisses, they never really settled anything, they always left it simmering.

Last time she had told him about her fight with the director, and asked him what to do.

—Director Zhao said he saw us in the park, followed us for two whole hours, and heard everything we said, she exaggerated.

—So what? With something like that, it doesn't matter what anyone says unless you're caught in the act.

Then he told her how he'd handle it if he ran into that sort of problem at work. What he said made her furious. He was acting stupid, she didn't want to listen. What she wanted to know was if he still intended to marry her.

—I love you, Keke. I can't believe you still don't trust me. Why get angry? Then he went to embrace her again.

She kicked, bit and shoved, but he didn't get mad at all. He fell onto the bed, and let her vent her frustration.

—*Strangle me, he said. Strangle me!*

He made it sound as though she was being unreasonable and forcing him to marry her. He had it so tough, he suffered so much. He not only had a wife, he had kids too. Didn't he keep saying he loved her? Surely that was enough?

She lay on his chest and cried, wondering how she'd become such a vulgar woman. But he forgave her, held her and rocked her like a small child, repeating what he'd said a hundred thousand times before. Then he churned up her emotions and fulfilled her with his unbounded passion, making her yield to him completely, her heart cracking with love.

Later, it still wasn't over. They argued several times more, and several times things were as good as they'd always been. Like an actress, she recited lines she'd rehearsed to him. First she poured out her troubles, then she yelled accusations through gritted teeth.

She said he was a shameless bastard, a cheat without a conscience. Why had he gone after her? He wanted to possess her. And why had he stopped being faithful to her? She wished she had claws so she could rip his face up. But that made it even clearer that she could not stop herself from loving him. He knew it too, and every time he held her pale, shining face and kissed her, her fury subsided, and she fell into his arms again.

She really didn't want to start that unfinished argument up again, but she did.

—*My brother asked me why I love you.*

—*What did you say?*

—*I said because I'm the only one you love.*

She stared into his eyes, hoping to find an answer. But he smiled and then avoided her gaze.

—*What else did your brother say?*

—*He asked me if you were prepared to get a divorce for me.*

—*Really? What else?*

—*He also said you were a bastard, that you were deceiving me.*

—*Really?*

She didn't know what his 'really' was really supposed to mean, she just felt the same old fury rushing the doors of her heart. If they weren't in public, she would have turned the table over; plates, bowls and all.

She didn't know how her temper had gotten so bad recently, or how her fury had become so great. She gritted her teeth and swallowed. She struggled against her anger like a firefighter. She was the one who had brought it up again.

She had noticed a little, light yellow sweater in his bag.

—*You bought that for your daughter. It's her birthday soon. How is she? Still pretty?*

He got the sweater out to show her. He'd never tried to hide the fact that he was a good father. However, she felt he was deliberately putting a distance between them.

—Maybe your brother's worried about you. How's that Students Association chairman of yours from your old school?

His voice was so different he sounded like someone else.

—He's not mine, he's got nothing to do with me! Her anger had resurfaced. She used to mention Nan Huang to him a lot, at first to remind him, later to get him mad.

—Do you love him? he would say, not a little jealously. I won't interfere with your relationship, but please don't mention him when you're with me.

But today he had brought Nan Huang up first. What was he up to? Maybe he was reminding her. He certainly didn't want her to dump Nan Huang, nor was he belittling her first love.

She really didn't want to go on talking to him. She didn't have the energy to argue anymore. He never lost his temper, but listened quietly and attentively to her endless railings. Still, she always lost. She began to feel stupid.

—You're despicable!

She spat it out at him, then got up and walked out of the restaurant.

—Keke, Keke! Wait! Wait for me!

She heard him coming after her, but she'd hopped on a bus.

She already realized that they were kicking an invisible ball back and forth. It was a meaningless ball, but it might break the bond between them. She decided someday she would have to talk it through calmly with him.

This time she wouldn't mention anything about marriage; they'd just talk about the unbreakable bond between them.

She hadn't seen him for several days, because she'd been busy with rehearsals. He'd phoned several times to say hello, and they had gotten along quite well, both of them carefully avoiding last time's unhappiness.

She decided to go to his home to see how he lived; maybe it would help her understand him.

—Oh, Keke! What are you doing here?

He cried out in surprise, and took her by the shoulders. Just then his little daughter's head popped out from the room. She felt a bit embarrassed and slipped away from his grasp.

—Dad! Have we got a visitor?

A woman's voice came from the south-facing room, which had a door curtain. It was his wife. She still addressed her husband the way they did back home. Without waiting for him, she lifted the door curtain and went in. She wanted to see her.

The room had two windows, and got plenty of sun. It wasn't a big room, but it was crammed with objects. Still, they were all organized very neatly, and everything was spotlessly clean. Even the books on the two sets of shelves along the outer wall were lined up straight and thoroughly dusted. There was a smell she couldn't quite put her finger on, a bit like vanishing cream, but also a bit like prickly heat powder.

In the middle of the room was a double bed, also neat and tidy. There were two pillows on top of each other at the head of the bed, small and hard. That was probably a custom from back home too. And his wife was there on the bed, half sitting, half leaning. It was a hot day, but she still had a big cotton quilt over her and a dark red scarf around her head. Apparently, she was ill.

She both hated and pitied her. She remembered something he'd said to her, and right away she was filled with pity for his wife.

—Come in and sit down, his wife said. Sit down. Don't stand on ceremony.

His wife greeted her as though they knew each other well. She wasn't bad looking, except her cheeks were a bit big. Her face was quite delicate, and her pouty lips were red. Although you couldn't say her eyebrows were full and her eyes large, her eyelids were as fine as lotus leaves. Only she was a little plump, and her enormous breasts were quite shocking. They pushed against her pretty white blouse like two loaves. Her feet, which poked out from the bottom of the quilt, were pale and small. She didn't know if they were plump or swollen, but they looked as though they'd ooze water if you squeezed them.

Nevertheless, her impression of his wife wasn't bad at all. That slight envy—or was it hatred?—she'd felt on the way went away completely.

—Get our guest something to drink, Dad. Don't just stand there.

The way his wife ended her sentences still sounded very rural, but she hadn't expected such a delicate little voice from that hearty chest. She sounded so fragile one gust of wind could finish her off. And why was she acting like a spoiled child towards her husband in front of a woman guest, if not to show off her wifely rights? Her husband actually did pick up a mug and go.

In her heart, she knew his wife had already started to do battle with her.

—It's no big deal really, but he won't let me move.

Apparently, she was reminding her of her illness.

She sat down on a chair between the desk and the bed. This was to get a sense of where he worked. The desk was very clean, the glass top gleaming like a mirror. Under it there were a few photographs; his son, his daughter, the whole family, and also some of the two of them. She was sure it was his wife who had put them there.

She noticed one yellowing little photo which she finally decided was the two of them when they were younger. His wife still had braids then, and you could tell she had been young and slim once too. He didn't wear glasses then, he looked a bit of a bumpkin. His hair was parted neatly on one side, not one strand out of place. He must have used at least a cupful of hair oil before the photo.

—That was taken when we were in love. Actually, we'd only known each other a couple of days.

They had been in love once too. He'd never mentioned that. She wanted to tell his wife when a man and a woman had only just met, that couldn't count as love, but she didn't. Suddenly, she realized his poems and writings were produced at this desk, his wife sleeping on the bed by his side. At night, under the light of this little desk lamp with its blue glass shade, his wife sometimes slept and sometimes woke, but no matter when, he was there before her whenever she wanted him to be. Maybe he looked at her from time to time too. When he'd finished writing, he'd climb in and lie beside her.

She was his wife, the mother of their children. I hate her and I pity her.

As she turned this thought over again, she felt strange inside. She wasn't sure if she understood him better or if she was more confused. Certainly it was more complicated, and that frustrated her!

Maybe she shouldn't put such heavy demands on him. After all, this family of his had been going for more than a decade.

—Daddy, come here! Come over here. His daughter's voice came calling for him from the other room.

—I'm coming! I'm coming!

She heard him answering hurriedly in the corridor as he rushed to her.

She breathed out and moved the chair back from the desk. She noticed that none of the drawers had a lock. What about my letters? Where's he put my letters? Although there was nothing outrageous in her letters and only he could read between the lines, they were still her letters, the most precious part of her life!

Without realizing it, she stole a glance at his wife. She was busy putting her red scarf back on again. When she finished, she didn't forget to pull a few bangs out from the cloth above her forehead so she'd look natural, and even primped them with her palm. She laughed at her paranoia. You, you're too sensitive, too suspicious. How could he put your letters here? Of course he wouldn't let anyone see them. He said he loved to read your letters, that he kissed them, just like he kissed your eyes.

—Keke, come over here. We'll sit in the other room. Mom's sick. He stood in the doorway holding a glass of water as he called her.

She followed him into the north-facing room. It was a terrible mess. The two children were doing their homework, each bent over one side of the table. A cartoon was showing on a color TV set on a bedside table.

—Off you go, go over to Mom, he ordered.

The boy was quite grown up already, and he headed off immediately, but the girl whined and didn't want to go.

—Be good now, he said. Do as Daddy says.

He patted her head, as though letting her know that he understood she wanted to watch TV, but there was no other way, and so he had to make her leave. The girl got up pouting and mumbling. She didn't forget to turn back and look at her just before she left, either. It made her feel like an invader.

When his daughter left, he closed the door. He came back and sat next to her, then embraced her. Reluctantly, she let him kiss her, then struggled free. She didn't feel like it; this was his daughter's bed.

—What's the matter? No one'll come in, they never interrupt when I'm talking with a guest. You're upset. Are you afraid I'm not really glad to see you? Don't be so silly. Didn't I embrace you just now when you came in? The way he spoke, you'd think she'd come just to hear that sort of stuff. Apparently he was letting her know his desire hadn't abated just because they were meeting in a different place.

She got up and walked over to sit on the little bed facing him, putting her hands flat on a desk piled high with children's schoolbooks and homework, hoping she could calm herself down. She didn't want to part on bad terms again.

She wanted to tell him calmly and honestly she wouldn't bring it up again as long as he loved her the way he had before, that they'd let their relationship be the way it was when it just began, okay? Let's continue on a basis of mutual equality and understanding, making no demands of each other. She wasn't the vulgar sort of woman who absolutely had to get married. He had said it was pre-ordained for women to get married, but she was willing to wait for him till he thought of a way out, even waiting till his children were grown up. Either way, she didn't want to go on kicking that invisible ball back and forth between them because of that issue, kicking it on and on until the understanding and feelings they'd suffered so much for were exhausted.

This time he didn't follow her. He just sat opposite, solemnly watching, with a hint of a smile. He seemed to be waiting for her to speak, but also admiring her. His deep and steady gaze calmed her. She knew that little smile so well.

—I've thought it through. I won't mention that matter again, and don't you give yourself a hard time over it, either. I finally do believe that you love me, she said slowly.

—You're so good, Keke, you're so good. I'm the one who's been unfair. I'm upset about it too, but I'm being pulled in too many different directions. I really have been unfair to you. But I love you, I love you! As he spoke, he stretched across the desk and gently took her hands, playing with her fingers. His eyes shone with boundless affection for her.

No, she couldn't leave him. He'd opened up a whole world for her, a vast world full of suffering and passion, a world she'd never known before. It had changed her outlook on the world, her whole aesthetic. He'd helped her discover and develop her own talents. He said her imagination and emotions really amazed him. He'd made her mature into a real woman. And from him, she'd also gained confirmation of her own attractiveness.

That moment was like warmth on a winters' day; she had found many long lost thoughts again, thoughts like a fine soft rain.

—Let's be like before, let's…

Suddenly she stopped. She simply couldn't believe her eyes but she was sure she wasn't hallucinating. What she saw on the desk really was an envelope. Although it was the back of an envelope and it was covered with numbers, she still recognized it. It was an envelope she'd made herself, folded out of a piece of thick white paper. It was the one she'd sent to him two days before. Inside had been a poem she'd published in the university journal that year, the poem he'd recited for her.

I'm a lilac tree on a summer night,
You're the wind rushing through the black night.
You're the wind rushing through the black night,
Knocking at my heart.

Ringing a million bunches of flower bells,
I sing for you tirelessly under the moon.
I sing for you tirelessly under the moon,
Courageously, lustily in full bloom.

You've plundered my mauve fragrance,
But you won't stay any longer.
But you won't stay any longer,
Abandoning me far away in the night.

She'd sent him this poem to make him remember when they were first in love; to make him take her in his arms and comfort her, saying he wasn't *that wind rushing through the black night, he was her earth, her firm and stable earth.*

—*Who knows if the poem's still inside or not? she thought, but she didn't dare pick it up, and she didn't dare ask. She was afraid of his explanation, even more afraid of his embrace. Maybe this is just an accident, maybe he's locked all my other letters away safely, she explained for him, knowing she was only deceiving herself. She thought it odd that this time she really wasn't angry. There was just a sort of emptiness in her mind, a clear, shining emptiness. It was just like a summer sky at noon, not the slightest breeze, no cloud at all.*

—*I'll be going, she said. She got up unhurriedly.*

—*What is it? he asked. Now what's the matter? He looked surprised, but he didn't try to stop her.*

She remembered to lift the door curtain on the south-facing room and say goodbye to his wife. The two children had crawled onto the bed, and were in their mother's arms, one on each side.

—*Take care. I won't see you out, his wife said, getting up politely, walking over, and leaning against the doorway. Look, I really haven't received you properly, but I've just had a little operation, and I'm afraid of catching a chill.*

When she'd finished, either to upbraid him or flatter him, she looked over towards her husband, and for some reason he suddenly blushed.

She understood everything. His wife had just had an abortion, and she was in the middle of the miscarriage now.

She didn't know how she managed to get out of the apartment and down the stairs. For a time it seemed her legs weren't attached to her body. She was so light she could have been hollow, blown along by the wind.

—*Keke, Keke, wait a minute. I'll see you out.*

He was behind her, calling after her. She stopped on the landing and waited for him, not knowing why she even wanted to see his face again.

—*Keke, listen to me. What is it? Don't run away like a puppy that has been smacked.*

He still had the nerve to crack jokes. However, apparently he sensed something, because he didn't dare touch her.

—*Keke, don't be like this. Listen to me. You don't understand. She cried, cried all night. There was nothing I could do. The children heard, Keke... You don't understand, Keke, he said. Listen to me. I, I'm really having a tough time. Keke...*

She didn't listen to him. She just felt her stomach turning over. She wanted to throw up. She didn't know where she got the strength, but she swung her bag to hit him hard across the face. He ducked, and it landed *on his left shoulder. Taken aback but not panicked, he straightened his glasses.*

That bastard, he's always so composed.

She rushed down the stairs and out into the midday sun. He didn't chase her any further.

She left him lightfooted and unburdened. She didn't know what lay ahead, or what was behind her. There wasn't a single tear; she didn't even want to cry.

8

The play was performed at last.

At first, it was just given a try out in the small auditorium, but it was quickly moved to a theater in the city for public performances. I had a stage role, too. In the last scene, I played the lead's shadow. Because the shadow had no lines and wore a mask, it didn't even get a credit in the program. The actors said it didn't amount to anything, and none of them was willing to take it, so I blacked up and hit the stage myself.

When *The Chair* was performed for the censors in the small auditorium, there was a lot of debate at first, and quite a few leaders opposed it, saying plays like this would destroy proper standards. It was Little Bull who took the initiative again, inviting that enlightened vice-minister along. He not only applauded enthusiastically, but also requested a picture with the cast, which was certainly a great boost for the whole troupe.

I hear the vice-minister told those who disagreed: 'We should support this sort of innovative spirit in young people, okay? Don't write it off just because of a few transgressions, okay? Don't take on a negative role during this era of reform, okay? Keep up with the new wave of the times, okay?'

I got all this from Little Bull that night. He not only had the vice-minister's accent down pat, but even stuffed my big pillow under his clothes for a potbellied look. I split my sides laughing. I hadn't laughed like that for ages. Nothing could get a laugh out of me. My colleagues were beginning to wonder if I hadn't had my sense of humor surgically removed. Except in rehearsals, I was always spaced-out and preoccupied. I just went along with everything. Sometimes even good-natured jokes left me at a loss for words.

The theater leaders held an emergency meeting all night long to discuss the public performance of the play. Arranging a big theater, printing programs, painting posters, getting new costumes made and so on; a whole range of big deal issues. Nobody raised any more opposition, not even that director, Zhao. He didn't want anyone saying he was a fly in the ointment.

The day before opening night, I went home. It was the first time in over two months.

I gave Nan Huang a call and invited him to come and see the play. There was no ulterior motive. I was just inviting him to see the play, which I'd said I would do before we split up. Nan Huang seemed genuinely pleased. However, he hesitated before hanging up, as if he had something else to say. I asked, but he said to let it wait until we met.

Apart from Dad, Mom and my brother, there was a whole pile of relatives and friends that it went without saying had to be invited too. I sat by the phone, dialing my finger to the bone. I told them one by one, saying the same things to each of them. If I'd known it was going to be so much trouble, I would have played a tape down the wires. Mom fluttered around like an old moth, helping me remember who I hadn't told yet. She was busy making dough, so she could make dumplings for me.

Dad sat by on the sofa, taking advantage of the gaps when I was dialing to tell me about his 'I remember when' again. When I started a conversation he stopped, and when I stopped he started again. He made me dial the wrong number quite often, but he seemed happy to keep me company as I went on dialing and dialing. I guess it was his hope for my success. Maybe what really mattered was that Dad hoped the perform- ance of the play would make me happy. Actually, nobody in the family had raised the issue since the last time my brother had spoken to me. I hadn't said anything, either. But I was sure they had been busy reading between the lines.

I didn't phone him, even though I thought of him every time I dialed. Twice I dialed through to his office without even knowing I was doing it. I knew the number too well. Of course, I hung up immediately. He'll come, I thought. The big billboard outside the theater gate almost hit the skies. There were ads in every Beijing newspaper too, and they'd been running for almost a week. Also, quite a few critics and reporters had seen the previews and written pieces. This evening the radio station's capital news program was doing an item too. Even if he were blind, he'd still hear it was going to open soon. He'll come, I was sure. He'd said that from the day he met me, he would take an interest in everything about me. I believed him; he'd never lied to me.

Today, the whole family was happier than they had been for a long time. It was all because of me. Watching Dad cheerily keeping me company all the way through my phone calls, I suddenly understood. I'd really done them wrong. But I didn't know if I could redeem myself. I was less willful already, but nothing could cheer me up. I was as numb as a lump of silicon—water-, fire-, cold- and heat-proof.

'Dad, I'll give you a piggy-back ride, okay?' Even I had no idea I was going to come out with something like that. I loved Dad giving me piggy-back rides when I was small, and even when I was ten I still wanted to climb up on to his shoulders. Mom would shout, 'Get down, get down right now. You'll squash your father.' But I never wanted to get down, and Dad wouldn't let me down, either. He would lope, yelling 'Dog meat! Dog meat for sale! Buy it today or it'll be off tomorrow!' He also said, 'Today I'm carrying Keke, but tomorrow Keke will carry me. Okay, Keke?' Dad would come to a standstill, waiting for my reply. I would laugh and agree 'Yes! Yes! Yes!' as I smacked Dad's head and yelled 'Giddiup! Giddiup! Giddiup!'

I carried Dad on my back. He was so light, no heavier than a child. Mom tried every which way but couldn't put another pound on him. It was true; with a daughter like me, how could he put on weight? I imitated Dad back by part-walking, part-jumping, and yelling: 'Puppy meat! Puppy meat for sale! Buy it today or it'll be off tomorrow!' Hearing Dad clucking like an old goose on my back, I felt so bad my heart shriveled to a pebble.

At the entrance to the theater in the evening, I became the center of attention. The people who came up to me were full of appreciation and congratulations, even though they hadn't seen the play yet. Our neighbor, Dad's old chess partner Uncle Chen, shook my hand vigorously, although I'd seen him at home half an hour ago. What was the 'long time no see', 'so honored to meet you' all about?

Nan Huang arrived, and the girl at his side confirmed my suspicions. He didn't introduce her, but he did introduce me, 'Hey, this is Keke.' He called her 'Hey'.

Nan Huang seemed to be in a good mood, his smiling face aglow. I guess it was love. The girl with him was very sweet and delicate. A pointed chin, short hair, a very slender waist, and a huge pair of glasses, so out of keeping with her delicate little head she looked like a cartoon mantis. She clung to Nan Huang's arm as though he were a kite that would blow away if she didn't hold tight. Nan Huang was quite willing to indulge her in this; apparently, they were deeply in love.

'Keke, you've lost weight. How could you have lost so much weight?' Nan Huang said.

'Must be age?' I felt my cheeks, putting bluntly what Nan Huang had said in a roundabout way.

How could I not have lost weight? How could I not have aged?

I'd cried a lot when I was alone, and sometimes in my dreams. My hair was falling out by the handful—I don't know why. In fact, I never had any regrets about the past, because he had neither deceived me nor dumped me. I had no excuse to indulge in self-pity.

To this day, I have never doubted that when we were together he loved me, truly loved me. No man on earth could fake that love and passion. But I also couldn't deny my throat felt like I'd had an injection to seal it shut; all day there was something blocking it, making my larynx small and thin, so that whether liquid or solid, everything was hard to get down. Whatever that something was, eventually it would block my weeping and wailing too.

Although I wanted to talk more with Nan Huang, I didn't like that girl by his side. Either that, or I didn't want to admit I envied her. I handed the tickets over and said, 'Hurry on in, the opening scene is very important.'

'What about you, I want to see you,' Nan Huang said.

'I'm a shadow, at the end.' Watching Nan Huang walk into the auditorium with the girl he loved, I had to admit they were made for each other.

He didn't come. I staggered about outside until the end of the first half. When I heard the applause from the auditorium, I felt it had nothing to do with me.

After that night, *The Chair* was on for twenty-odd days in the city, with more than thirty performances, moving to four theaters. I wandered around in circles at the theater door every day, but the fact was he didn't come. Someone came backstage looking for me, but it wasn't him. Although I had no desire to go back to the way we used to be, I still longed for him to come, and still believed he would. Come to see my play, to see my success!

Even if he didn't come, didn't phone, I could still write to him, but what would I say? I wanted to tell him, I never think of the past, and although I do hate you, I don't have any regrets. It's no big deal, just a fuss over nothing, and it's all in the past anyway. Maybe he was out of town on business, not in Beijing, I thought, trusting to luck. Didn't he often go off to do interviews?

Right until I was getting ready to take the play on tour with the troupe to Shanghai, Nanjing and elsewhere, I was still thinking, maybe I'll run into him out of town. But during more than three months touring outside Beijing, through three provinces and eight cities, there was no trace of him. Every day, when I saw the ad on the back page of the local paper I thought, maybe he'll see this newspaper, until in the end I had to laugh at my own refusal to give up.

However, I did see Little Bull and Meilun kissing. It was the evening before we left Suzhou. The Suzhou Municipal Theater and the theater dormitory were joined together. Just before I was about to go to bed after that night's performance, I discovered I'd left my watch backstage and went back to get it. As a result, I saw two shadows in the last set of wing curtains. They were holding each other so close that at first glance I thought it was one person. I didn't dare move any further forward for fear of disturbing them, and so in all the bustle of packing up and leaving the next morning, I forgot about going to get my watch again. It was left behind as rent for the theater. I didn't tell anyone about it.

To be honest, by the time we got to the end of the run, everyone was exhausted and even I'd had enough of it. It was almost as though I hadn't written it, but that some incredibly stupid playwright had forced it on us.

Finally, we returned to Beijing. Everyone was overjoyed. We each had five or six hundred yuan in our pockets, we'd brought ten or twenty thousand back for the theater and, most important, we'd made a name for ourselves. All the big shots and not-so-big shots from the Ministry of Culture, the Arts Bureau and the theater all came to the station to meet us. We were returning heroes.

I gave the gifts I'd brought back for the family, and everyone was so excited they grinned like monkeys. My little niece screamed and jumped up and down like a grasshopper.

That night, when everyone else was asleep, I sat in my own room and lit a cigarette. Normally, I wouldn't dare do that at home. My brother walked in without knocking, but when he saw the cigarette in my hand he didn't try to stop me.

'He got divorced,' he said, handing over a letter. It was his, his!

'Really?' I didn't open the letter in front of my brother.

'One child each. I hear he's giving the apartment, furniture and all his savings to his wife.'

'Oh.'

'He's remarried,' my brother said. 'He's remarried.'

I didn't ask who to or when. What did that have to do with me? Seeing I had no response, my brother left.

His letter was very simple. It just said he'd seen the play, how he felt about it, and some suggestions. He didn't mention his divorce, let alone his remarriage. But the last line in his letter was, 'I have to keep an eye on everything you do!'

I lay down on the bed, blowing smoke towards the ceiling. I didn't feel anything. I was neither angry nor happy, neither upset nor excited. I thought, that girl—and I was sure she was a girl—will be happy. They may have nothing for a time, but he'll be able to satisfy her completely. He really knows how to love, he's all love.

He'd gotten rid of what he wanted to get rid of, and gotten what he wanted to get.

The only thing I couldn't figure out was how it could have happened so quickly. How could he have remarried so quickly? Maybe he had lots of mistresses, and I was only the most sincere and the most stupid of them.

What Mom said was so wise: if you don't get punished for your sins immediately, it's because the time hasn't come, but when the time comes, you get punished for everything.

I turned off the light, then turned it back on again. Then I turned it off again. I didn't know if I'd be awake or asleep tonight.

I remembered seeing a newspaper on the train a few days before, *World Panorama* or something like that, I think it was. There was a paragraph that ran, 'The "Other Woman" is a phrase being heard more and more often in American society

today. It refers to single women in America who form relationships with married men. The phrase "Other Woman"
comes from a book by American sociologist Laurie Richardson, published by the American Free Press, and called *The New
Other Woman*. Over the last eight years, Richardson, 44, has
met with one thousand single women who have had relationships with married men and interviewed fifty-five of them, to
investigate how single American women of today pursue
love.'

I don't know what sort of experiences those women have,
but I'm sure they're similar to mine: the pursuit of love has a
lot to do with vanity. Although happiness for them may be
like an island in the Pacific, the Indian or the Atlantic Ocean,
it's an island you can't find on any map no matter how hard
you look. It only appears by chance, through countless,
crashing waves and endless, bitter seas. And because these little
islands of utter happiness may disappear again later, scientists
call them 'ghost islands'.

translated by Chris Berry

Black Cat

When will I ever break free from it and be done with these dirty tricks?

On the dark staircase landing, the moment I push open the door and enter the room, whenever I happen to look out the window—also, whenever I spin around to look behind me—every single time, it zips away, quick as lightning or, rather, a fart. So quick only I can smell it. But to this day the sheer strength and measured calm of its physical presence and those relentless, unfathomable eyes leave me fraught with anxiety.

If Asha hadn't had that cat, or if she'd had a cat but not gone to her mother's and taken her husband along, if she hadn't asked me to take care of her cat, if I hadn't so casually accepted her house key, maybe I'd be more normal right now.

Or you could stay at my place; it gets so lonely here all by itself, Asha says. She nuzzles the cat's ear, the picture of inseparability. I say no, but agree to keep it company when I have the time.

In our building, Asha and I get along the best, because we live nearest each other. When you go up to the second floor, the first door on the left is Asha and her husband's newlywed apartment. The second is the washroom, the third the toilet. The fourth, the farthest from the stairs, is my place. So Asha's abuts the washroom and mine the toilet. The door to the toilet, which is always open, is marked MEN, but if no one answers when I call out I use it too, because the women's toilet is at the far end of the third floor. A real pain in the ass.

Our two apartments are the only ones at this end of the hall; they face north. Of the three big rooms facing south, two are used for storage, though probably even the manager has forgotten what's in them. I've lived here three years and never once seen anyone go in. A guy I don't know lives in the third room; I've never spoken with him. He doesn't work in our unit,* and he's rarely here, except when he's with a woman. He's pretty good-looking; Asha and I call him Mr. Cool behind his back. We nodded to each other once in the hall recently and he said, 'Third World'. I don't know whether he was referring to the location of my room or if he'd figured out that I'm an old maid. It doesn't matter to me anyway; I've never much liked big social situations. Whenever I have to pass a human pile-up in the hall, I clench. I can't stand having eyes on all sides of me. I often think to myself how lucky I am that the room across from mine is storage, that the toilet and I are neighbors.

Actually, we've got our own sweetness and light right here—in Asha's newlywed apartment. Go in and have a look—it's a regular crystal palace.

Asha's husband is the handiest of handymen. He has decorated the whole room with mirrors and glass; he says that way the dust can't stick. I'm convinced that sooner or later he'll even cover the bed with a plate of glass. He's incessantly lighting sticks of incense and sticking them in the nail holes in the walls. Naturally, none of this interferes with their love for each other.

They've got this liquor cabinet with three shelves—no, four I think, or…? Anyway it's not important. The point is: every horizontal surface is glass and every vertical surface a mirror. So all those glittering crystalline bottles and stuff inside are multiplied so many times it makes your eyes swim. You can't tell which are real and which aren't. Think about it: bottles reflected in the left mirror are also reflected in the right, and the mirror in the back, in addition to its own task of reflecting the bottles in front of it, goes on to reflect the images reflected in the right and left mirrors as well—my god, I'm worn to a frazzle on behalf of those mirrors.

* Chinese society is divided into 'units'. A unit is something like a workplace, but it is also responsible for many of its members' social welfare concerns, including housing up to, and after, retirement.

However, I am of the opinion that everything has a will of its own, that all that glass and all those mirrors really can make Asha's home cheery and bright. Anything in her home can be multiplied: one lamp can become five lamps, a single braised chicken can become five chickens, and a measure of love can be quintupled too. Even Asha's cat loves standing in front of that liquor cabinet, shaking its head back and forth in wonder, now viewing its left selves, now its right. No wonder Asha said so smugly, just look at your place, dark as a mouse hole! If my cat ever got in there it would surely take you for a rat and eat you up. My spine chilled at the thought, as if hit by a draft. I had a premonition that such a day would come.

Asha's husband gave her the cat when they got married. As far as cats go, this one could be called pretty. It's black and white, a long-hair, with a squat face and a sweet temper. It waddles when it walks, yet somehow manages to retain a certain lithe agility. Asha's husband said it's descended from a line of Persians. Catching my look of doubt, he explained further: when it gets older, its eyes will change. My god, I split a gut laughing. Naturally, if such a possibility existed, I'd gladly wait a hundred years for those two big round blue-gray eyes to become one blue and one gray. Of course, this does not deny Asha's cat its pedigree; those desultory eyes and that fat butt attest to that.

Asha had no idea what a Persian was; she thought Persian was a kind of silk. But she says foreign women always watch TV with a cat in their arms. Asha's husband loves seeing his wife holding her cat. Whenever I go over, he always starts off praising the cat, saying how naughty it is, how well-behaved, how it won't even touch bread dipped in milk, how they can only feed it things like fresh fish or pork liver. Just look at them, don't they look just like sisters? He finishes off every cat spiel with that remark. That's his way of cottoning up to Asha. She cocks her head with mock annoyance and presses her cheek to the back of the cat in her arms. I fail to understand how being sisters with a cat could be such a happy affair. Especially when the cat's a tom.

I never imagined that my first time alone with Asha's cat would be so hard to take.

Following Asha's husband's instructions, I bought some pork liver, boiled it, chopped it fine, mixed it with rice, and added a little salt. Asha's cat was terribly affectionate when it saw me, probably because it had been alone all day.

I was barely in the door, still deciding where to put its dish, and it had circled me three times. It's funny—Asha is so skinny, but her cat has the ass of the amply-nourished. When I set the dish down, the cat didn't start right in; it gave my fingers an affectionate lick first. This cat really knew how to win a girl over.

Since Asha treats me special and says I can watch their TV anytime I want, I turned it on and sat down on the couch. I guess Asha's cat is used to lying in the lap of the lady of the house and being stroked whenever the TV's on, because it ever so naturally jumped onto mine and rested its two front paws on my forearm. I swear to high heaven I didn't mean to, and I still have no idea how I could have reacted so fast, but I was so startled I leaped up and threw up my arm and flung Asha's cat to the floor. I was covered with goose bumps.

Asha's cat yowled, probably in pain at hitting the floor. It was out of my hands now: it was probably the yowl that did it, probably in that very moment, but it made itself my enemy for life.

Asha's cat wasn't mad in the least over my flinging it to the floor so inhospitably, it just looked at me in bewilderment. When I sat back down to watch TV, it jumped tactfully onto the couch and settled in beside me. But I could not regain my peace of mind, and I grew increasingly, uncontrollably restless. The people on TV were talking and gesticulating. The man was gently smoothing the woman's sea-breeze-swept hair. The woman, head petulantly cocked, was pouring out her heart through lowered lashes. But all I saw was anxiety; all I heard was the cat's yowl.

So dark, so still. It must be night. Should get up, take off the shoes—better yet, wash the feet too. Shoes and feet are dirty and wet. Mama's sheet will get dirty, and if she comes back she'll have something to say about it. You think this, but don't move. You should turn on the light, get undressed, take a look at yourself there, at that place with the two small bumps, to see if they're really gone. You think this too, but still don't move. You don't want to move, to break this stillness, this stillness at last all your own. So much like lying in a hot bath. No, like lying in a little boat adrift on a boundless sea, drifting, drifting. Don't know what book that line came from, but then it's very fitting here, you think.

You do so love to think. Mama always said she never knew what was installed in that little head of yours to make you so good at thinking.

You are convinced that if you have to take one more step you'll never make it home. Because your cotton shoes are wet, every step you take makes a funny squishing sound. Especially loud going up the stairs. You open the door with the key hanging around your neck and collapse on your parents' big bed. When Mama was home, you wouldn't go on her bed even when she let you, you were too embarrassed. You felt you were grown up, a big girl now, but more important, you were afraid Mama would notice those two little bumps on your chest, silently rising, sore and itchy. Only when you were alone did you dare hide under your quilt to sneak a look at them. Now that your parents are gone, you climb onto their bed every day, press your face into the pillows, the quilt, trying with all your might to make out the scent of your mother and father. You have found this is the only way you can fall asleep.

But when you lie down on the bed tonight, you don't even have the energy to distinguish scents. You just lie here quietly, dazedly thinking. You didn't even go to Auntie Ma's for supper, but of course she wouldn't wait on your account.

Who's there? A faint sound outside the door. No one answers, but you are convinced the sound is nearby. Mama said you've grown dog's ears, you can tell who's breathing even in your sleep. The sound again. It really sounds like someone breathing. You don't dare make another sound. All you can do is hold your breath and listen, trying with all your might to make out what's out there.

God! At this moment, you wish whatever is outside is a bad guy, any old kind will do, even one with a knife in his hand—anything but *it*. But you already know beyond all doubt that what's out there is *it*. From the sound of those unrelenting, determined footsteps, from the sound of that unhurried, insistent breathing, you can tell—it's the black cat.

Because it only comes out at night, you know it's black. The black that is blacker than night, blacker than a coffin. You cannot describe its blackness, yet you believe that if its skin were stripped off for a rag, it could rub all the daylight you've ever seen into starless, moonless night. You have never ever seen it. But you know its black face has a pair of enormous eyes that shine with a speckled emerald light. Like devil's fire, or rather, green scum on a pond, pond scum smelling of piss and fish. One look and your scalp tightens, and you know its body is skinny and its two front paws are thick and fat. The pads beneath each long claw are as big as broadbeans. Its palms are nearly the size of checkers, just not as hard, they're soft, very springy. Only that kind of paw could work such magic. Your poor little Shasha.

You are thoroughly terrorized by all this. To get up and chase it off is completely out of the question; you don't even have the courage to turn over, so afraid are you it will discover you in the room. You are like a thief who has broken into someone's house, waiting for the owners to come up and nab you.

First the black cat saunters twice around the stairwell, breathing ragged like a man, its grandiose footsteps rasping. Then it stops outside the door and won't go away. It has surely discovered this door, perhaps even looked right through it and seen you with the multi-directional green rays of its eyes. You don't dare breathe, afraid it will hear. You don't even dare open your eyes, afraid it will see.

Oh no, did you latch the door? Yes. No. You didn't latch it, for didn't you collapse on Mama's bed the moment you came in? You still haven't taken off your shoes—how could you have latched the door? This means the black cat might come tearing in this very instant. Maybe it's latched after all, for the first thing you do when you come home is latch the door—Mama told you to do this time and again before she left. Oh god, you simply cannot remember whether you latched the door or not. Get up and check. No! You can't. It will notice the moment you move. Maybe you really didn't latch the door and it will pounce upon you in no time flat. Like a streak of black lightning, like a loud smelly fart. The way it pounced on Shasha.

When school was let out for lunch that day, you saw a crowd around something by the door of the steamed bun shop. You wanted to go around it and be on your way but were drawn by the sound of chirping. Squeezing in to see, you felt all the blood in your body surge. The big flat bamboo basket on the ground was filled with downy little chicks. Oh, how cute, bumping and rolling over and stepping on and nipping each other like bundles of sunlight. Twenty-five cents each, the old humpback said, never mind how small they are, they're strong and healthy. The old man's hump was as big as a hill.

Sir, I only have twenty cents, you said softly, feeling very ashamed. Twenty cents it is, then, take a small one, the old man said, lifting out a little yellow chick crowded trembling on one side and a little unsteady on its feet. You handed the old man the twenty cents you'd planned to buy steamed buns with, and there in the palm of your hand stood the little yellow chick. Just got a little cramped, that's all, nothing to worry about, take it home and give it some room and it'll hop about just fine. The old man was afraid you didn't believe him, but it was the one you liked, it was just the one for you.

Without even thinking about it, you skipped school. When you got home you found an old shoe box under Mama's bed. First you lined the bottom with a layer of cotton, then spread a handkerchief over it. Only then did you feel right about putting the little chick inside. This took you the whole afternoon. That night, under the desk lamp, you named it Shasha. You chose the name because its color was almost exactly the same as the blonde hair of a boy you once liked. That boy was a character in a children's book. He was a Russian named Alyosha. Alyosha was a good, clever boy with such pretty golden locks, and you always thought that if one day you ever saw him, you'd just have to reach out your hand to feel his hair. Later somebody burned that book. You were heartbroken then at the thought that if you ever did see Alyosha he would ignore you.

Shasha actually made it, and even turned out to be down-right frisky. One day when you came home from school, you were surprised to discover him gone from his box. You looked everywhere but couldn't find him—you even looked under the covers. Finally, when you could no longer fight back the tears, what did you see but Shasha, waddling out from one of Mama's high-heels, craning his neck and looking right at you with his shiny black eyes, as if to say, what were you so worried about, aren't I just fine? You cupped Shasha in your palms and kissed him over and over again.

Shasha grew too big for his box. He was always hopping onto the windowsill to look out, longing for the outside world. You washed down the balcony and made Shasha a new nest from a lidded basket. You told Shasha from now on he could play on the balcony, even spend the night outside in his basket. You knew Shasha was pleased, for he too wanted a world of his own, and liked having some quiet time alone to think.

You tied the basket lid securely with a length of twine. This is your room, and that is mine. You said good night to Shasha. You slept well all night long. But Shasha was gone, gone forever. First thing next morning, when you got out of bed and went over to the balcony, you saw the lid of the basket mysteriously open, the basket right where you left it, perfectly intact, but empty. All that was left was a single feather, already turned hard and white. Everything was the same as the day before, neat and clean, not even a trace of blood. But on the newspaper where Shasha slept, you discovered a paw print big as a checker. No use looking—Shasha had been eaten up, right in the new house you made for him, eaten up by a big black cat that only comes out at night. It happened so fast poor Shasha couldn't even cry out. The black cat's mouth was as black as a bottomless pit. Its paws were swift and powerful—it could spring straight from the ground to the second floor balcony and undo the tightly tied twine just like a person.

Yeow—the howl finally breaks the night, breaks glass, breaks the last line of defense in your heart. The black cat is opening its black bottomless pit of a mouth towards you too.

You clamp your hands over your ears, pressing against the sides of your head so hard your eyeballs hurt. But it doesn't do a bit of good. Yeow—yeow—the black cat is yowling steadily, straight from the diaphragm. Each yowl is more terrifying than the last, sharper, brighter, vibrating at an even higher frequency. Its big black ink-slab face must be braced on those two fat front paws, its emerald eyes trained on your door. Its whole body glistens with infinite rays of irrepressible black light.

Your heart begins quaking, quaking uncontrollably, quaking so hard your teeth are chattering, quaking so hard your hands and feet freeze, quaking into an old rag full of hundreds of holes on the verge of disintegrating into thousands of tatters. It is quaking so hard it has begun to make churning sounds, like a blackened old cast iron rice popper, just waiting for the final explosion.

It's a cat and you're a person, so what are you afraid of? Don't know. Dying? No. You're just scared, so scared you want to die. So scared you think you are no part of this world at all. You are scared of its yowl, its black, its green, its smell, its you-don't-even-know-what.

Yeow—yeow. The black cat has surely sensed your fear. It keeps yowling with its big black mouth, helping you quake your heart. It is as if it's got that tattered rag in its paw, shaking it around however it wants—now flinging it up, now hurling it down, now crumpling it up. You are helpless. You can only submit to its unbridled power to do with you what it will.

Finally you can stand it no longer. By now the yowling is not just coming in through your ears to intimidate your puny little heart, it is coming in through your every joint and pore. Those black rays have baked you to ash, your blood has turned into strands of gray-green smoke seeping out of your ears and nose. You crawl off the bed, facing the door, and kneel to it. You beg it to let you go. Your tears gush forth like a river bursting its dyke. Before long, you sense that even your mouth has swelled up, like a duck's. You kowtow frenetically towards the door, you don't know how many times. You know the black cat can see you, with its little pond-scum emerald eyes. Yes, it knows everything, controls everything. It is lord and master of the night. So you go on kowtowing like this, slowly now, not sure if the black cat has really stopped yowling or if it's just that you can no longer hear it, but it all seems to be quiet now, really.

Today is the Dragon Boat Festival. Auntie Ma is really something; I know she finished wrapping her zongzi* last night. I got one from her this morning before school. She didn't give me any sugar for it, and I didn't dare ask. I know she was pretending she forgot as she bustled off to do something else. Anyhow, they're still good even without sugar. There was a big red date inside, and I saved that for last.

Before Mama left, she turned me over to our downstairs neighbor, Auntie Ma. As Mama beseeched her, softly, meekly, she gave my big brother's beloved new pair of Energizer sneakers to her son Huarui. *Ai*, if I didn't feel sorry for this girl of yours, I wouldn't agree to it, Auntie Ma said. I've got a good heart, I have, Auntie Ma said as she took a hundred yuan from Mama. This was three month's food money Mama left for me. Yes, yes you do, Mama nodded repeatedly, agreeing to the goodness of Auntie Ma's heart. It's not as if the *child* has done anything wrong. We'll be living in the

---

* Zongzi consist of a red date or meat in sticky rice wrapped in bamboo leaves and are traditionally served for the Dragon Boat Festival.

collective dorm, and there won't be anyone to look after her, otherwise I'd take her with me. As she said this, Mama pried my hand loose from her lapel. My hand was as skinny as chicken claws, my fingernails bitten ragged as sawteeth. Auntie Ma, I'm really imposing on you. This girl of mine minds well, but she's always been sickly, so I'm afraid I have to ask you to keep a special eye out for her. She can eat whatever you all normally eat. But if your lunch hour's tight, you can give her twenty cents to buy something on the street. Take her to the bathhouse once a week, for ever since she was little...now...The tears in Mama's voice made me a little dizzy, like I wasn't getting enough oxygen. Okay, okay, enough already. Auntie Ma had grown impatient. There's no need to cry; she'll be just fine with me. Just put your worries to rest and concentrate on walking that big glorious road to self-reform.* Three meals a day, she won't go hungry with me. As she said this, Auntie Ma eyed me as if I had a bottomless pit for a stomach, as if all I ever did all day was eat.

When Mama left, I joined Auntie Ma's family. She never had a job before; it's just in the past couple of years that she's had temporary work with the neighborhood production team. Auntie Ma is fat—that kind of solid fat which makes her very strong. One time she took me to have a bath, and she said I stank all over. Actually, I could tell, she was the one who stank. Those shiny dark red bulges of hers looked really hard, and I really wanted to poke them to see if they would budge at all. Of course, I'd never dare do it, I just wanted to.

Auntie Ma pulled me by the hair under a steaming shower and held me there. Yikes—it was so hot I couldn't breathe. I bent over to look at my feet, which turned bright red in no time, even gave off steam, just like sorghum buns fresh from the steamer. Auntie Ma stood beside me, washing my hair with a bar of soap. I am convinced she yanked out a good third of my hair. I scrunched up my face; this seemed to lessen the pain somewhat. The folds of flesh in Auntie Ma's stomach made deep creases. That hot drain water stench had to be coming from those creases. And she said I stank all over! I stood there clenching my teeth as she yanked out my hair, defiantly watching her stomach.

---

* This suggests to any Chinese reader that this part of the story is set during the Cultural Revolution (1966–1976).

All finished? Auntie Ma asks. I nod, popping that sweet red date in my mouth like a piece of hard candy. Even though I eat at Auntie Ma's, I have never sat at the same table with them. Mostly she has me eat first, with my own special bowl and chopsticks, like I'm contagious. But I like it that way, for if I had to eat at the same table with her son Huarui, I'm sure I'd never manage even a mouthful of soup.

Thank you, Auntie Ma, I say, as my mother taught me. I shoulder my satchel and start to leave. Today's the Dragon Boat Festival, have a chicken egg. Probably my good manners stirred her pity, for Auntie Ma is spooning me up a hard-boiled egg from the pot on the stove. But I can tell—it's not a chicken egg, it's a duck egg. Chicken eggs are the kind with red shells—and Auntie Ma slipped right by those with her big iron spoon. She spoons me up a slightly bigger white egg with a bluish cast to it. I want to tell her it's a duck egg, but I don't. Mama told me, don't be a picky eater, eat whatever Auntie Ma gives you. I hold out my handkerchief to take the egg. What a good girl, your hanky is so clean, Auntie Ma says, wanting to act as if she hasn't noticed at all whether the egg she is giving me was laid by a chicken or a duck. So clean and tidy, she says, patting me on the head. Your clothes can be dirty, but your hanky's got to be clean, that's what Mama taught me.

I amble off, waiting for the duck egg in my hand to cool. It's still a bit early for school, because Auntie Ma is always having me eat before her family. I find the granite post by the big gray wall in the lane. It's probably an old road marker. I really like it. When I see it on the way home from school every day, I always let out a sigh of relief, feeling safe, feeling I have made it home. I crack my duck egg on the post and peel it carefully, bit by bit. But no matter how careful I try to be, I don't do a very good job—it ends up pocked and ugly. Little chunks of the white have come off with the shell.

I've had duck eggs before, but they were always the ones our old nanny made, preserved in mud and salt in a little crock. You don't need to peel that kind. All you have to do is poke a little hole in the fat end and then pick out the inside bit by bit with a chopstick. What I like best is to poke right down to the middle and get a blob of the orange creamy yolk on the end of my chopstick—it's really good. I've never ever had a plain hard-boiled duck egg that wasn't pickled. I can't imagine

what it would taste like. I don't know why, but looking at
that pocked duck egg in my hand, I feel a bit queasy. But I
am still hoping to reach the yolk in one bite, to see that bright
orange cream.

I take a deep breath, open my mouth, and take a big bite.
God! This duck egg doesn't have any bright orange cream at
all, but a sticky soupy yellow that sticks in my mouth, all over
my hands. The egg is not cooked all the way.

My mouth is filled with the taste of stinky piss. I don't dare
spit it out, for I fear Auntie Ma will see me—I sense her eyes
behind me. But I dare even less to chew, and before long my
mouth is full of spit. There isn't enough room for it all, and
it leaks out the corners of my mouth. It feels like even my
own spit has come from the butt of a duck. I can't stand it any
longer. I straighten my neck, shut my eyes, and swallow the
whole bite like poison.

Eyeing the rest of the egg in my hand, I suddenly remember
what Mama once told Nanny a long time ago: You've got to
hard boil eggs all the way done or else you can get blood fluke
fever, and your belly swells up. Oh no! I'm scared out of my
wits. I can feel my stomach getting bigger and bigger.

I feel like no matter where I dispose of the rest of the egg,
Auntie Ma will find it. She could show up right beside me at any
moment. I don't know when I'll be able to get over this
sneakiness of mine. I'm always scaring myself to death with
it—my heart stops, my muscles twitch, my whole body freezes.

Pretending to tie my shoelace, I squat next to the big gray
wall and quickly dig a hole in the ground with a little piece
of glass. I come up with this on the spur of the moment. I
don't dare look up for fear someone else is here. For I've
always believed that if I can see others then they are surely
looking at me. Actually, I've already sensed a pair of eyes
staring at me. But come hell or high water I put the egg in the
hole and cover it with dirt. Uh-oh—I have barely stood up,
not even lifted my head, when Auntie Ma's son Huarui shows
up, standing right in front of me with a crafty smile on his
face, as if he has just caught a traitor planting land mines. I
close my eyes, waiting for him to hit me, but all he says is,
Okay, just you wait! And leaves. He walks off on his toes,
leaning forward, for he is wearing my brother's beloved white
sneakers. My brother used to say he could jump right over my
head in those shoes.

I walk ahead slowly, keeping to the wall. I know that going on will only bring disaster, but I have to go on.

I began, for no reason whatsoever, to set myself against Asha's cat. Eyeing its patches of black fur, wondering if there were any similarities between Asha's cat and my old foe, looking for a blood relationship between them that simply wasn't there, I began to wonder if I would still be so afraid of it the next time I saw it. But right then I couldn't stand Asha's cat. I despised it.

I knew that Asha's cat, having been alone all day, was anticipating my arrival. Anytime there were footsteps in the hallway, you could hear its plaintive mewing from Asha's room. I could hear it frantically scratching the door. But I intentionally ignored it. I let get all worked up on purpose. I deliberately made it lonely. I put the key in the hole, turned it twice, and pulled it out again. I jiggled the doorknob back and forth a couple of times. But I didn't open the door. I let it know I didn't want to see it. Listening to Asha's cat desperately hurtling into the door, I felt my heart swell with joy.

For two days now I hadn't gone inside, I'd just opened the door a crack and shoved its food in, then quickly shut it again, giving it no chance. I knew that what Asha's cat was waiting for wasn't food, but people, something alive. By this point even a fly would have sent it into a frenzy of delight, but I didn't even let it see my face. I of all people know what loneliness feels like—you try it for awhile. The pathetic mewing of Asha's cat was music to my ears. I jumped for joy in the hall, though I'd never reach that fifteen watt bulb unless I stood on a chair. But I knew Asha's cat could see my every move. I've always believed that cat's eyes can see through anything.

On the third day, I decided to go inside, not to see the cat but to change its litter. Asha's husband told me to change it every three days. He imagines this is a pleasurable task for an old maid like me.

As soon as it laid eyes on me, Asha's cat started rolling around at my feet with such excitement that it was actually somewhat touching. It flung itself at me with such force it nearly knocked me down. I couldn't take a single step. I kept nudging it away with my foot, but it just thought I was playing.

This cat was doing everything it could to ingratiate itself with me, sparing nothing in its frantic attempts to win me over. No man had ever treated me that way. It contorted its fat ass as it comically started chasing its own tail, although of course it would never catch it. It kept this up till it had made itself dizzy, hit its head on the floor with a yelp, and collapsed. It struggled to its feet again with its front paws curled under, took a few steps on its back paws, and fell over again. It was hilarious. It was clearly no use pretending to ignore it, for its determination that I pay attention to it far exceeded my own resolve not to. There's no denying Asha's cat was cute and smart, a cat anyone would love.

I couldn't help but feel a twinge of regret; at the very least I wasn't being much of a friend to Asha to treat her cat this way. I bent over and stroked its head. To my surprise, it closed its eyes in bliss and held its breath, as if intoxicated.

Mewing coquettishly, it sniffed my hand with its cold wet nose, and then flopped over on its back and batted my hand with its outstretched paws. Then it grabbed my hand with its front paws and brought my fingers to its mouth, where it proceeded to lick them one by one with its little red tongue. It's as if that thin, pliable, soft yet sturdy tongue is covered with tiny thorns—it made my whole arm tingle. I scratched its belly and hind legs with my other hand. Its whole body was limp as it lay there letting me stroke it. Perhaps because I inadvertently hurt it, every now and then one of its back legs would twitch, but it didn't do anything to stop me, returning immediately to its languid position. Meanwhile, its front paws were still playing with me; again it took my fingers in turn to its mouth, nibbled on them with its pointy little teeth, knowing all the while the strength of its bite, and not hurting me in the least.

There's a saying in China about losing oneself in bliss. Either I had made Asha's cat too relaxed, or else it just couldn't stand being so happy, but it leaped to its feet. All of a sudden its neck was craning, its squat face stretching skyward. The sudden force behind this motion turned its face in that instant mean and savage. Like a hideously threatening human face. While I'm at it, I might as well mention that I've always considered every ugly face squat. Asha's cat was clawing the floor with its front paws, its claws fully extended, which made its paws far bigger. With its butt in the air, it had contorted itself into an S, its once roly-poly belly now stretched thin. Worst of all, it was facing me, opening those blue-gray eyes at me, its vocal cords squeezed flat as it let out a long howl.

How could it be like this too? I don't know what came over me. I just felt my whole body shaking and a vile taste rose in my throat, under my tongue, as if I were sucking on a piece of green copper. I sprang up, one foot flying, and kicked Asha's cat a couple of meters into the air. As it hit the opposite wall with a resounding thud—before it even had a chance to yowl—I was already out the door and turning around to lock it tight. I bounded to the sink room, where I rinsed my mouth over and over with icy water. But that vile taste seemed to stick in my throat. I couldn't spit it out.

The black cat is not going to let you off after all. Having for the last time contorted its body into an S and let out a long howl, it begins to wield the power of its big fat magic paws. It leisurely extends those claws hidden between the broadbean pads and tufts of black fur, and begins to claw at your door. You think its claws must be some color between yellow and black, their shape and length right up there with the Cixi Empress's fingernails. There was a picture of the old witch in your big brother's history book that sent chills down your spine the first time you saw it. After that, your brother would hold up that photo every chance he got to scare you. It made you scream and run around the room to get away from it, feeling if that hand reached out from the page, it would claw your skin and pierce your heart. One time you were so scared you actually started crying. Mama scolded your brother, but he said you were only scaring yourself.

The black cat is still clawing at the door. To keep out the winter drafts, Mama had pasted layers of thick white paper over every crack in the door before she left. Right now, the black cat is clawing at that paper. Those sharp claws must be tearing it to millions of shreds tinier than grains of rice. You think.

The scratching is punctuated every few swipes with a yowl. You are by now beyond pleading, beyond kowtowing, beyond tears. You have cried your tears dry; even your throat is so dry it sticks with every painful gasp. As if scratched by one of those claws, your tongue is stuck, either straight out or to the top or bottom of your mouth. Your eyes are swollen to slits you cannot open. And your heart? Your heart has stopped quaking, but only because it can no longer muster a quake, only because it is utterly incapable of quaking. It has even stopped churning, incapable of exploding now, as it has been wracked dry by the yowling, the blackness, the stench. It has lost every last ounce of elasticity, every last drop of moisture— like a rock. Just like the rock that came flying through the classroom window, that cobblestone—like a duck egg.

During the bouts of extreme terror, the pause between heartbeats lengthens. The brain alone mounts the final arduous, sluggish resistance, like a dilapidated old water wheel on its lumbering haul.

You lie there, helplessly, as the black cat rips open your chest with its sharp claws. Your ribs, mere slats of bamboo, are no match for the steel claws of the black cat.

The black cat finally rips your heart out. It stares at it with its speckled emerald eyes. It opens its black bottomless pit of a mouth to eat it. But it cannot bite into it, for it has forgotten that it has squeezed this heart flat with its night, the whole black night. All it can do is scratch it with those claws whose color falls somewhere between yellow and black. Again and again, until the surface is covered with white scars. It feels like the deep-boring pain has shredded your entire body to mincemeat. Like the shredded paper on the door.

As bit by bit you die, bit by bit you lose awareness of the pain.

As you are dying, you are gasping out for life with your last iota of consciousness. Knowing that if only day would break the black cat would go away, you cry out for daylight with your last strand of consciousness. You know beyond all doubt that this is the longest, blackest night in human history.

But it is no use, no use at all. The black cat has held the night fast; the black cat won't let day break. Night can only stretch on like this, endlessly, interminably. The black cat is lord and master of the night.

The room is no longer the room it was, it has become a smelly, suffocating crock. Your minced flesh has been pickled there; it has turned as black and smelly as the black cat itself.

While the whole building, or rather, the whole world, is sound asleep, something flickers dimly in your mind, and in this space you know—you can feel it—something strange is about to happen.

Class Two, Grade Three, listen up! No more class for today, it's time to practice the welcome ceremony. Everybody report to the playground. And girls, don't forget to put on your pretty skirts, the lady teacher says. Her neck is often covered with deep purple bruises from a home remedy that calls for simultaneous pinching and pulling of the skin. They pop up and down like rubber bands whenever she speaks with conviction. It's too cold today, Teacher. The girl who says this doesn't have a pretty skirt—hers is gray, like a rag. Wear them over your pants for now, and roll up the legs right before the ceremony. The elastic in Teacher's neck pops up again.

All the girls are in a flurry of excitement, for we rarely get such a chance to show off. We only get to wear pretty skirts at a welcome ceremony. A chorus of desk tops slamming shut fills the classroom. Okay boys, leave the room, the girls need to change into their skirts, Teacher says. At this, the boys have to whoop it up for awhile before they'll go. All that just for rolling up pants legs?

Of course, I don't even have the right to roll my pants legs up. You stay here and clean the classroom; sweep it clean and mop the floor. As I stare at Teacher's jumping rubber bands the words I dread most pop out at last: And let Zhang Yuzhen wear your skirt. Teacher, it's too small for her. I try to protest, to make Teacher realize that Zhang Yuzhen is too big around the waist for my skirt. She is, after all, fourteen, and I'm only ten.

Let her try it on, it won't hurt it. Teacher shoots me a dirty look. Zhang Yuzhen's father is the leader of a Worker's Mao Zedong Thought Propaganda Team. Zhang Yuzhen has never passed math, and she was held back. But whenever our teacher sees her father, her eyes brighten with deference and she crooks her arm through Zhang Yuzhen's, elevating her butt and bust in one brisk motion. No! I say in my mind as my hands are handing over my skirt. No! I won't let you wear my skirt! I keep saying this to myself as I watch my skirt going over Zhang Yuzhen's big gray pants. Oh my pretty skirt, stretched so tight not a pleat remains, just like a broken umbrella that will never close again. It feels like every organ in my body is being stretched right along with it, heart, liver, lungs—even my nostrils and eyelids.

Everyone leaves. I start to work, with a vengeance. I push all the desks neatly against the back wall, sweep all the dust and debris in the front of the room to the back, then move the desks to the front and sweep the back. This is how Teacher has us do it when the whole class does a general cleaning. I'm not after an award or anything, it's just that this is the only way I can stop thinking about my skirt and hold back the tears. All the dust I've kicked up is making me cough. But the whole thing is damn satisfying. I fling the dust and debris towards the ceiling with all my might. A tornado couldn't do worse. As long as I'm at it, I throw in a flood for good measure, and why not? The classroom is all mine. One pail, two, ten pails, eleven. Swish, swish, swish go my cotton shoes in the cold dirty water—it's lots of fun. My stretched organs are starting to come back down to size.

A warm welcome to Prince Sihanouk! Welcome! Welcome! Wel-wel-come! The sounds of the welcoming ceremony rehearsal come in through the window; they've got it down pat.

But what's wel-wel-come? I find it hilariously funny, imagining Zhang Yuzhen swinging her gross umbrella of a butt, and those rubber band bruises on our lady teacher's neck.

Once I stop, my whole body feels limp as a noodle. My legs are quaking uncontrollably in the water, shaking so hard the bellies of my calves are swinging around to my shins. I can't even hold on to the rag. My heart, on the other hand, is swelling with a kind of masochistic delight that follows being bullied, the kind of mental and physical calm that follows extreme exhaustion. I even hope to pass out, or die. I lie here at peace on the wet floor; it's a bit chilly, but decidedly relaxing. I pretend I am the revolutionary heroine Jaing Zhuyin after her torture, or Vera, the girl they executed in that Albanian movie, *Death Before Surrender*. My imagination knows no bounds. Through these fantasies, I achieve a sense of contentment that borders upon happiness.

In the end, though, even this happiness is snatched away. Those clouds of my fantasies slow to a halt, suddenly pasted over with faces that scare me out of my wits.

After Huarui left me on the road to school, I truly regretted having buried the duck egg. I even wished he'd come back and make me eat it. For I was so frightened by the unexpected disaster ahead that I nearly peed my pants. I had just reached the corner when a boy bolted out from the side and crashed into me. If not for the wall there, I would have fallen down. I know this boy, he's in our class. He sits three desks behind me. Because his face is covered with ringworm, everybody calls him Whitey. I've always considered him a pretty decent guy.

You...I say, but only get that one word out, because in the gang of boys behind Whitey, I see Huarui. At this moment, his face looks more cruel and unfamiliar than anyone's in the world. As I cringe for mercy, his derisive air and cocky stance make me feel like dirt.

They—they pushed me, says Whitey, grinning shamelessly, rubbing the ringworm on his face. It's enough to make your hair stand on end. They—they said your daddy's got green hair and red eyes, heh heh heh. They—they said...But before Whitey can finish, the big boys behind him are piling on top of me. Huarui just stands there, giving the orders.

As these hoods slump into me, they are sniggering. All I can do is press into the big gray wall for dear life, or rather, bore inside it. How I envy every last ant in the cracks! My heart is quaking like litter on the street blown spinning every which way by the wind.

My heart has been quaking a lot like this lately, as if every last blood vessel has been yanked loose, every last inch of protective membrane gone. At its most severe, I can't even breathe. All I hear is a churning sound in my chest, like the blackened old cast iron rice popper the old man shakes with his hand, ss-sssh ss-sssh ss-ssh-ss-ssh-ss-sssh, just waiting for the final explosion.

Look, out the window, there they are, that gang of hoods. I've already decided to fight them to the death as I pull from my pencil box the little knife I use for sharpening pencils. Oh, my undependable heart, why are you quaking again? Why don't they come in? What are they up to?

What's that sound? My heart shattering? No, it's not the sound of a heart bursting—that would be more of a splat. This is glass shattering, in the classroom. A stone as big as a duck egg doesn't split my head open as they'd hoped, but it does hit me full in the chest, knocking me right off my feet. My head slams into the corner of a desk, and it must be bleeding, for it feels like hot worms are crawling all over my face.

The funny thing is, the gash in my head doesn't even hurt. In fact, I'm not even worried about it. I am just clutching my chest. I never imagined it could hurt so much. The skin's not broken or bleeding, but it hurts so badly I'm seeing stars. It's the kind of pain that shoots out from the heart, from the bone. The kind of pain that spreads from the blood out, from the soul out. A desperate pain. And in this pain I have but one thought: It's all over, done for, they'll never grow now. They have been killed, and they'll never grow. Those nights, I would secretly look at them, even touch them, but not too much, lest they not grow. I could sense them slowly rising through a sort of gratifying ache; that pleasure born of timidity, pride, anxiety and smugness was something no one else would ever experience.

But now it's over, completely doomed. They have died.

For a whole day, I found myself listening for sounds of activity whenever I passed Asha's door, but there were none. Asha's cat was beyond pitiful mewing. Now when it heard my footsteps—for I knew beyond all doubt that it recognized my step—it tightened its throat and let out a long yowl. It could only make that ghastly sound when it contorted itself into an S. The bastard knew how much that sound scared me, and how much I hated that pose.

When I jiggled the doorknob, it didn't rub up against the door with pettish impatience; what I heard instead was frenetic tearing around the room crashing into things. Like a racket of birds startled by the bowstring. Sure enough, when I opened the door, Asha's cat was clinging to the windowsill, despondent and fraught with anxiety. The pair of blue-gray eyes watching me seemed to be coated with a film. Asha's cat no longer trusted me at all.

I was planning to trick it. Come on down now, I've got a treat for you, I said, ever so softly and speciously, squelching my disgust, and held out my hand to it. Asha's cat jumped down from the windowsill only half trusting me and waddled over, swinging its big butt. I reached out with false affection and petted it like I had the last time. And, just like before, it rolled over on its back, letting me stroke it, looking just as relaxed as before. But I could tell it wasn't relaxed at all—its belly and hind legs were tense, for the little creep knew how to be vigilant too.

As before, Asha's cat was playfully batting its front paws at me. Just as I was putting the finishing touches on how best to deal with this cat, it suddenly clamped my thumb in its teeth, damn viciously, and it hurt so bad I screamed. By the time I'd freed my thumb and was ready to let loose a strong kick, it had zipped up to the three-meter-high ceiling, where it clung for dear life with all four paws to Asha's dark green floor-length drapes, whirring the wire on which they hung. The squat face it turned towards me was brimming with smugness. The little bastard had seen right through me, and I had actually been stupid enough to fall for it.

Asha's cat's glare of pure enmity declared to me: don't even think about it, thank you very much. Now that we understand each other, let's show our true colors. After all, you're human, I'm a cat. Probably as a result of this mutual understanding, I actually stopped hating Asha's cat.

I jabbed its butt hard with a bamboo pole as it clung for dear life to the top of the drapes. It wouldn't come down; it didn't even yelp. It just stared at me with those blue-gray eyes, sending chills down my spine. Once again I feigned conciliation and beckoned to it. Its reaction was to snort at me in disdain. Those eyes could see right through to my bones; that cat had been on to me all along.

My rage having reached the point of all caution thrown to the wind, I leaped onto the bed and grabbed Asha's cat by the tail. I don't know why, but the instant my hand made contact with its fur, my heart filled with terror, an inexpressible terror. Clenching my teeth, I yanked with all my might. At first, the cat acted as if it would never come down, even if it meant losing its tail. By the time my whole body was virtually hanging from its tail, its claws loosened, and, suspended in mid-air, it snapped its head around and bit down on my wrist. The jolt of pain made me scream. My scream sounded to me like something else. Like a cat, an arch-backed cat.

Even though I had seen Asha's cat's sharp white teeth sinking into the flesh of my wrist, even seen my blood seeping between its teeth, I didn't let go, because the courage it took to hold on to its tail was a hundred times greater than the courage required to conquer the pain.

I flung the cat onto the couch. I clenched its face between the thumb and forefinger of my right hand and squeezed, forcing its mouth open. I pinned its hind legs with my shin, rendering it unable to struggle free. Then, with my left hand, I stuffed piece after piece of the raw pork liver I'd prepared for this right into its mouth.

I'd bought the pork liver from the cafeteria. It was fresh as the devil, purple-red and bubbling with blood, as if still producing blood, emitting gusts of stench. Asha's couch is right across from that liquor cabinet, and all those mirrors were multiplying the antagonism between me and her cat. Its two front paws were flailing, scratching my hands as if fighting to the death. Before long, the backs of my hands were covered with white scratch marks, upon which bits of tender pink flesh intermittently appeared, followed by droplets of bright red blood. Viewed dispassionately, it was as if someone was inlaying the backs of my hands with strings of red agate.

Probably because the pieces of pork liver were so big, the stench was overpowering. Asha's cat was jerking its head back and forth and spitting them out, refusing to swallow. Like an obstinate boy refusing to take his medicine. The cat was flinging that unbearably disgusting purple-red mush, spitting it out all over my face and body, turning me into a murderer. Two clumps stuck to the edge of my mouth, tasting no different from the raw duck egg I'd swallowed back then. The base of my tongue stiffened with nausea. I opened my mouth to exhale lungfulls of air, hoping against hope to expel the stench that kept penetrating my entire body. I dare say that stench had seeped right into my hair. Determined not to quit, I kept stuffing the liver Asha's cat was spitting out right back into its mouth. Its ribs were heaving beneath my hand; my own ribs were heaving. That's because my heart had begun quaking again. This time around I couldn't tell if it was quaking in victory, or from nausea, or, when you get right down to it, terror.

Asha's cat finally grew too weak to struggle any longer. I noticed that the front paws scratching me had essentially lost their strength. Yet I still wouldn't let it go—I wanted to go on torturing it, getting back at it. I thought this viciously. I reached out and whipped off Asha's TV cover, a piece of cloth printed with a profusion of unidentifiable flowers. In no time I had Asha's by now completely limp cat wrapped inside it, the corners of the flowered fabric clasped together in my death grip, standing straight up like two pair of rabbit ears.

I thought I must be mad to be doing something like this.

I tied the big flowered bundle containing Asha's cat to the long bamboo pole, and swung it around like a battle flag to the limits of Asha's room. Ever since I was little, I've always been afraid of swings. One time my brother pushed me really high, and as I swung up and down, it felt like all my guts were being yanked out through my anus and navel. I imagine Asha's cat was going through pretty much the same thing about then.

That air of compressed pain accumulated for so many years beneath my sternum, that compressed stench, that shadow hounding my body, that shadow of black night concentrate, now seemed at long last to have left my body, left me suddenly lighter and looser by far. I was leaping, shouting, swiping all kinds of bizarre shapes and patterns through the air with the pole in my hand. Listening to the cat's cries, now strong, now faint, each one more wretched than the last, my heart was so joyous it seemed to fly from my body. Actually, my spine was coated with icy sweat, but I was body and soul positively swimming in an utterly exhilarated bliss. This was a bliss I had never experienced before.

In the end, the bamboo pole could no longer bear up under such a load; I was wearing it out. It reached the limit of its flexibility in the midst of the last swipe and snapped in two. After the flowered bundle slammed into the ceiling, it fell, heavy and utterly lifeless, to the cement floor.

The sudden stillness stunned me. Asha's cat had not made a sound, yet alone yowled. My heart was enveloped by that stench and shadow again. And in that moment it dawned on me in despair that I had not only failed to free myself from any of this whatsoever, I had turned around and compounded it all. I didn't dare breathe, didn't even dare move, not even to blink. I was pierced numb by goose bumps all over my body.

At this point, whether Asha's cat was truly dead or only faking it was enough to scare me to death. I knew, no matter what, that Asha's cat would never let me off.

You have died. But more important than your sense that your heart has long since left your body is your unmistakable discovery that you are undergoing bizarre and monstrous changes. You have grown whiskers, four clumps in all, a total of thirty-two hairs, no more and no less. You have learned to bare your teeth fiercely. Your fingers have become five fleshy pads and the sheaths have grown thick, yet long and pointy, claws that measure up to the black cat's in every way. Patches of fur are growing rapidly all over your body, prickly and sticky and unspeakably filthy. It scorches your whole body beyond endurance, itchy beyond compare. You want to shout, this isn't me! I don't want to be like this! But what tears from your throat is the yowl of a black cat.

Well, your premonition has finally come to pass. While everyone is silent and still, you have turned yourself into a cat—a real, live cat. You have joined the ranks of the black cat.

You have triumphed at last. You despise what you've become, but you are also delirious with delight over your victory. Now you can stop fearing the night, fearing the black cat. Now there is nothing at all to fear. Now you can even go scratching at other people's doors.

It's really something—everyone is still sound asleep. They are like dead fish, pale bellies up or fresh off the hook, randomly tossed on each bed. They are utterly defenseless against the black cat, so what's going to happen to them? Will the cat let the fish go? Fish people, unless you hurry up and turn into cats too...You know that by doing this you will scare them to death. They will take cover in their rooms, or crawl under their beds babbling what's gotten into you? What are you doing? What can you be thinking? What is the meaning of this? Why are you saying these things? What the devil are you after?

Yeow—yeow—you jump down from Mama's bed. Not on two feet of course but all four paws at once. You stand in the middle of the room, facing the door, deferentially imitating the black cat's yowls, now high, now low. And outside the door, the black cat responds, sounding surprisingly elated, as if it has found a soulmate.

Yeow—you feel your yowl doesn't quite make the grade. Think about it—perhaps your posture's off. With your front paws braced against the floor, you extend your neck upward and arch your butt for all you're worth. Now you've made yourself into an S too. *Yeow*—sure enough, that's more like it. Sharp and piercing, palpably vibrating the air. Maybe this isn't going to be so hard after all. After all, long before humans can talk they are innately able to wail. You are so excited over this achievement of yours that your fur is standing on end.

You've subdued the black cat for sure now. Its yowl has perceptibly weakened, and now it is pacing anxiously outside the door. Inside, you continue arching your butt and yowling. Relishing every sound you make, you begin leaping and prancing. Chairs knock over, the coffee table upends, and the thermos, after arcing through the air, actually bounces a few times on the floor before it explodes like a firecracker. You are dancing with joy, tearing off your clothes, hurling yourself at the door, scratching it with your claws. But the door on the inside hasn't been pasted with paper, which leaves you most unsatisfied. Your ears crave the sound of your own claws scratching. You crawl beneath Mama's big bed and pull out a pile of yellowed newspapers. It seems like Mama once said these were Daddy's articles. But what does that have to do with you? You're a cat, a cat who can yowl.

You spread the papers on the floor and scratch at them with your claws, yowling as you go. Drops of blood ooze beneath your fingernails, but you don't feel any pain. You're a cat, and you like yowling to the sound of scratching paper. At the sight of sheet after sheet of paper ripped to shreds like snow, you are delirious with delight.

The black cat is silent now, but you know it is crouched outside the door listening intently. You can even hear the sound of its breathing—no, its heartbeat. That heart is drumming away like crazy. Quaking. It is utterly terrified. Look, even its body is quaking like it's got malaria. Finally, the black cat can't stand it anymore and—suddenly, uncontrollably, totally—breaks down into one long desperate howl. But that sound has completely lost its metallic sheen; it is instead muddy, moldy. And then the black cat shoots off like lightning. You don't know in which direction—all you hear is a clanking sound, as if someone has tossed a broken basin to the ground from a great height. And then there is nothing at all. You are sure you have scared the black cat to death.

I get up from the cold wet floor of the classroom. My only desire now is for a pack of dynamite, like the revolutionary hero Dong Cunrui's. Of course, it's a good thing I don't, for actually I only have the guts to push over a desk.

Welcome, Welcome, Prince Sihanouk, Wel-wel-come! With one last look at those disgustingly tacky skirts wriggling around on the playground, I leave school, convinced I will never be back.

I've developed a fever, but don't know if it's from being hit with the rock or frozen by the cold water. I feel my temperature creeping up bit by bit, and behind my ears it's sore and itchy where a row of red bumps has appeared. This must mean I'm getting sick. The breath from my nose has become hot, and everything I see is covered with a steamy film, as if it's just been ladled from the steamer. All the way home I keep to the wall. That way, I can insure at least one side is safe, from flying rocks or whatever. I've been taking this route to school for three years now, but today it is longer than ever before. Even my book bag is against me, as heavy as if stuffed with bricks, not books.

The sound of a bicycle comes up behind me; somebody riding by slowly brushes past me. It might be a man, because all I see are his feet. They are skinny and narrow, but very long, stuck inside a pair of black cotton shoes with white soles. With my head down, I keep walking and see the granite post that was once a road marker, which gives my heart some modicum of comfort. Now somebody riding by brushes against me again, and it seems to be the same guy—long narrow feet. The man says something, but I can't make it out at all; I think he mumbled on purpose. I press on for dear life, my head down, my heart inexplicably starting to quake. This heart is so sensitive by now that I've reached the point of wanting to rip it from my chest.

Even so, my heart was right. I can't go on, all I can do is stand here, for a pair of feet is blocking my way, a pair of long narrow feet wearing black cotton shoes. I can't make out a word of whatever he's saying; his voice is as smeary as the raw yolk of that duck egg this morning, sticky and smelly, enough to make you sick. From his feet up, I raise my eyes.

I'm stunned. The man in front of me—I don't know when—has dropped his pants below his knees. His thighs are skinny and white, just like two fleshless bones. He's holding the handlebar of his bike with one hand and the other hand is fiddling with something between his legs. I don't make out what it is—no, I didn't even see it at all! I just sense that his five fingers are icy and wet and slimy, five live loaches. His face is pale and gaunt, nearly bloodless, and his flappy ears are paper thin. When I see the expression in his eyes, which is smeary as his voice, I make out what he is saying. He is having me look, and something else too. His hand is still going at it.

In my entire ten-year-long life, the only lower part of a man I've ever seen was on Maomao, the eighteen-month-old son of Auntie Li who lived in our compound. He was so cute when he peed, straightening his little belly, sticking his little pecker up high. I held him when he was even littler and he peed on my clothes, but I never thought that men could be like this, so repulsive, so filthy, worse than a monster for making me so dizzy and dazed. Before my very eyes, the whole world is quickly falling over, collapsing in on me.

The loaches are twisted together, wriggling around. My heart is so loud I can't hear a thing, and my ears are stuffed full of those smeary words. They are wrestling with each other inside my ears, making jolts of racket worse than raw alternating current. My legs are stuck to the ground like nails, utterly incapable of any function but rattling. The acrid taste of green copper swells beneath my tongue, fills the spaces between my teeth.

The world is still swiftly falling over on me. Since it hasn't crushed me to death, all I can do is close my eyes and hold my breath. I decide to suffocate myself. I think if I don't breathe then I didn't see.

Probably I don't belong in this world. Or even if I do, I don't want to be a person, let alone a fly or whatever. Of course, a wolf would be best, or a wild dog. Then I'd pounce and bite it off. All that thing deserves is to be torn off by a pack of mad dogs and wild wolves.

I don't know when the man left; actually he was probably only there in front of me for thirty seconds, maybe less. As I struggle to move my feet, all I feel, along with the toppling world, is that smeary voice, those cold slimy loaches, and that unbearably vile stench boring into my body, stuffing my mouth, my nostrils, my ears, my eyes, every hair on my head. I kneel down, wanting to puke, but after retching forever all that comes out is some acrid gluey spit. Any sound of a bike behind me will once again turn my legs to nails that can do nothing but rattle. This condition persisted for five or six years or more.

In that moment I seemingly instantaneously understood many things I shouldn't have known. He raped me, of this I have no doubt. Will I have a baby? I remember a rag doll of mine; she had a broken arm and an eye that never closed. I shouldn't go on living. I should kill myself. Hang myself, take sleeping pills, jump off a building, cut my throat with the little knife I use for sharpening pencils. As I drag my rattling legs along I make these plans for myself.

I don't dare go near that surging flowered bundle of flesh, nor do I dare leave it. I'm afraid Asha's cat is alive, even more afraid it has died. If alive, it certainly won't surrender to me; it would fight me to the death, and I couldn't beat it, for it

is stronger than I. Even dead, it won't let me off. I imagine
it has become a ghost, opening one filmy eye, battered blind.
I am in the light, it in darkness. It will harm me minute by
minute so I'll never have any peace my whole life long. I fall
apart. Eternal remorse sets in. I wish it was still alive so I
could beg its forgiveness.

I kneel down and meow at the big flowered bundle, trying
to rouse it. I meow shamelessly, like a she-cat in heat. When
the bundle finally wriggles slightly, I let out a sigh of relief,
but am still a bit uneasy. Screwing up my courage again I
stretch out my hand and give the flowered bundle a cat-like
poke. A sound comes out. So happy I nearly kowtow, I scurry
over on my hands and knees to it and tremulously untie those
rabbit ears.

Asha's cat sticks its head out of the cloth. It is still in a state
of shock, unable to stand. I want to take it in my arms over to
the couch, but I don't dare. I can't tell if its grogginess is
genuine or fake. I continue meowing, tenderly and submis-
sively, and move its water dish over to it, but it still won't
open its eyes. Suddenly, I have an idea. I open the glass door
of the liquor cabinet and pull out a bottle of some kind of
alcohol or other—all their booze is name brand. At any rate, I
pour out a small glass, open Asha's cat's mouth and dribble it in.
I learned about giving alcohol to shock victims from a foreign
movie. Sure enough, Asha's cat opens its eyes, even sneezes. Ha!
It's out of the woods now. I scramble over to the bed, pull off
Asha's pillow slip and cover the cat with it. Then I crawl towards
the door, knowing that if I stood up and Asha's cat recognized
me, it would pounce ruthlessly, straight for the jugular.

Only when I've locked the door from the outside do I dare
stand. I nearly bump Mr. Cool in the chin. The devil only
knows how long he's been out there listening. Catching the
flicker of a smile in his locked stare, I meow at him for good
measure. I know he is trying to decide whether to send me to
a mental hospital or the zoo.

I crawl and roll my way back to my room, sensing the
moment I close the door that Asha's cat has surely followed
me in. I fall on the bed and close my eyes, feeling once more
as if Asha's cat is staring at me. Oh well. All I can do is get up
and light a cigarette. But I put it out again after a few puffs.
Because I find that the strands of smoke I've blown from my
mouth are limp cats; even though they're somewhat bizarre

and misshapen, I can nonetheless concretely distinguish their heads and tails, even their extended claws. They are running for every nook and cranny in my room. My mouth has become a cat-producing cave.

I need some human contact, the sound of a human voice. I wish I'd invited Mr. Cool in for some company. I turn on the radio but all the local programming has already gone off the air; the hiss and sputter of the static sounds like a cat breathing. At last I find an overseas station, on which a Japanese geisha is singing. God, she sounds just like a she-cat in heat, sending yet another chill down my spine. I collapse on the bed, determined to lie there with my eyes wide open till dawn.

Dim light is casting on the side wall by the head of the bed, and my attention is caught by the yellowed water stains on the wall. I'd never really noticed them before, but now they look as if someone meticulously drew them there. Their curvy lines are now fine and fluid, now rough and rigid, but it doesn't take long before I find something in this dizzly-dazzly landscape. Say no more, of course it's it. It raises its squat face towards me and arches its back, as if it knows just what effect this pose will have on me. One of its legs is a bit loose, broken maybe, but this does not prevent it from extending its long claws towards me. Tensing my every nerve, I fix it unrelentingly in my stare, for I know that I've only to blink and it will come raging to life.

My intellect tells me: you must exert your will to control your fantasies. But I can't do it, and this pains and saddens me considerably. My eyes—better off blind—willy-nilly continue the search. I find my own shadow and—my god, it has blended into that broken-legged cat. How did my ears end up on top of my head? Have I really become a cat?

At last there is a knock at the door. It can't be the black cat, because you've already scared it to death. It is Auntie Ma and her son Huarui. They're afraid you're dead too, right?

Come on child, be a good girl now and open the door, okay? Come on now, open up the door, or at least just say something. Auntie Ma is nearly pleading. You never thought your whole life long she could use this tone of voice. But how can you open the door? You're a cat. Curling up your four paws, you lie languidly in the little bed you've made for yourself from old newspaper. I'm not in the mood for them. I'm a slovenly cat. You've given yourself these attributes.

Come on child, you haven't eaten in three days, aren't you hungry? Auntie Ma's made you some nice food, come on now, open the door. Auntie Ma and her son are just afraid you've died and they won't be able to explain it to your mother. You meow at the door a few times to let them know you're still alive; you've just turned into a cat, that's all. But Auntie Ma and her son won't let you off so easy; they're still calling and knocking. Annoying as hell. Unable to suppress your rage, you raise your head from your bed of papers, arch your butt with all your might and let out a long vicious howl as you begin expertly clawing the papers all over the floor. Haha—sure enough you've scared this mommy and her boy away. It sounds like they are tumbling down the stairs. Now you can relax in the peace and quiet of your little bed again.

Unfortunately, before too long they are back again, this time with stuff like hammers and pliers. They have started prying open your door, scraping and scrunching; who knows how much longer the lock can hold? You have no desire to involve yourself in their tripe; the inside of your head is blanketed with haze, like a lazy old goldfish swimming back and forth. So you just close your eyes and let the stupid idiots break your door down.

So they've made it inside, panting and wheezing. Like you're a bomb on a timer.

It is Huarui who carries you to bed, and you notice your brother's white sneakers—he's already gotten them dirty. You're sure you must be no heavier than a cat. Huarui lifts your head and rests it against himself. Open her mouth, Auntie Ma commands. Huarui obeys, but his touch is very light. Auntie Ma puts a warm spoon up to your lips—it's a carefully made wonton and smells great. You open your mouth. There's a good girl, Auntie Ma says.

The meat filling of the wonton is chopped tender and fine, but when it has slid into your throat, try as you may, you are unable to swallow it. With a wave of nausea, you spit it out again. And clamp your teeth shut, refusing to open your mouth no matter how Auntie Ma pleads or Huarui tries to force it open himself. You're sure they've chopped that other stuff—raw duck eggs, loaches—in with the filling. You shake your head and flail your hands for all you're worth, knocking Auntie Ma's bowl over with a clatter.

What're we going to do with this girl? Auntie Ma isn't scolding you, just babbling. Mom, what's the matter with her, Huarui asks, his voice tearful, as if he's just had a couple of teeth pulled. Auntie Ma whispers something into his ear. You don't hear it, and don't want to; this fat lady's got a bad habit of coming up with mean ideas, and god only knows if she'll ever change. Having spoken, she leaves.

So you lie on the bed in a daze, using your will to direct your breathing. Because if you don't, you will forget to breathe, and never be able to breathe again. You know Huarui is still at your side, hasn't left for a minute, as if you might escape in the time it would take him to pee. From time to time he wipes your dirty face and hands and feet with a hot washcloth, and it is very soothing.

That big stray cat fell into your water crock and drowned. I got rid of it for you and I smashed the crock. When you're all better I'll get somebody to get you a new one. Huarui is kneeling at the head of your bed, saying these things over and over, for the umpteenth time. Quite unconsciously, you open your eyes, listening to his every word, but they go in one ear and out the other. You just wish he would turn into a cat too. That way, you could have it out with him. Of course, he's being very nice to you right now, but you won't let him know this is what you're thinking if you can help it. Maybe you should be thanking him. With great effort you open you mouth and meow at him a few times. It looks like his jaw's gone out of whack from sheer terror. You wrest a hint of a weak smile from your heart.

Are you dreaming? No. You hear a voice from far, far away, a voice familiar yet strange—is it calling you? Little one, my little one, it's Mama. Open your eyes, Mama's here!

That's right, you remember now, this is your mama's voice. But how come you aren't even the least bit happy? You want to reach out and touch Mama, but you don't have the strength. So you want to cry out, to tell Mama you are no longer her beloved little one, you have turned into a cat. But you don't. If Mama knew, she would die of a broken heart. Little one, my little one, it's your mama, Mama's back, Mama's right here. Mama says these things, non-stop, with her mouth to your ears, nose, eyes, hair. Her lips brush your face, tickling you.

You don't want Mama to despair, so you muster all your strength to open your eyes. You see Mama's face, you see her eyes. Mama's face is drawn with worry and there are dark circles under her eyes. She looks a lot older, but still as beautiful as ever. No one can take her place.

She wraps you in a blanket, cradles you like a baby in her arms. Little one, my little one, let me hear you say Mama, let me hear you say Mama for me now. Mama is pleading, her eyes glistening with tears. She still doesn't know that you've become a cat, a filthy, stinking cat. You open your mouth but nothing comes out, for you know you can no longer say Mama—any sound you make will be a meow. You think, I can't! I can't let Mama hear my voice; I can't let her find out that the child in her arms is a cat. I'd rather die, right now. You close your eyes. Your thoughts are bobbing in confusion. You desperately want to piece together everything that's happened, but it's no use; you lost your capacity for thought a long time ago.

Beads of water, fat and warm, are falling on your face. Mama's tears. You lick them with your tongue—they're salty and bitter. At last you feel yourself melting, ever so slowly melting. In Mama's arms, you've become a drop of water.

Hardly a moment goes by when Asha's cat is not entrenched in my brain. I simply cannot discern the moments when I'm consciously thinking of it. It sways before my eyes all the time, only sometimes it's distinct and other times blurry.

It's been two whole days since I crawled out of Asha's room, but I don't dare go back. Each time I feed Asha's cat, I just open the door a crack, stick the dish inside, and quickly shut it again. Most of the time now Asha's cat and I are spying on each other. It's just that it's on one side of the door and I'm on the other.

I know that at this moment it is listening for the sound of the doorknob turning; it is waiting for the target of its attack. It has been saving up its strength these past two days, honing its military maneuvers. I keep hearing outbursts of noise from in there, as if two big hulks are fighting it out. I'm sure Asha's cat has broken every last bottle in the liquor cabinet and lapped up all the booze from the floor, because in all the chaos of the other day, I forgot to close the cabinet door. Pressing my face to the crack of the door, I can smell the alcohol wafting out. Having drunk all that liquor, Asha's cat has begun acting crazy drunk, jumping way up in the air and slamming into the mirrors of the liquor cabinet, for it has mistaken its own reflections in those mirrors for me. It is biting and scratching at the mirrors, single-handedly obliged to handle so many at once—front, back, right and left. I hear it panting with exhaustion. Christ, listening in on Asha's cat's every move has become a form of recreation with me.

Yoohoo! I'm back! Asha throws an arm around my neck from behind, scaring me to death—for a minute there I thought she was her cat. As far as I'm concerned, if Asha hadn't come back soon, her cat and I both really would have lost our minds. Noticing that what lies in the food dish I am holding is, believe it or not, a whole fish, Asha hastens to ask brightly, Hey, how's my precious baby? Alive, I say.

Upon pushing open the door, all we hear is a whoosh— Asha's cat has flown to the top of the drapes, and then turned around and pounced down again, fast as lightening. Fortunately, I've steeled myself by standing the whole time behind Asha and her husband, ready to flee at any moment. Asha's cat is savvy to the situation; upon noticing its owner, it hesitates. As I expected, the room is in a shambles.

My little sweetheart, I missed you to death. Once inside, Asha ever so sweetly holds out her hand to it. But the cat isn't having any of it; with its blue-gray eyes fixed on me, it charges helter-skelter and yelping towards Asha. I know the little shit is reporting my crimes. Don't waste your breath, Asha will never know a thing. She's human and you're a cat, don't forget. This I say silently to Asha's cat.

Come here, my precious baby. Asha takes a couple of steps towards her cat, not expecting it to arch its back in fury and reach out and scratch her. Even white lines quickly appear on the back of Asha's hand. Asha screams and jumps back, lifts her leg and kicks. Damn you, are you out of your mind, she shouts. But her foot doesn't even brush the cat's fur, for the cat's been on guard and has bolted into the liquor cabinet. Its smug little face is instantly multiplied five or six times. Asha's cat is now completely incapable of accepting that sort of tenderness of word and deed. Is Asha's face ever red.

Never mind, never mind, it's just a little shy; before long it'll jump into your arms. Asha's husband hastens to take his wife's hand in both his own. Asha is fine again. Presents? Where are the presents? Asha asks her husband.

God, can you guess what they brought me? A big porcelain cat, exquisitely made. Asha holds it in both hands right up to

my face. It is smiling at me through bared teeth. One eye is
blue, the other gray, and it is white all over with four black
paws. In the back of its head there is a black, black hole, as if
someone has stabbed it with a knife. Asha says it's for putting
change in.

No, no thanks, really, I couldn't. I am pushing Asha's hands
away. Come on, take it, you don't have to be so polite with
me. Asha won't stop shoving the porcelain cat into my arms.
And dammit, I can't not take it.

With the porcelain cat in my arms, I go back to my room.
I don't know where to put it. Within an hour, I've moved it
several times. I can't do anything, because I can't keep my eyes
off it. I feel like that face with its fake smile is moving, sizing
me up. I keep feeling like I'm being incredibly stupid, but at
the same time I can't stop myself from thinking like this. I
have no choice but to shove the porcelain cat under the bed,
trapping it for good measure beneath a wash basin, thinking
I've just got to return it to Asha tomorrow, or else give it to
somebody else.

I seem to have calmed down. I lie down on the bed with a
book, but after one short story I realize I haven't retained a single
word. I have no idea whether it was about people or dogs. I don't
even know if it was a Chinese book or a foreign one. The reason
I've calmed down is because I am listening, perking my ears for
any sound of the porcelain cat. Trying to hear what it's doing,
what it's thinking, whether it is preparing to tear free from the
basin. As I listen and listen, my heart starts quaking again.

Since I'm utterly incapable of controlling myself, I get up
and get dressed. Lying on the floor, I first meow at the basin
a couple of times before I dare to lift it off. The porcelain cat
seems trustworthy enough—it hasn't moved an inch. It is just
watching me with that phony smile. I grab a piece of old
newspaper, wrap it up, and creep out the door. With all my
strength I clutch the porcelain cat to my chest; the fingernails
of both hands ache to the quick, but I feel that if I don't hold
on this tight it will run away. Once outside the building, I
don't dare look back, for I feel a pair of righteous eyes staring
at me from every window. I feel like an executioner about to
assassinate a revolutionary, I feel like...Dammit, I don't feel
anything! I warn myself.

Holding the porcelain cat this way, I race through several
streets at random before finally finding a red brick garbage

area—I could smell the vile stench of rotting vegetables several meters away. I suck in a deep breath, take a running start, and hurl the porcelain cat onto the garbage pile with abandon. Crash! As the porcelain cat shatters, this is its final cry. Not daring to look back, I run all the way home.

Once inside the building, as I pass Asha's, I hear her scream. I know that cat will never be the same. Asha's right—it has lost its mind. It has gone completely insane, driven there by me. Sure enough, the next day Asha's husband gives the cat away. Asha hasn't been feeling well these days, always hankering after something tart to eat. That cat was too much trouble; I'm going to get her some goldfish, Asha's husband says.

Are you pregnant? I ask Asha. Asha nods happily.

God, what's she bearing there in her belly—it wouldn't be a cat, would it? Another chill runs down my spine, as if a draft's come through.

translated by Cathy Silber

If You Were Still Alive

It's nice out today; that matters for people who get up early to go out and exercise. You shove on your shoes the minute your eyes are open and run outside. Who cares how you look at that time of day? The drowsier you look, the stronger your willpower seems. The courtyard's pretty full already. Whether it's fatties trying to slim down or skinnies trying to beef up, the quest for a long life has a powerful hold on everyone. Exercise has become an essential part of modern life. Nobody wants to die young.

'Xingxing, phone!' Someone's calling me from inside. At this hour. What a nuisance! And I was just getting ready for a jog.

'Hello?' I pick up the receiver and sit on the table in the mail room.

'Where've you been? I've been worried sick!'

It's my friend, Grease Bucket. We all call him that because he's short and fat. 'Well, then, go ahead and worry yourself silly!' I tease.

'Cut it out. Something's up. He's done for.'

'Who is?' I jump down from the table.

'Wang Fuling. He's dying. In fact, he may be dead by now!'

'You're kidding!' Even as I speak, I know it's true.

'Really, I swear! It was a cerebral hemorrhage. That's when one of the veins in your head splits—no, bursts! Know what I mean? Wait for me and we'll go to the hospital together. Maybe we can still see him one more time.' Click.

182

Without even giving me a chance to ask more, Grease Bucket hangs up. I guess it must be true.

I met Wang Fuling last fall at Grease Bucket's. I'd just graduated from university. 'Xingxing lives off her imagination; all her thoughts begin with *if*.' That's how Grease Bucket introduced me to a young man I'd never met before.

'Imagination is more important than knowledge,' I said. I was pleased with Grease Bucket's opening remarks.

'In that case, why did you go to university?' the stranger grinned. You might as well sit at home imagining, that was what he meant.

'It's a quote from Einstein,' I shot back. When it comes to a match of the mouths, no one can out-talk me; I learned a whole heap of famous sayings by famous people when I was in school.

He smiled broadly but he didn't take up the gauntlet, so I calmed down and took a good look at him. When I'm in the middle of an argument, I don't look too closely at my opponent's face. His eyes weren't big, but they were deep-set. His eyebrows were thick and dark and almost joined together. His forehead was clear and broad, but his thick, coarse hair made him look like a bit of a peasant.

At this point, Grease Bucket said he was a new friend; a 'philosophical young man', a 'new literary figure.' He was full of sincerity, but he came over like a secondhand car salesman. As always, I chatted away quite informally as soon as we met. I found out his name was Wang Fuling. He'd been in the military, and now he was back working in his home town outside the city. He'd come into town because some editorial board in Beijing had asked him to write a novel. He told me this very earnestly, as though worried no one would believe him, which left him without the ironic manner a modern young writer should have. Later, when Grease Bucket mimicked his country accent in front of everyone, he blushed to the base of his neck, and after five or six minutes of tight-lipped silence, dashed out without so much as a glance at anyone. What a guy! He was a bit too proud. He was among friends, and we all thought it was a bit much to take a joke so seriously. Actually, if he'd been a bit more friendly and laid back, if he hadn't been so eager to prove himself that he'd laid out every last detail of a project that wasn't even on for sure, to me, a girl he'd only just met, and if he hadn't been so earnest when he spoke, (his slight country accent didn't bother me at all), I could have trusted him, admired him even. However, he didn't understand young city folk at all.

One day, Grease Bucket came looking for me. 'Come on, we're going out to eat!' he said.

'You're paying? Where'd you get the money?'

'Wang Fuling's paying. What? You've forgotten him ... That's right, he's the writer. He's made it big; his book's been published. He made me come especially to invite you.'

'I'm not going! I can't even remember what he looks like.' I broke away from Grease Bucket's grip.

'It doesn't matter. Strangers at first meeting are old friends next time around. Fuling's not the type to play games, so you'll be refusing a free meal for no reason at all.'

I went with Grease Bucket after all, and I didn't forget to dab on some perfume just before we left, either. 'How old is he?' I asked Grease Bucket on the way.

'About thirty, I guess. All grown up,' Grease Bucket kidded, as though that was another reason for Wang Fuling to celebrate.

'Is he married?'

'Yes, country people marry early. I hear his wife comes from his home town.'

'What does she do?' For some reason I wanted to know more.

'I never asked. Wang Fuling's a bit strange; he doesn't like to talk about himself.'

While we were eating, I discovered Wang Fuling didn't like to laugh, either. He'd invited us, and he did order a table full of whatever was expensive, until I began to wonder if he wasn't just trying to show how rich and generous he was. However, apart from that, he just didn't play the host at all. He didn't say much, and he didn't eat much either; just puffed away on his cigarettes, and let Grease Bucket and the guys stuff their mouths and then shoot them off. He'd respond with a few chuckles, but his laugh was dry and forced. I didn't understand why he'd invited us because, apart from Grease Bucket, none of us really knew him well.

I don't know if it was deliberate, but as we came out of the restaurant, Wang Fuling said he had something to do which meant taking the same route as me, and so could we walk together? Grease Bucket and the guys took their leave, happily wiping their mouths as they went.

'Would you like to come in for a moment?' I asked Wang Fuling when we got to my place. I was only being polite, but he followed me in.

The room was a mess; the clothes I'd changed out of before I left were still all over the bed. I smiled awkwardly at him.

'Much better than I'd imagined,' he said, his eyes sweeping across my face. God, he'd imagined it! We barely knew each other.

I thought he'd only followed me in for a moment to be polite, but he lit up a cigarette and showed no sign of leaving. Somehow I understood; this was the something he had to do.

'Do you despise me?' he asked out of the blue, taking the glass of water I'd poured him.

I was taken aback. What was he getting at? Was it because Grease Bucket had made fun of his country accent? Or because he spent so much money inviting people he didn't even know for a meal? Or did he mean coming to my place? It was really weird.

The room was silent for a moment, then it was full of Wang Fuling's cigarette smoke. I realized he didn't actually expect me to answer, and that his mind had already moved on. He sat on the edge of the bed flipping through books, but not reading. I couldn't figure out how to break the awkward silence. I was already regretting inviting him in.

'I come from a very poor family, completely uneducated.' As he spoke, he stared at his drifting smoke rings. 'They were so poor, they sold my school clothes the same day I changed out of them into military uniform. I've still got those blue army trousers. Wore them three winters; they're really old now. Dad's a stonemason. Mom had nine kids, but only my younger sister and I lived. She was even keener than Dad for me to do well…'

He spoke as though reciting from memory, his voice flat and colorless, as if he was talking about someone else. He stared at the floor, so I couldn't see his eyes, although at that moment I really wanted to.

'Are you smiling?' He was really strange, coming out with something like that all of a sudden, and in a tone clearly mocking me.

'I wasn't smiling!' I was a bit annoyed by his sensitivity, and I couldn't keep a note of irritation out of my voice.

He laughed at my protestation, but out of relief, and when he went on talking his voice was a lot more relaxed. He even started gesticulating. He talked about the big mountain of rocks outside his family's front door, about the little girls he'd secretly been sweet on when he was a kid in the village, and the world he'd seen after he joined up. He waved his hands about as he spoke. Those hands—the backs were dark as though sunburned, but the palms were pale, and there was a clear line separating them.

I smiled along with him, like we were old friends. He looked a lot cheerier than during the meal, but he kept staring at the floor, or else somewhere else. Either way, he was avoiding me, and so he seemed to be searching for something.

'A film studio has asked me to adapt the novel I published, so I'm living in the dorm there. Will you come over and visit?' he asked as he was leaving.

Agreeing, I saw him out. He gestured for me to stop with the hand he was holding his hat in. 'Don't see me out, don't come any further. I've taken up so much of your time, really…'

'Okay, I won't see you out, then!' I said, leaning on the door jamb. His sudden politeness and diffidence had turned the relaxed atmosphere we'd established back to caution and reserve, so I went along with it and hit right back. Falseness is the one thing I just can't forgive.

I didn't go to the studio to visit Wang Fuling. I'm lazy, and I was busy. I remembered for awhile, but then I didn't, and later I forgot about it altogether. I didn't like his evasive qualities, like his eyes.

It was probably about a month later. No, it was more than a month. The first light snow had already fallen in Beijing. It was winter. It wasn't late, but it was so dark outside you couldn't make anyone out.

I was lying on the bed listening to light music on the radio. Maybe you could call it jazz. Some genius had taken the music from the spot where Yang Zirong chases the tiger up the mountain in the revolutionary opera, *Taking Tiger Mountain By Strategy,* and set it to a disco beat. It didn't sound like the detective hero was chasing a tiger anymore; it was more like he was after a mouse.

Somebody was knocking at the door. 'Come in,' I said, not breaking away from the music. 'Oh, it's you!' I hadn't expected it would be Wang Fuling for a moment.

'You're really busy!' He brought a blast of cold air in with him.

'No, no, I've been meaning to visit you all along, but once I got busy…' I was lying and he could tell. I didn't blush, but he did.

'It doesn't matter. I was just passing by again. I wasn't going to come in, actually…' He stopped abruptly in mid-sentence. There never was any need to explain. If he'd come on a visit, then he'd come on a visit. Why did he have to be so worried about his image? I was happy he'd come on such a lonely winter night!

It wasn't five minutes since he'd come in and said hello, that he was looking at his watch for the third time already. He always made other people nervous along with him. 'What time is it?' I ventured. He went blank for a moment, then lifted his wrist again. Those other looks at his watch had only been stage movements. He was uncomfortable, not sure whether to sit or stand, even more awkward than usual.

'I've got to go, there's nothing up, I was just passing by.' He tried hard to sound casual, but his voice was all over the place, just like his eyes.

I didn't say anything, and I didn't try to stop him. That was deliberate; it's just the way I am, direct and to the point. All that covering up and sounding out—wasn't it just because of that pathetic pride of yours? I pretended not to understand, but I could tell he'd regretted it the minute he walked in. His hand was twisting the doorknob back and forth, but he didn't open the door.

'Sit down for awhile if you don't have anything else to do.' Saying that was worse than saying nothing at all.

'No, no, I was only passing by.' He explained himself again, and opened the door.

I understood. He wanted to live life to the fullest too, but when opportunity was staring him in the face he hesitated again. Out of pride, or because he despised himself? I couldn't help wondering.

It really was cold out, and the snow on the ground had turned to ice now. The wind wasn't strong, but it still cut to the bone. He'd come such a long way to see me; the round trip probably took two or three hours. Even if he was passing by, it was still a testament to his sincerity.

'Careful!' When we got to an icy patch, I reached out and took his arm. 'It's so late, where were you going?' I asked.

He didn't answer, but grabbed my hand, grabbed it tight, stopped dead, and said decisively, 'I'm not married.'

His tone and manner were so abrupt I nearly fell flat on my face.

'Really, I'm not married,' he repeated. And he stared straight into my eyes in a way he'd never done before. He was very firm, and when he finished speaking, he let go of my hand, made rock-hard fists and clamped his jaws shut so tight his cheek muscles popped out. I dare say if I'd shown the slightest disbelief at that moment, he would have beaten me to a pulp.

'You're not married.' Although I repeated what he'd said, inside I was puzzled, scared even, and when I calmed down enough to meet his gaze again, I found he'd already moved away from me. I ran a few steps to catch up with him.

'I'm really not married,' he said for the third time. 'When I was living at home, Mom did fix a bride up for me, but I never acknowledged her, so how can that be called marriage?' Was he asking me, or was he answering me?

'That's an arranged marriage!' This time, I responded prompt as could be.

He laughed, I guess because he thought I was oversimplifying the problem. 'You don't love her,' I went on.

He shook his head. 'That's beside the point. I don't even know her.'

I understood. Like a million others I'd read about in books, he was resisting a traditional Chinese marriage. Scenes from any number of tragedies came promptly to mind. Without even realizing it, I'd developed a sort of respect for him. I respected his courage and his trust in me. I even respected his personal tragedy.

'If you don't love her, you absolutely mustn't force yourself, or the result will be dreadful. Take advantage of the fact that you haven't been through the formalities yet, and be sure to explain this terrible situation clearly to your parents. Explain it to her, too. You can't keep her hanging on.' I advised him as though I'd been through the same thing myself.

'You're right, that's how it is.' He nodded seriously. Of course, he was only acting, because somehow I knew what I'd just said was worthless to someone with so much buried pain.

'So how come Grease Bucket told me you were married?'

'He was only guessing. He asked, but I didn't explain. I wanted to save myself the bother. Anyway, I'm not looking for a sweetheart at the moment, so it doesn't matter what they say about me.' After a moment, he continued, 'But whatever you do, you will keep all this to yourself, won't you? Don't tell anyone.'

Although 'looking for a sweetheart' was a rather quaint way to put it, I swore not to tell a soul. He breathed a sigh of relief, and his eyebrows unknitted themselves a bit. As though an invisible warm current were passing between us, we both felt happy from the trust and understanding we'd established. He let one bus go by. I wanted to spend a bit more time in his company too. Maybe that way I could share some of his unspoken bitterness and pain.

However, I still didn't see that he had to build such a prison for his emotions. 'Not looking for a sweetheart' did cut down on trouble, but wasn't he being too hard on himself? Why did he have to be so mean to himself?

I stood with him like that, leaning on the railing at the bus stop. It was quiet, and there was no one around anymore. Maybe he wanted to tell me more. Somehow it dawned on me that he'd come to see me on this cold night just to tell me he wasn't married. When I realized that, I panicked a bit, and I didn't dare look him in the eye again. I concentrated on the other side of the street, but I could sense he was sneaking glances at me. He kept it up as long as I didn't look back at him, and he even drew a little closer.

'Why didn't you come to see me?' he asked, very softly.

'I...I was afraid you were busy. Writers hate being disturbed when they're busy writing more than anything else, I know. If you...' I was babbling.

'But you agreed. I was waiting for you almost every minute, you know. Whenever anyone knocked on the door, I always thought of you first. I kept thinking you'd be there all of a sudden, like the stars. But in the end...' He sighed. It was hard to make his expression out under the lamplight, but those roving eyes were flashing now. I could feel his breath getting short and rough. I heard a heart beating, but couldn't tell if it was his or mine.

'I...' In the end, I could not stand the silence any longer. The black night was pressing down on me. I was even finding it hard to catch my breath.

'You...you really are...' Suddenly, he flung his arms out towards me. I don't know if I was taken by surprise or if I was waiting for it, but I closed my eyes at once. He put his hands on my head, pushing them through my hair. It was cut short like a boy's. 'It'd be great if you were a boy,' he said. 'Then you could be my little brother.'

'Here's the bus.' I dipped away from his hands. He actually rested one on my shoulder, like I really was a boy. Still, I could sense those hands of his were thinking, hesitating over whether to let the person in front of them go or to pull her into an embrace. I really didn't mean for him to leave, but he got on the bus. He didn't hesitate for a moment or even glance back; it was almost like he was running away.

Had I got myself out of a sticky situation? No, it was more like I'd been taken by surprise, and even more like I'd lost something but couldn't quite figure out what.

I didn't see Wang Fuling again, but I did get a letter from him. It was extremely short and the tone was formal. He addressed me as 'Comrade Xingxing'. He said he'd already gone back home to the country to work. 'I wrote almost nothing in the city,' he wrote. He didn't even mention when he'd be coming back or whether we'd meet again. He didn't give me a return address, no doubt because I despised him so much I wouldn't write back anyway. The way I saw it, maybe cold-shouldering me was self-defense. Next time he came looking for me I'd ignore him. However, that same evening I called Grease Bucket to ask where he was, but Grease Bucket didn't know anything.

This time, he'd won.

'Xingxing!' It's Grease Bucket come to get me, and I rush out after him. Grease Bucket looks very serious, and says he's never been through anything like this before; such a close, young friend, and all of a sudden you hear he's about to leave the world. I tell him I've never been through anything like this either.

I pedal like crazy after Grease Bucket. It's a long ride, and we don't say anymore, each thinking our own thoughts.

'Red light! Red light, Xingxing!' If it wasn't for Grease Bucket, the policeman would have been forced to confiscate my bike for sure. Perhaps because he figures I'm more upset than he is, Grease Bucket keeps an eye out for me all the way.

I never did tell anyone the things Fuling told me, except for Grease Bucket. That was because somehow he had worked out that Wang Fuling and I had set up our own line of communication. Maybe I told Grease Bucket those things because I wanted to explain our relationship, but I begged him to keep them secret. Of course, I left out the business at the bus stop. Grease Bucket felt it was a bit odd, but he believed me right away. After turning it over in his mind, he said, 'Looks like Wang Fuling's keen on you.' I swore at Grease Bucket for talking rubbish, but I couldn't get it out of my mind for a long time. Wang Fuling was someone I really understood, and also someone I couldn't understand at all.

God! I can't believe he's really going to die. I pedal with all my might, as though my efforts might prolong his life.

I imagine a big hospital, with white gowns, white hats and white masks everywhere. Of course, I'll beg those men in white to please, please try everything to save him. I'll tell them his life has not even begun yet. They'll believe everything I say.

I also imagine a ward quiet as death, with pure white everywhere, the smell of lysol filling the air. Fuling lies on a hospital bed, his face ashen, and that broad, intelligent forehead of his even whiter, although very calm of course. That's because he's so proud. I imagine myself tiptoeing up to his bed, and quietly calling out, 'Fuling'. I've never addressed him by his first name before. Then I pick up his listless hands and clasp them to my bosom, and at that moment, of course he opens his eyes a little. Are they still roving all over the place? Of course not, but he recognizes me, and he can look at me. Two big, shiny tears appear at the corners of his deep-set eyes, tears because he can't bear to leave life, friendship, his career and love. Then, I lean closer to him, and if he says he loves me, no, if he says thank you, if he just fixes those black eyes of his on me one more time, then I ever so softly but passionately throw caution to the wind and kiss his forehead, that beautiful white forehead like a slab of marble. Seeing his clearly hewn lips trembling, I begin to weep. Let my tears drip slowly onto his forehead. He smiles gratefully at me, at everyone in the room, at the whole wide world, then closes his eyes, exhausted yet content, and waits for death. As I imagine these things, a mysterious and tragic mood sweeps over me.

'We're here, this is it.' Grease Bucket leads me quickly to the ward. The hospital corridors are tatty and loud, and there are pronounced water stains on the walls and floors. I knock on the door a couple of times, but nobody answers. Grease Bucket pushes it open and takes a look inside, then beckons to me. Once inside, before I even have time to see clearly what's in front of me, a smell hits me full in the face and chokes me. It's not lysol as I had imagined, nor some medicine—it's an indescribable mix of decay, oxygen starvation, and poison, and at once all the things I imagined are stifled and suffocated by it. Yes, it's death, the smell of death. And it's coming from the lungs of the man on the bed in front of me.

It's Fuling; he's lying on the bed nearest the door. There are two more beds in the ward, but they're separated off by an old screen. The other patients want to maintain a distance from the dying, to make it clear they're not in the same category.

He bears almost no resemblance to the figure in my imagination. Neither his face nor his forehead are a bit white. In fact, they are much darker than before, as though blackened by thick smoke. His cheeks and his temples are terribly sunken, and they make his whole face look like a brown death's head. Even his body beneath the white sheets seems shrunken. His eyes are shut tight, and although they are still very deep-set, the eyeballs protrude. I am overcome with despair at once, because I realize those eyes will never open again, never weep again. What's a bit odd is that his moustache and his hair are as black, long and vital as they always were. Everything else is headed for death, but they are stauncher than ever.

Grease Bucket and I stand by Fuling's bed, looking at this him that doesn't look like him. Two long rubber tubes lead out of his nostrils, calling to mind an elephant's trunk, and his breathing is labored, like someone who's just run a marathon. All this is about as much use to him as a rowing boat is to a drowning paraplegic.

I repress my physical revulsion, and take one of Fuling's hands from the side of the bed. It's very light, it's hard to tell exactly what color it is, and even the clear line which used to divide the back of the hand from the palm has disappeared. His hand doesn't respond to my touch at all; there's no sign of either displeasure or comfort.

Perhaps the last warmth in his hand has moved into mine and on into my heart, because a warm current is sweeping unstoppably through my breast. Truly, if I'd known this day was coming, I certainly would have gone to visit him at the film studio; I would have sought him out actively, and wouldn't have let him injure his head just so he could be with me for awhile. I would have thought of a way to get a letter back to him, and I would have used warm, sincere language, because it was only his pride that made him call me 'Comrade'. I would even...I'm so moved by my own chain of 'if's' I don't notice when another woman comes into the room.

She's by my side already, and using her arm to block me. She looks about twenty-eight or twenty-nine, or maybe a little younger. Although her eyes are red and swollen and her hair is a mess, she still has a quiet dignity about her. She's carrying a bedpan which has been washed very clean, and she smoothly places it under the patient's body. He's naked; I see that when she pulls back the sheet. Then, for a moment, the woman caresses Fuling's body with her face. Only then does she look up at me, saying 'You're here'. God, she knows me! And apparently quite well.

Do I know her? Of course I do, but not so well. I recognized her just now when she blocked me.

I don't avoid her stubborn glare. We're both waiting for the other to speak first.

'You are...?' Grease Bucket asks the question I should be asking.

She doesn't reply at once, but stares at me, as though asking me to answer, or waiting for me to ask a question. However, at this moment my mind is blank; no imaginings and no question marks at all. Of course, this is all completely beside the point, because everything is clear as day, and all words are utterly meaningless.

'I am his wife.' She speaks, and in an instant her eyes are brimming with tears. They break through their invisible wall in no time. She puts her head on my shoulder and silently, without hesitation, begins to weep.

Things couldn't be any simpler. He's lied to me, but he hasn't lied to her, because she is his wife.

'He was always talking about you at home, so I recognized you at once. You're called Xingxing.' She drew closer, as though something bound us together.

Why had he had to do this? Was it to give her a hint, or to confide in her? I wasn't sure.

'He so wanted to be the best,' she's calmed down a little, 'so determined to outdo everyone else. He said he'd had a bad start, and he was far behind you all, so there was no other way but to struggle like crazy. He wrote and re-wrote night and day. But I never expected that early the day before yesterday he would pass out and never open his eyes again. If...normally he won't let our son pester him while he's writing for fear of losing his temper. Now how am I going to explain to our son when I get back home...'

'Your son?!' I'm shocked and let go of her arm without even realizing it.

'Didn't he tell you we had a son?' she asks sharply. She's very clever; she doesn't let any hostility show at all.

'Yes, yes, he told me.' I nod my head a bit too sincerely; 'He mentioned your son; he's very cute. He said he liked giving him piggyback rides.' I congratulate myself that I can deal with emergencies, and say all this so fluently and naturally.

'Yes, he loved our son dearly. The boy's just over three but he never even smacked him once. What he liked to do most was feel the boy's head with both his hands.' Her voice isn't too loud, but her tone is proud and confident. She takes a cotton ball soaked with rubbing alcohol from a little bottle on the bedside table, puts both her hands under his sheets, and gently cleans every part of his body. And like an obedient child, Fuling lets her move him about. Her tears and her snivel stream onto his face, his hands and his body.

Everything between them is so natural, familiar and taken for granted. She's not scared of Fuling's deathly smell, and she doesn't find his death's head face hard to look at. She is his wife. They have a son. He belongs to her. That was how it was when he was alive—he's all hers. She turns to look at me again, and her sadness is mingled with embarrassment, also pride. It is as though she's let outsiders see something particularly intimate between the two of them.

She's a good wife. She's already prepared to take on all the burdens he may have left her. The doctor says Fuling won't make it through the night.

I say goodbye to her, calm inside, though it's all very strange to me. It's as though I'd always known it would turn out like this.

Grease Bucket's watching me, and I know full well why. You don't need to look at me; I don't hate Fuling at all. He never harmed me. Whenever we thought of him, we always acknowledged he was a good man, and we always will. This is what I want to tell Grease Bucket, but not today of course.

On the way back, I don't say a word to Grease Bucket until he cannot stand it any longer. 'Do you feel you've been conned?' he asks.

I don't answer, because I don't know how I should answer. I'm thinking that Fuling actually did fool me, but I don't have the feeling of being hurt and humiliated the way one does after having been conned. I don't even mind that Fuling mentioned me to his wife, or told jokes about me.

'Don't take it like that,' Grease Bucket continues, since I don't say a word. 'Maybe Fuling himself didn't know what made him do it. At the very least, it means he liked you.'

Grease Bucket does his best to console me according to his understanding of the situation, although in fact there is no need.

Really, I don't hate you, I don't blame you, and I don't hold anything against you. Fuling, I will still mention you to other people as though I'm talking about a best friend. I understand you. I've never been this way before, this way I'm being towards you; so willingly and selflessly trying to understand someone. I understand that you didn't want to abandon your wife and family; on the contrary, you loved them very much, and were very frank with them. You just wanted to enter a different world, and make yourself a member of that world. But you were wrong. If you were still alive, if God gave you another moment of consciousness, if you saw her and me standing together before you, what would you do? What would you think? What would you say? Of course this is all conjecture, because you're dead, and there isn't even time for you to think anything anymore because your thoughts stopped long ago.

The journey back hasn't seemed as long as the journey out. Somehow, I didn't notice before that one side of the road is lined with budding little poplar trees, all glimmering green, and the other is lined with old, deep green pines. You mustn't just think of both trees as green when the contrast between them is so great.

When we get to the turning where we go our separate ways, Grease Bucket asks as he rides along, 'Are you still coming to see the modern art exhibition tomorrow morning?'

'I said I would, so of course I am!' I nod in agreement, but Grease Bucket's already turned off onto the main road.

translated by Chris Berry

The Angry Kettle

To say he was annoying would be unfair, because he was always flashing smiles like winter sunlight in the city. In fact, he was the sort of man whose honest, decent appearance would make a woman relax right away. Still, I have to admit he was weird, because I will be damned if I know why he spent three hundred and ninety-nine dollars and ninety-nine cents on a kettle, a plain old kettle for boiling water.

'It's an excellent kettle,' Michael said the first time I went to look at the room. He was fingering the short, fat spout and playing with the little whatsit on the end of it. That little whatsit, it was very unusual, a bit like the cups we use for drinking shots in China. 'It's beautiful, isn't it?' Michael asked, putting the little whatsit back on the end of the spout.

'Yes, it's very shiny,' I said. 'It's almost as shiny as a mirror,' I continued after a pause, because that was the only positive thing I could think of to say.

'Of course! You won't find a mirror shinier!' he insisted.

In that case, why do people look in mirrors? They could just as well look in the kettle. That was what went through my mind but only through my mind, because I did not want to have a disagreement with him before I even moved in. Besides, I liked the room; it had high ceilings and orangey-beige walls that made it sunny day and night. The landlady was a sweet old soul with a soft voice and silent steps, as if she was afraid of scaring someone. She did not live on the premises, and so, all in all, although the rent was a bit steep, it was attractive.

'You can use it, but you must keep it clean,' Michael generously offered me his kettle, which he was holding in his hand, the day I moved in.

'Thank you. But, to be honest, I still don't see why it's worth three hundred and ninety-nine dollars.' I nodded sincerely and expressed my doubts sincerely at the same time.

'You can't express the value of something as good as this in monetary terms.'

'Sorry,' I said shamefaced, as I tried to fathom the meaning of Michael's deep thoughts. When I looked back up at the kettle, it was with an almost worshipful attitude but then I couldn't stop myself from laughing, because my face reflected in its side looked like a rock melon.

I got along well with Michael. He was a lawyer. He had his own practice, worked hard, and lived simply. We met most mornings or evenings in the kitchen. Every time he picked up his kettle, Michael made a gurgling noise in his throat. At first I thought he had a headache, but then I realized he was expressing appreciation, as though it was full of honey, not water.

Michael was very eager to correct my English mistakes. I was delighted at first, but it soon became unbearable, because he always interrupted me the minute I opened my mouth. If it was not pronunciation, it was grammar, and if it was not either of those, then it was to praise my command of the language. Five interruptions for every ten words would make anyone forget what they were saying. After awhile, I tried speaking like a machine gun to stop him from interrupting me, but it was no good; no matter how fast I was, he was faster, and if he couldn't get a word in or I wouldn't listen to him, he started drumming on the table with his fingers. Damn it, he drummed away until I couldn't get another word out, and then he would correct my mistakes for me from the beginning.

His behavior only made my English worse and worse when I was with him. I was nervous before I even opened my mouth, not because I was afraid of making mistakes, but because I was afraid he would interrupt. The English he spoke to me was more difficult than a philosophical treatise, and I even began to wonder whether he was using real words you could find in a dictionary at all. I know he meant well and was doing his best to help, but every time I found myself watching his little smile and wondering when I would finally be able to escape. However, he must have read my mind, because he started pouring out his sentences without blinking or pausing for breath, like a tap with a broken washer.

I used Michael's kettle a few times, but quickly decided never to use it again, even if it meant dying of thirst. If I used it to boil up some water, I had to stand there and keep an eye on it, then turn the gas off at the first puff of steam. Otherwise, the little whatsit would perk right up and start to scream through the apartment like a missile searching out its target. The sound was high and piercing, like a conquering hero determined to flatten everything in his path. Whenever I heard it, I panicked, torn between going to turn the gas off and sticking my fingers in my ears and fleeing. I stumbled at the kitchen door once, twisting my ankle so it swelled up like a bun and I could not wear high heels for over a week. I even heard it in my dreams, howling like a wolf.

It had another trick, and that was burning me. Because it was all metal, the minute I turned the gas on, it got hotter than the flame itself, and whether I went to pull that screaming little whatsit off or pour the water out, either way I stood a good chance of getting burned. I'm not exaggerating; I've still got the scars to prove it.

'Let's use my kettle today.' I dreaded that more than anything, because although I cleaned it thoroughly every time I used it, Michael was never satisfied. I began to wonder if the kettle was not telling tales on me.

'Didn't you say I could use it?'

'Yes, but I said you have to keep it clean.'

'I can't see that I've left any marks on it.'

'This is your fingerprint,' he pointed with his long finger.

I did not argue any further, because it was mine. However, I was thinking he should use a rope and pulley system to lower it onto the stove. Michael bought seven or eight different cleaning products all for the one kettle, and every Sunday he rotated through the red and green fluids cleaning it. I could not stand to be in the kitchen a minute longer than absolutely necessary, and although I was scared of Michael, I was more scared of his kettle. At least I got to see Michael's smile every morning, but apart from making me jump out of my skin, that kettle was only good for making my face look like a rock melon.

In the end, the day came when even Michael's smile disappeared.

When I went to the kitchen in the morning, I saw the kettle had been put in the middle of the table, and its master was sitting on the edge. Not only was there no trace of a smile on his face, but he was also drumming all ten fingers on the table top. My instinct was to bolt, but too late, he had called me to a halt already.

'It's dirty,' he said. 'It's been dirtied.' He was pallid and there were dark circles around his eyes. He spoke as though he was making a public statement that his beloved had been violated, although it was only a kettle and not a person.

'I haven't used it,' I said. 'I haven't used it for a long time.' I congratulated myself on not having even laid a finger on it recently.

'But you've dirtied it.'

'I haven't touched it.'

'But I've told you, it has to be kept away from oil, and when you cook, you use oil.'

'It's at least ten feet away from where I cook.'

'But it isn't shiny anymore, it's all blurry.'

'Maybe, but I can't stop eating just because of that kettle.'

'You could eat a sandwich.'

'But I'm Chinese.'

'Do Chinese people have to eat fried food?'

'Do Australians have to treat their kettles like sweethearts?'

'If you don't like sandwiches you shouldn't have come to Australia.'

'If this kettle is worth so much to you, you should take it to bed and hold it tight, not leave it in the kitchen.'

'I will.'

'Thank God for that!'

That was the longest exchange I ever had with Michael without him correcting my English mistakes.

Although I still heard its scream sometimes, I never did see that kettle in the kitchen again. Walking by Michael's room one day, I saw it sitting proudly on his pillow, its whole body shiny and glowing. What a coward I was; I barely had the guts to look straight at it, as though it might whizz after me like a missile and drill a hole right through me.

Early in the morning a week later, to the accompaniment of the kettle's happy scream, I moved out.

translated by Chris Berry

Ding Xiaoqi was born in Shenyang, China in 1959. The Cultural Revolution brought her formal education to a halt at the age of nine. Separated from her parents, who were sent down to the countryside for re-education, she grew up more or less alone in an empty apartment full of books. She graduated from the People's Liberation Army Art Academy, and held the rank of Vice-Battalion Commander while working as a stage director and lyricist for the Navy Song and Dance Troupe. During this time, her songs, poetry, film-scripts and plays won many awards. She began to write fiction in the mid-eighties, resulting in two acclaimed collections of stories, one published in 1986, the other in 1989. The stories of *Maidenhome* are taken from these two collections.

Maidenhome is the first collection of Ding's stories available in the English language anywhere in the world.

Ding left China shortly after witnessing the notorious Tiananmen Square massacre of 1989 and immigrated to Australia. In 1990, she was appointed a Visiting Fellow in the Cinema Studies Division of La Trobe University in Melbourne, Australia. Two of her plays about the lives of Chinese students, *The Gate to Paradise* and *Kiss Yesterday Goodbye* (for which she received an Australia Council award) have since been produced. Translations of her stories have been published in a number of literary journals.

Recently Ding has started her own business in Melbourne where she lives with her son.

Chris Berry

The Translators

Chris Berry currently teaches Cinema Studies at La Trobe University, Melbourne, Australia. He is the editor of *Perspectives on Chinese Cinema*, and met Ding Xiaoqi while working as a translator and sub-titler for the Chinese film industry in Beijing.

Cathy Silber is a Ph.D. candidate in Chinese Literature at the University of Michigan. She has published translations of Chinese fiction and poetry in the United States, China and Australia. She is writing a dissertation on *nüshu*, a script used exclusively by women in Hunan.

aunt lute books is a multicultural women's press that has been committed to publishing high quality, culturally diverse literature since 1982. In 1990, the Aunt Lute Foundation was formed as a non-profit corporation to publish and distribute books that reflect the complex truths of women's lives and the possibilities for personal and social change. We seek work that explores the specificities of the very different histories from which we come, and that examines the intersections between the borders we all inhabit.

Please write or phone for a free catalogue of our other books or if you wish to be on our mailing list for future titles. You may buy books directly from us by phoning in a credit card order or mailing a check with the catalogue order form.

Aunt Lute Books
P.O. Box 410687
San Francisco, CA 94141
(415)558-8116

This book would not have been possible without the kind contributions of the *Aunt Lute Founding Friends:*

Anonymous Donor
Anonymous Donor
Rusty Barcelo
Diana Harris
Phoebe Robins Hunter

Diane Goldstein
Diane Mosbacher, M.D., Ph.D.
Elise Rymer Turner
William Preston, Jr.